The *Prince* of *Bagram Prison*

Alex Carr

An Orion paperback

First published in Great Britain in 2008
by Orion
This paperback edition published in 2009
by Orion Books Ltd,
Orion House, 5 Upper St Martin's Lane,
London WC2H 9EA

An Hachette UK company

1 3 5 7 9 10 8 6 4 2

Copyright © Jenny Siler 2008

A CIP catalogue record for this book is available
from the British Library.

ISBN 978-0-7528-8448-6

Printed and bound in Great Britain by
CPI Mackays, Chatham ME5 8TD

The Orion Publishing Group's policy is to use papers that
are natural, renewable and recyclable products and
made from wood grown in sustainable forests. The logging
and manufacturing processes are expected to conform to
the environmental regulations of the country of origin.

www.orionbooks.co.uk

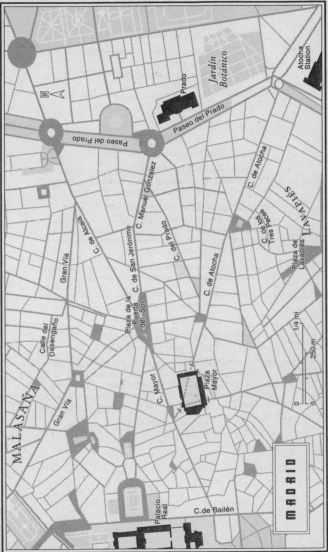

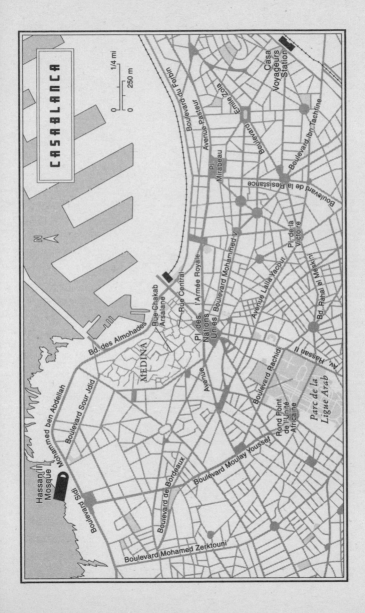

The *Prince* of *Bagram Prison*

othing was as Manar had imagined it would be. Her mother should have been there, and her two aunts. Her older sister, whose hand she had held through two births and who had pledged to do the same for her. There should have been clean sheets and basins of warm water, someone with a cool cloth for her forehead. And, on the other side of the house, the men regaling Yusuf with stories of their own children's arrivals, so that when the time came he would be awake to say the *adhan* and perform the *tahneek*, the first sweet smudge of dates in the child's mouth.

But there was none of this.

The room smelled of blood and feces. Manar's mostly, but other women's as well. Old blood, and on the once-white walls the stained remnants of past catastrophes. Birth or death or both.

On the far wall, Hassan II hung in stiff portrait. An aging playboy performing the role of beneficent king in an expensive French suit and a red fez. Polo player, racing-car driver, epicurean, Manar thought, looking at his slim fingers and European face. Torturer, murderer, rapist.

In the stark light of the prison infirmary, the doctor's round forehead glistened like the grease-laden haunch of a lamb on a spit. Four in the morning, and Manar could smell the stale liquor on the man's breath, the sweat stink of the whore he'd left to come here. He was the same man who had examined her the night they'd brought her in, who had grudgingly confirmed for her jailers what she'd been trying desperately to tell them all along, through the first round of beatings and humiliations: that she was pregnant.

The doctor had not dared look her in the face then, and he didn't now.

"Put her feet up," he said to the nurse, and Manar felt the woman's hands on her ankles, the cold steel of the stirrups on her bare feet.

A contraction hit her, faster and harder than the previous ones had been. Manar took a deep breath and shifted her hips to absorb the pain.

"Do not let her move," the doctor snapped.

His hand was inside her now, as if she were an animal. She could feel his wrist against her pubic bone, his meaty fingers on the baby. And the pain—greedy, ravenous, wanting everything she had and more. She turned her head and retched, emptying the thin contents of her stomach onto the filthy floor.

"Do not let her move!"

The nurse took Manar's hand and smiled weakly, a conspirator's smile, and Manar thought, There is nothing between us. Nothing. How could you even dare?

"He is turning the baby now," the nurse said. "You must stay still. It will all be over soon."

For a moment, it was. Manar's abdomen relaxed and she felt the baby shift inside her, felt the doctor's hand slide out from between her legs.

Please, God, she thought, taking that single moment of calm to offer one last prayer. Please take the child now, before it is tainted by any of this. Then another contraction hit her, and with it the undeniable need to push.

"This is the easy part," the nurse told her.

To Manar's surprise, the woman was right. After fifteen

hours of submission to the pain, the agony of pushing was a relief.

When the baby finally came, the doctor did not give it to Manar but handed it to the nurse while he cut the umbilical cord. The baby was still and stunned, his skin dark as a bruise. For a moment, Manar felt a sense of profound relief that her prayer had been answered. Then the child cried out and she realized that he was not dead.

He cried out and Manar could not help herself. At least he will be my reprieve, she thought selfishly, as she had that first night, when she had naïvely consoled herself with the presumption that they would not rape her while she had a child in her body. Even they, even these animals, she told herself now, would not harm her while she had milk to give.

She put her arms out to take the boy, but the nurse shook her head. "I'm sorry," she whispered. "You must have known."

"The *adhan*," Manar pleaded, understanding that she had been completely forsaken, that neither of them was to be spared. Her child would live and she would die. "Please, in the name of Allah, I must say the *adhan*."

The baby shrieked in the nurse's arms, and Manar felt his desperation in her entire body. "He is mine!" she yelled.

The woman stepped forward and laid the child on Manar's chest. He was naked and bloody, his eyes wide open, dark as two wet stones.

Manar put her lips to his right ear and smelled him, her smell and his together. Blood, like the earth, like the mud from which God had fashioned them all. Behind his ear was a small red stain, a single blemish on his still-purple skin. An imperfection, Manar thought, like that which a pot suffers in the kiln, a mark of what he had suffered inside her.

"God is great," she whispered.

"I testify that there is no god except God.
I testify that Muhammad is the messenger of God.
Come to prayer.
Come to salvation."

Then she turned him to say the second prayer, but the nurse was already taking him from her again.

ONE

"So, then, Jamal," the American said, resting his hands on his knees as was his habit. "How's everything going?"

He was a tall man, his arms and legs too long for his torso, his head square, with a neatly shorn cap of blond hair, pale eyelashes set in a pale face. Justin, he had insisted more than once that Jamal call him. But the boy could imagine nothing more awkward than addressing him this way.

It was evening, still barely light outside, and through the open window Jamal could see into the apartment across the street, where the woman in the pink *abaya* was cooking dinner, as she almost always was during these meetings with the American. *Harira*, Jamal thought, smelling the heady odor of garlic and spice. Last week there was lamb. And, the week before, the pleasant aroma of sugar and cinnamon. The promise of seeing her was the one thing about these weekly meetings that Jamal did not dread.

"There are some very important men coming to see you," the American announced, not waiting for a reply to his earlier query, apparently not wanting one. "They're going to ask you some questions about Bagheri."

Jamal's mind raced anxiously back through everything he had said. He had not meant for it to come to this, and now he wasn't quite sure what to do. Somewhere in the building, a baby was crying. A baby was always crying, though whether it was the same baby or different ones Jamal could not say.

"From Washington?" he asked, trying to conceal his panic.

The American nodded, the gesture somehow both encouraging and unkind. "Just tell them what you know, what you've told me, and everything will be fine."

Jamal thought for a moment. "Will Mr. Harry be there?"

The man sighed, clearly exasperated. "We've talked about this, Jamal. Harry—Mr. Comfort, that is—doesn't work with us anymore. But you have me now." He conjured a smile, leaned forward, and handed Jamal a scrap of paper with an address scrawled in black ink. "There's a safe house in Malasaña. We'll meet there at midnight tomorrow."

Jamal took the paper. "And after I tell them about Bagheri I can go?"

"Of course." The American shrugged, pressed his hands against his knees, and unfolded his long body from the chair. "You can go right now if you'd like," he said, not understanding.

"No." Jamal followed the man's face as he rose. "I can go to America?"

The man paused to recover himself. Clearly he had not expected this, and his mouth was suddenly grim in the room's fading light. "Yes," he said at last. "Yes, of course. We'll talk about that later."

Jamal nodded, sensing that this was the right thing to do, though he knew the American was lying. He had seen this same look many times before. Not pity but guilt. Shame at what had been done, at what was about to be done.

"Trust me," the man said. Pulling his wallet from the back pocket of his pants, he slipped a hundred-euro note—much more than the usual payment—from the billfold and handed it to Jamal, then turned for the door.

Jamal could hear the American's footsteps as he made his way down the stairs, the scrape of his leather soles on the gritty concrete. Then, far below, in the building's foyer, the front door slammed closed.

Give me five minutes, Mr. Harry used to say after he and Jamal had played their usual game of gin rummy. He'd had an easy way of talking, as if it was all just a game, a joke between the two of them. *Make them think we've been up to something in here.*

But Jamal was in no hurry to leave. After the American left, he sat alone in the apartment and watched the woman cook. It was not something he had ever permitted himself before, and though she was neither young nor beautiful, watching her felt somehow unclean. Pornographic. Jamal could not make himself stop.

Emboldened by the darkness, he inched his chair closer to the window. In the kitchen's halogen glare the woman's *abaya* was bright as a pomegranate, the fabric shifting as she moved from one task to another, stirring and chopping and setting out the dinner dishes. She was so close, the space that separated them so narrow, that for a moment Jamal forgot himself and was there with her. Then someone passed in the street below, a singer unaccompanied except by one too many glasses of sherry.

He could always go back, Jamal told himself, contemplating his slim options. To Tangier or Casa. Ain Chock, even. He did not think the Americans would come to Morocco. If they did, it would not be easy for them to find him. Though even as he thought this he knew that going back was not something he could bring himself to do. Not yet.

And the truth? *Never tell them the truth,* Harry had cautioned him once. *They'll just use it against you.* Suddenly Jamal missed the man with a desperation he rarely allowed himself. If Mr. Harry were here, Jamal thought, he would know what to do. They would sort this out together. Though, of course, if Harry were here things would never have come this far.

Below in the darkness the singer passed, the twelve-count rhythm of the Verdiales fading into the quarter's crooked street, the words slurred beyond recognition. For a moment everything was quiet, then the baby started up again.

No, Jamal told himself, fighting back tears as he fingered the hundred-euro note in his hand. He had started it and he would have to see it through. If he played things right, he might even come out on top. Now that he understood just how much Bagheri meant to the Americans, he would be asking for more than the usual handouts.

TWO

It was barely eight by the bar clock at the Kings Cross Coopers. Just enough time, David Kurtz thought as he watched Colin Mitchell shoulder his bag with his good right arm and make his way to the bar, for a quick pint before the next train north.

The Coopers was not a place to linger, yet there was something to be said for the unapologetic grubbiness of the establishment. A good station pub wasn't meant to be pleasant. Squalor was part of the allure, a distraction from the open shame of the patrons, men on their way to places they didn't want to go, medicating themselves for the trip.

From his seat at the back of the room, Kurtz watched Colin squeeze into one of the few free spaces at the counter and bark his order over the din. It had been two years since their last meeting, since that night at the Bagram Special Forces camp. Hardly long enough, Kurtz thought, for time to have taken such an obvious toll on the other man. Yet it had.

The barman set down a full pint and Colin hunched over the glass, looking up at the television, trying, Kurtz knew, to avoid his own reflection in the bar's mirror, the sight of his stiff left arm hanging awkwardly at his side. Hand and wrist and elbow that, after two years, obviously didn't feel like his own.

But there was more to Colin's transformation than just the loss of his arm. His entire body seemed diminished by the injury, as if the absence were not merely a physical one. Watching his graceless gestures and slumped back gave Kurtz a sense of overwhelming satisfaction, as if some kind of justice had been achieved.

Colin ducked his head and turned away from the television, letting his eyes wander across the room. It was a motion Kurtz was familiar with, cautious and searching, the look on his face that of a man who felt he was being watched. And Kurtz, wanting his presence known, allowed himself to be found.

Colin's gaze slid toward Kurtz and stopped, his expression shifting suddenly from confusion to contempt. It was the same way he and the other soldiers had looked at Kurtz so many times before, their disdain indelible. And this time Kurtz, thinking of what was to come, couldn't stop himself from smiling.

"Mitchell?" He raised his hand and waved, forcing surprise—an old acquaintance caught off guard by an unlikely meeting—then stood and jostled his way through the crowd toward the bar. "I thought that was you!"

He was not good at false sincerity, never had been. "Buy you a drink?" he proposed, wedging himself next to Colin, patting him on the back for the benefit of whoever was watching before signaling the bartender for a fresh round. "For old times' sake."

"Save your money," Colin told him icily, looking up at the television again. There was a rugby match on, Hull at St. Helens, the teams locked together in comic futility, like a group of drunks staggering home from the bar on a gusty evening. "I've got a train to catch."

"Just five minutes," Kurtz said, knowing full well that the Edinburgh train wasn't leaving for another half hour.

The barman set two fresh pints on the counter and Kurtz paid him. "I never could understand rugby," he observed, motioning to the game with his right hand, fingering the vial in his breast pocket with his left. Minutes, he reminded himself. Once he takes that first sip it will be a matter of minutes till it's over. "Same with cricket. Here, for instance. Was that a goal or a try? I can never remember which is which."

Colin's skin was sallow in the nicotine-dulled glare of the pub's lights, his face that of a junkie in need of a fix. Yes, Kurtz thought as he moved his hand across Colin's glass, letting the contents of the vial drop as he did so. Here was a man whose death would be a surprise to no one.

Kurtz slid the empty vial back into his pocket, then lifted his own glass and admired the contents. "You still in touch with Kat?" he asked. "She was somewhere in Virginia, last I heard." Like picking an old scab.

Colin shrugged, took a long, slow sip of his bitter, then turned to face Kurtz. "You here to make sure I haven't gotten cold feet?"

"Something like that."

"Well, you shouldn't have bothered. I'm not planning any sudden changes of heart, and neither is Stuart. So unless your Mr. Bagheri decides to make an unscheduled appearance at the court-martial, you've got nothing to worry about."

Kurtz laughed. Just a bit too easily, he knew, but it didn't matter now.

Neither of them spoke then, and for a moment it was almost as if they were, in fact, what they appeared to be: two old acquaintances passing in transit, two men making a truce. All of it behind them now, al-Amir and the Iranian. Kat, even.

Colin finished his beer and glanced at his watch. "Time's

up," he said, hefting his bag with his good right hand. He moved to push himself back from the bar, but his prosthetic hand slipped on the wet counter and he pitched awkwardly forward.

"You okay?" Kurtz asked jeeringly.

Colin struggled to stand. His face was damp, his mouth open wide, his breathing ragged.

Kurtz slipped Colin's arm across his shoulder and helped him up, steering him away from the bar and toward the bathroom. A woman lunged at them from the crowd, her mouth a sharp red slash, her fat face smeared and stained. A drunk recognizing her kin. She fell against Colin, pawing him sloppily. Disgusted, Kurtz shoved her away and kicked the bathroom door open with his boot.

Colin stumbled out of his grasp and into one of the doorless stalls, dropping to his knees before the toilet, retching up beer and bile.

Kurtz locked the door behind them. "That last pint must not have agreed with you," he sneered. Pulling a pair of black leather gloves from his jacket pocket, shoving his hands into them, he reached for Colin's bag and unzipped it, shuffled through the meager contents. Dirty underwear and T-shirts. A few toiletries for the overnight to Portsmouth.

"Open up!" There was a flurry of impatient voices from the other side of the door, a barrage of fists.

Kurtz paused briefly. "Fuck off!" he barked over his shoulder, then he pulled Colin's half-finished bottle of morphine sulfate from the bag.

"You know," he remarked, nodding toward Colin's bad left arm, "this was supposed to have happened at al-Amir." He dumped the remaining pills into the toilet, then set his boot on the steel lever and flushed. "Don't worry," he added. "It'll be over before you know it."

THREE

It was just past midnight when Jamal started across Puerta del Sol. Late already, he thought, glancing up at the clock tower on the Old Post House, not bothering to pick up his pace. The Americans would wait for him, he reminded himself. They would have to.

It was a warm night, early fall in all its perfection, and the outdoor cafés that ringed the plaza were filled to overflowing. The crowd was mixed, Madrileños and tourists both, all young and attractive. Bare shoulders and legs, skin burnished and dark from the August holidays.

In the center of the plaza a fountain washed elegantly onto itself, the water lit from beneath, lucid as blown glass. This other Madrid, far from the dank streets of Lavapiés and Jamal's room above the halal butcher shop, the sounds and smells of slaughter. This city Jamal so seldom saw, in which he would always be an outsider.

Picking his way through the crowd, Jamal crossed the plaza and headed north toward the Gran Via. He had been to Malasaña, the city's unofficial red-light district, before, on more desperate occasions than he liked to admit, always looking to make some quick cash. This wasn't his purpose tonight, but he could feel the fist of apprehension in his stomach all the same, fear of what he knew was to come.

Fifteen Calle del Desengaño. Jamal repeated the address to himself as he walked, trying to focus on the task ahead, on what, exactly, he would tell the Americans. He had not gone back to his room the night before, but had stayed at the apartment on the Calle Tres Peces, working his story over and over in his mind until he'd almost believed it himself. Then, sometime just before dawn, he'd finally fallen asleep.

Jamal could feel the angry stares of the whores as soon as he turned off the Gran Via and onto the Calle del Desengaño. These women had all been in the business long enough to know a threat when they saw one, and though Jamal wasn't trolling for tricks tonight, there was no way of convincing the whores that this was the case.

As Jamal passed, one of the women, a stocky brunette in a red bodysuit and scuffed gold boots, leaned out of her doorway like a grotesque cuckoo announcing the hour. "Look at that pretty ass, girls!" she called. She was short and thick-waisted, her midriff bulging against the bodysuit, her bare right thigh marked by a fist-size purple bruise.

Jamal forced his head down and kept walking, one foot in front of the other, the address the American had given him humming like a mantra in his head. Fifteen. Fifteen. There was something repulsive about the way the women showed themselves, Jamal thought, something frightening about their lack of shame, all their bodies' faults on display.

Someone hissed from the doorway behind him and Jamal looked back to see a man leering out, dark eyes and ragged chin, bare arms dotted with scabs and sores.

Nineteen, Jamal counted, scanning the numbers on the opposite side of the street, stumbling away from the apparition, the entire force of his will working to keep himself from running. Seventeen. He stopped briefly in front of the next door and glanced up at the building's grimy façade, searching for a number and finding none.

A plaque on the plaster wall read HOTEL DE LA LUNA, and beneath the name, a single filthy star. It had obviously been some time since the establishment had seen its last paying customer, even longer since it had earned the star. The foyer was dark, the glass in the front door webbed with cracks.

Jamal's eyes ranged forward along the street. Thirteen. Nine. Yes, he told himself, this would have to be the place. He climbed the three front steps and tried the door, half expecting it to be locked. But it swung open easily, and in an instant he was inside, blinking to make out the lobby's sooty contours, fighting the combined stench of cat piss and death.

Just tell them what you know and everything will be fine, Jamal heard the American say. And how, the boy wondered, could he possibly explain that it wasn't what he knew but what he didn't know that was the problem?

Home, Jamal thought, surveying the hotel's dark lobby. Home, and not a pleasant one. How many nights had he slept in places like this, grateful for the shelter? In how many cities, terrified of who might discover him? There was a small reception desk in the far left corner of the room, and on the wall behind it a tartan of pigeonholes dotted with unclaimed pieces of mail. To the right of the desk, a narrow staircase wound upward toward the second floor, from whose depths a scrap of light was visible.

Stepping carefully to avoid the discarded syringes that littered the floor, Jamal crossed to the stairs and started upward. His stomach was suddenly light against his ribs, his nerves taut. But now that he had arrived, now that the meeting with the Americans was imminent, he only wanted to get it over with.

He reached the second floor and paused, letting his eyes adjust to the relative brightness. There was no hallway to speak of, just a small landing and the staircase to his immediate right, curving upward to the dark third floor. A handful of rooms opened off the landing, and it was from the farthest of these that the light emanated.

"Hello!" Jamal called, leaning forward and peering through the doorway closest to him, catching a shadowy glimpse of the worn furnishings. Collapsing armchair and dusty wardrobe, bedclothes stained and frayed by years of illicit occupants— some animal, some human. Some both or neither, Jamal thought, the line in this place blurred to the point where it was impossible to tell one from the other.

The only answer came from overhead, paws scrabbling across the floorboards.

"Hello?" he called again, and this time there was human movement, a body shifting in the doorway of the lit room. A man stepped forward onto the landing, an unassuming figure in a long dark coat. He was older than Mr. Justin by quite a bit, his face haggard and hollow in the eerie light.

"Where's Mr. Justin?" Jamal asked, gripping the stair's iron railing.

The man smiled, but it was a jack-o'-lantern's crooked leer. "Looks like he's running late. I imagine he'll be here soon."

"Yes," Jamal agreed, though he knew this to be impossible, knew without a doubt that Justin had never been late for anything in his life.

The kind who blamed you, he thought, sizing the stranger and his appetites up instinctively, as years of self-preservation had taught him to do; the kind who hated you for what they had just done.

Down below, the hotel's front door creaked open, and Jamal saw the man's eyes shift past him.

"Must be him now," the stranger remarked, forcing a smile, and Jamal smiled back.

This, he told himself, was the kind of man for whom contempt and desire were inextricably linked.

A foot touched the first stair below and Jamal took a deep breath, propelling himself upward. The stranger lunged, grabbing Jamal's pant leg. When Jamal turned to look behind him, he caught a glimpse of the room at the back of the hallway, and of Mr. Justin sprawled, open-eyed and doll-like, across the bed. Jerking his leg with all the strength he could muster, Jamal pulled free and scrambled up the staircase.

The roof, he told himself, taking the steps two and three at a time, the blueprint for every squat or drug den he'd ever been in laying itself out in his mind. There was always at least one back way out, more in a place like this.

Jamal reached the fourth and uppermost floor and paused. He could hear the man below him, and a second voice. A hushed exchange and then quiet, the sound of someone climbing cautiously up.

"Jamal!" called a voice, the second man. "It's *okay,* Jamal. We just want to talk to you." Arabic now, with a thick accent.

Jamal blinked, his eyes battling the darkness as he scanned the landing, looking for an exit. Though scant, the light from the second floor provided just enough illumination for him to make out the contours of the space. The walls were shorter here than on the lower floors, the ceiling slanting sharply toward a handful of garret rooms. In coming this way, Jamal had hoped for a door or a hatch that might lead to the roof, but he could see none.

"Jamal? We're friends, Jamal. Just like Mr. Justin." It was the second man again, his accent the same as the first man's.

Bagram, Jamal thought. That was where he'd heard the accent before. It was the same awkward Gulf Arabic the American soldiers at the prison had used.

A loose board groaned somewhere below, and Jamal ducked into the room to his immediate right and eased the door closed behind him. The whole building reeked of feral cats, but here in the cramped space the stench was overwhelming. Jamal pinched his nose and took a shallow breath through his mouth.

Moving quickly to the window, he pushed it open and peered out, reading the topography of the surrounding buildings, assessing his dwindling options. The rooftop opposite was his best bet, but it was a full story lower than the window where he now stood, with a meter gap between the two buildings. He was a good jumper, light enough to fly and strong enough to handle the punishment of the drop, but this was a stretch even for him.

There was a noise on the landing, one footstep and then another. Jamal climbed up onto the windowsill and squeezed his body through the squat opening. His hands were shaking, his legs unsteady beneath him, his entire body shot through with adrenaline.

Gripping the outside frame of the window, Jamal forced his legs up and leaned forward slightly, imagining the spring in his feet, the distance to be covered. A meter and a half for measure, the boy told himself, and then he jumped.

FOUR

The sun was just up, the Blue Ridge blushing hazy pink, the morning hot already, the air saturated, heavy in Kat's lungs as she rounded the last curve through the pines and started down the hill toward campus. On the road below, a pack of cadets were working their way up through the trees. Two weeks, Kat thought, fourteen days of predawn runs and abuse. This was when the ones who weren't going to make it started to break.

There were some three dozen cadets in the pack, each nearly indistinguishable from the others, even the few women, their hair cropped nearly as short as their male classmates'. As it was meant to be, Kat reminded herself, moving to the shoulder of the road to let them pass. She'd joined the reserves and been through boot camp at the same age as the cadets, had been to war, even, and she understood the necessity of these first few months. But these kids seemed different to Kat, more naïve and at the same time more cynical than she and her fellow recruits had been, and she found herself wanting to protect them.

The bulk of the pack passed Kat, then the last few runners appeared, their breathing labored as they struggled up the hill.

F/2154796

Kat knew from experience that it was from this group that some of the most determined cadets came, the ones with something to prove.

"You gotta want it!" One of the upperclassmen had circled back and was hounding the stragglers, his abuse focusing on a lone female cadet at the very tail end of the group.

Kat recognized the girl, a soft-spoken and obviously capable young woman, from her first-year Arabic class. She was close to tears, her gray T-shirt and red shorts wet through with sweat, her face nearly purple from the effort of trying to keep pace with the others.

Kat met the girl's eyes and smiled encouragingly. There were few enough female cadets at the school, and Kat took their successes and failures personally. But the girl didn't return Kat's smile. The look on her face when she glanced back was a mixture of anger and fear, as if Kat's sympathy were a threat to her very survival.

Kat turned her head away and picked up her pace, stretching her legs out for the last half mile of her run, down into the ravine that marked the back edge of campus and up the last torturous hill, then across the parade grounds. She was breathing hard when she reached her front door, her clothes soaked through. When she stepped into the air-conditioned chill of the foyer, goose bumps rippled across her wet body.

There was a message on her answering machine, the red light blinking insistently, as Kat was certain it had not been when she left for her run. Colin, she thought, unable to imagine anyone else it could be at such an early hour. Calling to offer the day's first consolation, though this hardly seemed like something he would do, especially now, with the way things had been between them. Whatever it was, Kat told herself, feeling guiltily relieved that she hadn't been home when he called, it would wait until she showered.

Making her way into the bathroom, she turned on the taps, stripped herself of her sodden clothes, and stepped into the tub. Three years to the day, she thought, to the minute almost, and she could see her brother doing the same thing in his apartment in Astoria. An early run and then a quick shower before taking the train to work.

Afterward, when she had gone alone to collect his things, his running clothes had been there on the back of the bathroom door. Shorts and jock strap, salt-stained shirt that still reeked of him.

She rinsed herself and toweled off, then slipped into her robe and padded into the kitchen, punching the answering machine's playback button on the way. There was a short beep, then a male voice, a familiar Scottish brogue:

Katy?

Katy, it's Stuart.

Kat stiffened. Not Colin, then, but his best friend. Stuart had been staying at Colin's off and on since their team came back from Afghanistan. He and Kat knew each other tangentially, in the awkward way that people in their situation usually did. Both envying the other more than they should, jealous of what one offered that the other couldn't. Though, Kat couldn't help thinking, there was no longer much reason for Stuart to be jealous, hadn't been for some time. Since those first frenzied weeks at Bagram, her and Colin's relationship had been entirely chaste.

Sorry to call so early, he apologized. *I was hoping I might catch you before you got off to work. Can you phone me as soon as you get in? I'm at Colin's.*

Something was wrong, Kat told herself, ducking back into the living room and replaying the message, trying to gauge the timbre of Stuart's voice. Something had happened to Colin. Aside from the obligatory cordial exchanges that were an inevitable consequence of their respective relationships with Colin, Kat and Stuart did not speak, and they certainly did not call each other in the wee hours for a friendly chat.

Ticking off all the worst possibilities, Kat punched Colin's number with fumbling hands, counting five hours ahead to British time. Past noon in Scotland. And on this side of the world she was five minutes away from being late for the day's first obligation.

"Pick up," Kat whispered impatiently.

On the other side of the Atlantic, the phone rang and rang, but there was no answer.

THINGS ARE GOING TO GET UGLY. Harry had said. It was March 13, their first, confused meeting after the bombing at the Atocha station, and things were already ugly. By now everyone knew it was a group of Moroccans, not ETA, who had carried out the attacks, and the cafés and mosques of Lavapiés were teeming with civil guardsmen. But this wasn't what Harry had meant.

They'll be sending me home now for sure, Jamal. Do you understand what that means? No more gin rummy. No more pink abaya. Harry had motioned out the window toward the apartment across the street, and Jamal had felt himself blush.

Jamal could always tell when Harry had been drinking, and he was drunker than usual that afternoon. Jamal had consoled himself with this fact, and with the hope that Harry's dark prediction was nothing more than his usual drama. But two weeks later Justin was there at the apartment on the Calle Tres Peces and Harry was suddenly gone.

Jamal's ankle was throbbing when he finally made his way across the Calle de la Magdalena and into the thicket of tenements that was Lavapiés. He'd landed badly on the rooftop, wrenching his foot beneath him, and the pain was more agonizing with each step he took. A bad sprain at least, maybe worse, but there was no time to tend to it now.

He turned off the Calle del Avenida Maria and stopped short, scanning the block ahead of him. The butcher shop was dark, the metal security gate pulled across the windows and locked for the night. A figure moved in the doorway that led up to Jamal's room, and for an instant the boy felt his heart seize up. Then the person stepped onto the sidewalk and Jamal realized with relief that the man was his neighbor, one of the dozen or so Somalis who occupied the cramped room across the landing from his.

Jamal watched the Somali turn and amble restlessly down the street, then made his way cautiously to the doorway, glancing over his shoulder as he went. That he'd lost the two men at the hotel was little comfort to the boy. The Americans knew about his room above the butcher shop. If someone wasn't there already, they soon would be. Jamal would have to work quickly.

He let himself into the dark foyer and balanced for a moment on his good foot, letting his ankle rest, listening for any anomaly or counterfeit in the familiar sounds of the building. Jamal had spent most of his life in places like this—prisons and orphanages and refugee camps—and he was intimate with the habits of men living in collective solitude. Above him in the darkness there was a sudden, sharp cry of pleasure—the dream of a wife, or the sleep-shod gropings of one body imposing itself on another. Part of a long litany of humiliations, shames they all shared and yet never spoke of. From behind the door of the Somalis' room came the low hum of African music. The same tinny tape Jamal had heard a hundred times now.

Confident, for the moment at least, that he was alone, Jamal limped upward. The cheap padlock he'd installed on the door to his room was undisturbed, but still, Jamal's hands shook as he slid his key from around his neck and let himself inside.

He let the door fall closed behind him, then made his way forward, navigating the simple furnishings: bed and table and chair, single electric burner on which he'd cooked two years of meals. All of it shoddy and worn, and yet he'd been happy to have it, had cried that first night, realizing that it was his. After so long without privacy, it had taken him some time to get used to the luxury, and now he desperately didn't want to give any of it up. But it was no longer safe for him here, would not be so again.

Crouching on his good leg, Jamal pushed the bed aside and ran his fingers along the bottom of the wall, searching for the loose seam he knew by heart, popping the baseboard free. He'd discovered this makeshift safe several months after moving in, its contents left by some former inhabitant. Faded pictures of a woman and three children. A letter in a language Jamal had been unable to read, its creases worn to loose fibers from constant folding and unfolding.

Jamal stuck his hand into the blind niche and pulled out the small metal box he'd stashed there. On the rare occasions he had extra cash, this was where he kept it. But since Harry's departure there had been fewer and fewer of these occasions, and there was no money in the box now, just a ragged scrap of paper, a string of digits in a drunken scrawl. And the letters ES KEPLER, the print bisected where the paper had been torn away.

If you're ever in real trouble, Harry had said as he scribbled the number in the thumb-worn book he always carried in his coat pocket—*My Koran,* he'd called it. And then, as if suddenly realizing what he'd done, *I can't promise anything, you know.*

Moving quickly, Jamal stuffed the paper into his pocket, then gathered a change of clothes from the cardboard box that held his belongings. Everything else he would bequeath to the room's next tenant, as the former inhabitants had done for him.

He headed back out onto the landing and down the stairs to the foyer, then down one more flight into the building's dank basement. Suleman, the butcher, slept here sometimes, when his wife kicked him out, but Jamal was relieved to find the narrow cot behind the stairs empty tonight.

Switching on the bare overhead bulb, Jamal lifted the mattress from the cot's frame and pushed aside Suleman's stash of magazines, searching for the spare shop key he'd seen on previous visits. *You like?* Jamal could hear the butcher, his fat face flushed and sweaty with expectation as he displayed his collection to Jamal, his teeth sharp as a jackal's. And Jamal had nodded, understanding perfectly what was required of him.

Jamal took the key and unlocked the door that led to the butcher shop's basement storeroom, then stepped inside. There had been lambs here just days before, and their odor still filled the room—the pungent smell of lanolin and shit, the sourness of adrenaline and fear.

Choking back panic, the boy groped his way forward through the darkness. Out into the basement abattoir and up the narrow stairs to the shop. It was a thief's work, a trade he knew well, but he hadn't come to the shop to steal, knew from experience that Suleman never kept money in his battered old register.

Jamal skirted the butchering tables and moved toward the front counter, inhaling the death stink of the shop. Rancid fat and curing flesh. Bleach in the mop bucket. The light from the street filtered in through the metal window gates, casting a checkerboard of shadows across the hulking refrigerator case, the bloody and tongueless lambs' heads laid out in a neat row on the bottom shelf.

Jamal had never made a phone call, not once, had never had a reason to, and he was nervous as he set his hand on the heavy black receiver and pulled the paper from his pocket. He lifted the receiver to his ear, as he'd seen others do so many times, then put his finger on the key pad and punched in the numbers.

There was a tone in his ear, and another, each ring long and flat. And then a voice, so much closer than Jamal had imagined it would be. Not Mr. Harry but a woman.

"Hello?"

Jamal hesitated, suddenly flustered. He hadn't expected this, hadn't prepared himself for the possibility that someone besides Harry would answer, and now he didn't know what to say.

"Hello?" the woman repeated.

"I speak to Mr. Harry, please," Jamal blurted out.

"You've got the wrong—" the woman began, but Jamal didn't wait for her to finish.

"Mr. Harry," he insisted, and then, glancing down at the scrap of paper in his hand, "You are Es Kepler?"

There was silence on the other end. For a moment Jamal thought the woman was gone, then he heard her laughing.

"Of course. Mr. Harry," she said, leaning hard on the "mister."

"Please." Jamal took a breath and gathered himself, trying to piece the words together so the woman would understand. The phone was much more daunting than he'd thought it would be, his normally steady English failing him fast. "Please," he repeated. "It's important. Real trouble here."

"Yeah?" she said, suddenly bitter. "Well, if you find Harry, tell him there's real trouble here, too."

NOT EVERYONE HAS IT *as easy as you do*. It was the last thing Kat had said to her brother, at least the last thing of any real substance.

It was July of that summer, his last summer, and Kat, facing a six-hour layover at JFK on her way to Paris, had suggested they meet. They'd never been particularly close. Max was six years younger than she, the product of her mother's third marriage, one husband removed from Kat's father. Normally, Kat wouldn't have thought to tell him she was passing through, but just a month earlier their mother had announced that she was getting divorced for the fifth time. When Max e-mailed, obviously wanting to talk, Kat proposed a rendezvous.

They met in Brooklyn, at a Greek diner halfway between the airport and the city. It was a weekday, midafternoon, and Max had left work early to come. He hadn't taken the job at the Trade Center yet but was temping at an office in midtown. He had a girlfriend, he said, and was making enough money to pay the bills.

Kat wanted to be happy for him, and she told him she was, but there was a mean part of her that hated him for the ease with which he navigated life. Part of it was the luck of the draw, the fact that his father had money, while Kat's did not. That while Kat had paid for college with ROTC scholarships and part-time jobs, Max had skated through without so much as a student loan. But there was an effortlessness to Max and his dealings with the world that had nothing to do with wealth, a facility Kat simply did not possess, and for which she could never forgive him.

"So what are you doing in Paris?" he asked at last, then added, "I almost forgot. This'll be your first time out of the country, won't it?"

"I finally downgraded to ready reserve," she explained, conscious of the fact that Max had spent an entire year abroad after finishing college. "I thought I'd do some traveling. Maybe try to pick up some teaching jobs along the way."

"You're planning to stay in Europe?"

"Europe. North Africa. Egypt. Turkey. Who knows?" Finally finished with her dissertation, freed from the yoke of her weekend and summer reserve duties, Kat was hoping to become acquainted with the world with which she had fallen in love from afar.

"Sounds ambitious," Max remarked. "I've got a friend in Cairo who runs a language school. Guy I met in Essaouira. Now, that's a beautiful place; you should really try to make it down there. In any case, I'll e-mail you his information if you want it. I'm sure he could find work for you."

Kat shrugged. She knew he was trying to be helpful, but she felt patronized by the offer. "Sure," she said. "Whatever."

When they finally broached the subject of the divorce, Kat found herself defending her mother's actions, not out of reason but out of spite. Wanting, she knew, to beat her brother down.

"Not everyone has it as easy as you do," she'd told him, cruelly, after he'd expressed his concern.

Max had let the comment go, but they had parted soon afterward, Kat insisting that she had to get back to the airport, though she still had two hours to spare. They had not hugged, as siblings—even those who were angry with each other—might have done, but shaken hands. Then Kat had climbed into a cab, leaving her brother standing alone on the sidewalk outside the diner, looking uncharacteristically ill at ease.

THE COMMANDANT OF CADETS shook Kat's hand and gave her a stiff little bow. One of the many obligations of her grief, Kat thought, the terms of which were not hers to dictate. She nodded in somber acknowledgment, as she knew she was expected to do, then watched the man turn and make his way to the front of the chapel.

From the walls on either side of her, the dead and dying looked down. The faces of young men in battle preserved on canvas. Wounds in garish crimson, the artist's hundred-year-old brushstrokes visible still, the violence with which he had painted the scene.

During the Civil War, the school's cadet corps had been called to the aid of a badly diminished Confederate unit, and had ended up winning a key battle against Union troops. Some fifty boys had died in the fighting, and had been rewarded here on earth with permanent residence in the school's pantheon. The myth of the battle was invoked at nearly every school gathering. Each year on the day of their deaths, the cadets' names were read at the roll call and places were set for them in the mess.

The commandant took his place at the pulpit and began the brief ceremony. Then the school chaplain gave a sermon about God and righteousness, about the courage of those who had died and the cowardice of their murderers, and God's mercy at the end.

Kat had heard it all too many times before, and she let her eyes wander across the mural as he spoke, over the faces of the cadets charging determinedly forward. She knew for a fact that the artist had not been there that day, but had reenacted the scene decades later, using his own son as one of the models, and that the charge then had been on a hill of sweet pea and clover, with nothing but the breeze pushing them back. She also knew that the artist had returned years later, after his son had gone to Europe to fight in World War II. And that cadets had found him late one night, trying desperately to erase the boy's image from the canvas.

"Judge me, O Lord," Kat heard the voices behind her say in practiced unison, the first words of the Twenty-sixth Psalm. "For I have walked in mine integrity: I have trusted also in the Lord; therefore I shall not slide."

Kneeling, she ducked her head and glanced back at the rows of cadets, the sea of gray uniforms and bent shoulders, heads stubbled like those of newly hatched chicks.

Examine me, O Lord, and prove me:
try my reins and my heart.
For thy loving-kindness is before mine eyes:
and I have walked in thy truth.
I have not sat with vain persons,
neither will I go in with dissemblers.
I have hated the congregation of evildoers;
and will not sit with the wicked.
I will wash mine hands in innocency:
so will I compass thine altar, O Lord.

FIVE

"She's awake?" Dick Morrow asked, watching Marina set the kettle on the stove.

The woman nodded, then turned away from him and busied herself with Susan's breakfast tray. A pot of tea and two sturdy mugs. One of those horrible canned shakes. Chocolate this morning, Morrow noted, remembering Susan's fondness for the truffles at Fauchon and wondering how she stomached these drinks.

"Today, maybe good day," the old nurse remarked with characteristic Russian grimness, as if this scrap of positive news served only to remind her of the bad days to come.

It had been Susan's decision to hire her. This woman, out of all the nurses they had seen. It was almost, Morrow concluded, as if Susan had chosen the Russian to punish him.

I suppose you want the pretty Filipino, Susan had snapped when he'd questioned her choice. And Morrow had thought, no, any of them would be fine. Anything but this beast.

He'd even gone so far as to have Marina checked out through the old channels. But, to Morrow's disappointment, she'd turned up clean, the product of American evangelicals who sponsored believers from the former Soviet Union. Just a nurse from Leningrad who'd whored herself to God for a plane ticket and a green card.

And now here she was in his house, a ghost of all the Russians he'd known. Grim-faced, suffering the burdens of life. The two of them knocking into each other in the early-morning stillness that, by all rights, should have been his alone.

The kettle shrieked, and Marina's knobby hand sprang for it. She filled the teapot, spooned a generous dollop of blackberry jam into each mug. The jam was hers. She had canned it herself, for all Morrow knew. The first time he'd seen the label-less jar on their kitchen counter, Morrow had thought immediately of Moscow—of the horrible little grocery store near the embassy, half-vacant shelves stocked with sticky bottles of fruit syrup and conserves that looked as if they'd been fabricated in some babushka's kitchen. Misstamped cases of Cuban peanuts one week, moldy Syrian oranges the next. Leftovers to feed an empire.

Marina lifted the tray and turned back to face Morrow. "You take?" she asked.

Goading him, he thought, already fully aware of his answer. He shook his head. "She's expecting you."

"Yes," she agreed. But as she moved past him she grunted just slightly, as if to remind him of the boundlessness of her contempt.

Morrow listened to her trudge down the hall, then poured himself a cup of coffee and climbed the stairs to his office. The second floor was his, and his alone now. Susan couldn't climb the stairs, and Marina wouldn't, having made it clear from the beginning that her services were for Susan alone. When she'd first arrived, Morrow had made the mistake of slipping a shirt into Susan's laundry, and Marina hadn't acknowledged him for a full week afterward.

The kind who would have fingered her own mother to the NKVD for a bag of sugar or a week's ration of toilet paper, Morrow had thought then. *Yes, Comrade. The woman is a traitor, Comrade. I have seen it with my own eyes.*

Morrow checked his watch, then picked up the phone and dialed Peter Janson's home number in McLean.

"Hi, Dick." Janson's wife, Anne, answered before Morrow had a chance to speak.

The miracle of caller ID, Morrow reminded himself, quelling decades of habitual suspicion. Yet another battle Susan had won. *For chrissakes, Dick, I want to live like a normal person for once.*

"Good morning, Anne. Is Pete still around?"

Morrow heard her move the phone from her mouth, call out, "Pete! It's Dick Morrow." Then she was back. "How's Susan doing?"

"She has her good days," he lied.

"I've been meaning to come by," Anne offered.

Silence, then the merciful interruption of Janson's voice. "I've got it up here, Anne."

"Tell Susan I said hello," Anne said hastily.

Morrow listened for the click that told him she had hung up, then waited a moment more before speaking. "Any word on the boy?" he asked finally.

"Nothing since Andrews and Damien lost him. They're pretty sure he's bolted. It looks like he cleared some stuff out of his room."

"Any idea where to?"

"It's anyone's guess. But he's a smart kid. He won't stick around Madrid. I'm thinking he may be heading home."

"To Morocco?" Morrow was skeptical. It had been more than four years now since the boy left, with less than nothing to go back to.

"He's scared, Dick," Janson offered. "And it's close."

"Anything more on Bagheri?" Morrow asked.

"Nothing." Janson was silent for a moment. "I've been looking at the kid's file," he said at last. "There's a woman. One of the interrogators from Bagram. Apparently they were pretty close."

"Agency?"

"Army," Janson answered. "She teaches Arabic at a military college out in the Shenandoah Valley."

"She's retired?" Morrow asked.

"Ready reserve," Janson said. "So technically she's still ours." And then, as if anticipating what Morrow was about to say, "I feel good about this, Dick."

"Well, I don't. We'd need someone on her, in case she actually finds the boy."

"Andrews and Damien are still in Madrid."

Morrow thought for a moment. "The boy saw them?"

"Andrews, yes. Damien, maybe."

"No. We'll use Kurtz. I assume everything's cleared up on the London end of things."

"They might know each other," Janson reminded him. "From Bagram."

Morrow thought for a moment. A bad idea, and getting worse, he told himself. But then Kurtz had as much to lose as the rest of them. More, in fact. "Fax me what you have on the woman," Morrow said. "I'll drive out to see her this morning."

A DECADE PREPARING FOR THIS MOMENT. Kat had thought as she stood at the Tangier ferry dock, paralyzed by fear. Ten years of study, and now that she was facing the place she wanted nothing more than to turn and run. She had expected a different Morocco altogether, Africa and Islam tempered by years of colonial rule into something pleasantly and unthreateningly foreign. But for this—the formless women in their black chadors, the grubby children who would not be put off, the frightening men with their leering offers of assistance—she had not been prepared.

Europe. North Africa. Egypt. Turkey, she could hear herself say, *Who knows?*

That first night, humiliated by her own weakness, recoiling at the filth and desperation of the place, she had gratefully allowed herself to be driven past the squalor of the medina, past the African prostitutes ranting outside the Bab el-Marsa and the mass of child beggars at the port entrance, to a tourist hotel in the *ville nouvelle*.

Later, safely ensconced in her room, with its beige furnishings and fleur-de-lis wallpaper, she had assured herself that her discomfort had been a product of exhaustion; that, once she ate and slept, the panic she'd felt since stepping off the ferry would fade. The next day she would get up early and have coffee at one of Burroughs's little cafés on the Petit Socco, then hike up through the crooked streets of the old city to the casbah.

But in the morning, after sleeping late, she ordered room service instead: strong French coffee and croissants, with two fried eggs. Sustenance, she told herself, for the day ahead. And what did it matter if she lingered? She had weeks here, months if she so chose.

By the time she showered and dressed and left her room, it was early afternoon on the eleventh of September, the world she was about to enter and her relation to it already utterly and irrevocably changed.

Downstairs, a small group of guests were huddled around the lobby television watching the first disturbing images of the attack on the World Trade Center. The second plane had not yet hit, and the early consensus was that there had been a terrible accident. But even in those first confusing moments Kat had known otherwise, had understood that she would be going home. And despite herself, despite the horror of what had happened, she had been relieved that this was the case, that she would not have to venture any further.

She had not known about Max then, had not even imagined that her brother might be there in the towers. It was almost three weeks before she called her mother and learned that he was among the missing.

A week later, while Kat was still in New York sorting through the detritus of Max's unfinished life, the official notification came through, informing Kat that she had three days to pack her bags and close up her own life before reporting for duty. Two months after that, she found herself on the frigid tarmac in Karshi-Khanabad, waiting for the C-130 that would take her and the rest of the interrogation team to Kandahar.

KAT KICKED HER FRONT DOOR CLOSED behind her and lunged for the phone, slamming the receiver to her ear without bothering to look at the caller ID.

"Hello?"

Stuart's voice was so much like Colin's, their lowland accents so closely matched, that for a moment Kat was fooled into thinking everything was fine.

"Colin?"

He hesitated before correcting her. "No, it's Stu."

"What's wrong?" she asked immediately.

"It's Colin. I'm so sorry, Katy."

She knew without asking that she had been right. "What happened?"

Stuart paused, struggling audibly to keep his voice together. "Overdose," he said. "Morphine sulfate. The stuff he'd been taking for his arm. They found him two days ago in a pub bathroom in King's Cross."

"So it was an accident, then?" Kat heard herself say. "No, Katy. I don't know all the details, but evidently his prescription was time-release. He'd sped up the dosage somehow. Mixed it in with his drink." Another pause, and that struggle again.

Kat said nothing. She'd known Colin was unhappy. Losing his arm had been hard for him—beyond hard—but it had been three years now, and she had sensed from their last few conversations that he was finally moving on.

There was Stuart's trial coming up, of course. He'd been charged in the death of one of the Bagram detainees. Colin had been the only other member of their team to witness the man's death, and his testimony at the court-martial would weigh heavily in the case against his friend. But they all knew that the proceedings were merely a formality. The man had been asthmatic, something Stuart could not possibly have known, and had died under interrogation as a result of his illness. If anything, Colin's testimony would mitigate Stuart's responsibility.

"Are they sure?" Kat asked.

She felt numb, removed from herself. An accident she had been prepared for. A fall while climbing in the Cuillins or a wreck on his old Triumph. Trying to prove to himself that he was still the same person he'd been before al-Amir. But this, this she could not have imagined. It was a choice she would have thought utterly foreign to the person she had known and loved.

Stuart cleared his throat. "He knew what he was doing, Kat."

Neither of them spoke then, and for a moment Kat thought Stuart was crying. She wouldn't have been surprised, had seen more than her share of tough-as-nails Special Forces guys break down at makeshift funerals at Kandahar and Bagram.

"There will be a service of some sort," he offered at last. "I expect his parents will be arranging it. I can let you know. . . ."

"Yes," Kat told him, grateful for something concrete to focus on. The requisite motions of mourning. "Of course."

"I'm sorry," he said again. "I'm so sorry."

Then there was nothing more to say.

IT WAS THE SPRING OF 2002. and the Guantánamo facility had finally opened, bringing a merciful end to the operation at Kandahar. After four inhuman months at the southern base, defecating into barrels and subsisting on MREs and dust, Kat and the other interrogators had happily welcomed news of an impending transfer north to Bagram.

Kat was one of the last of her team to go, and one of the few not leaving Afghanistan. "That's what we get for being part-timers," one of her fellow reservists had complained when the orders came down. "Stuck here full-time." But Kat had thought, At least it'll keep us out of Iraq.

Kat had four days of R&R coming to her, and she'd chosen to head to Oman before settling in at Bagram. Kandahar was a virtual ghost town by then, and Kat found herself the sole passenger as she hustled her gear onto the C-130 that would take her north to K-2.

"Bet you've never flown on a private jet before." The air-force crewman winked as he secured Kat's gear for the flight. He was younger in looks than in years, with a wily Texas smile and oversized ears. "It's the milk run today. We've got to stop at Bagram and drop off some supplies." Another wink. "Give you a chance to check out your new digs."

Reports of a virtual Club Med in the desert had been trickling south for weeks. Hot showers and real meals. Uzbek beer and sunbathing on the roof of the interrogation facility. But as the C-130 finally dipped low for landing, skimming the jagged terrain, Kat's first view of Bagram through the plane's right portal was of a sprawling city of war.

Dirt revetments branched off the airfield like suburban cul-de-sacs; jet-size bunkers burrowed into the rocky, upchurned earth. A bleak neighborhood of tents blanketed the land along the main runway, the makeshift military structures mingling with the larger, Soviet-era buildings. All of it hunkered in the footprint of some two thousand years of bloodshed and defeat.

As the plane braked to a stop on the runway, a handful of scraggly soldiers appeared, as if from nowhere, and scrambled up the massive cargo ramp. Like most of the Special Forces soldiers Kat had encountered in Afghanistan, the men were not in uniform, at least not in the traditional sense. Their clothes were an improvised mix of standard Afghan attire and Western military wear. Mushroomy *pakols* and knee-length *chapans* paired with army-issue camouflage. The men's faces were shoe-leather tan, their beards long and unkempt.

At first, seeing their Colt M-16s, Kat mistook them for Americans, but when the Alfred E. Neuman staff sergeant hustled back to greet them Kat saw one of the men raise a small Velcro flap on the arm of his jacket and flash a Union Jack.

Not asking permission, Kat had thought at the time, for the fact that these men didn't need permission was something she had come to understand early on during her tenure in this strange place. That in a world where a pair of new socks required the signature of a senior officer, these men could hop a plane without answering a single question.

Kat didn't pay much attention to the soldiers on the flight up. The deafening roar of the C-130's engines made conversation impossible, and most of the men had taken the opportunity to sleep. But as the plane banked toward the landing strip at K-2, Kat looked up and saw one of the men watching her.

It was Colin.

SIX

David Kurtz turned off Whitechapel Road and headed north along Brick Lane, letting his ears bathe in the cacophony of languages. Friday prayers at the Jamme Masjid had let out not long before and there was a preponderance of Arabic on the street, along with the usual mix of Bengali and Urdu and Hindi, and the odd remaining snippet of cockney English or Hebrew.

Women in full *hijab* ducked past him on the sidewalk, some in groups of three or four, some walking just behind their husbands with small children in tow. Little boys in suits and preadolescent girls in ruffled dresses. The newest arrivals, Kurtz thought, watching the shrouded figures navigate the sea of Westernized flesh, skirting second-generation Bengali girls in hip-huggers and high heels, Hindu women in midriff-baring saris.

From the front window of one shop, racy Bollywood film posters looked out on the passing crowd, offering glimpses of dark-skinned women in suggestive poses. In the neighboring storefront, dour *abayas* and chadors hung crookedly behind the glass. And farther along the street the old Jewish bakery

perfumed the air with the smell of freshly baked bagels, sustenance for the cabbies and clubgoers who would make their
way to the East End much later in the evening.

Even in the mismatched crowd, Kurtz was glaringly con-
spicuous, his physical stature and blond hair marking him in-
delibly as the other. And yet there was nowhere else in
London, and very few places in the Western world, where he
felt so comfortably at home. Moving with the gait of someone
who knew exactly where he was going, Kurtz crossed Han-
bury Street and ducked into a doorway marked KENSINGTON
COURT.

*Not to be confused with the Kensington on Cromwell Road,
I assume,* Peter Janson had joked when Kurtz first gave him
the name of the hotel. And Kurtz had thought, No, not in a
million years, thank God.

"Message, sir." The Bengali proprietor flagged Kurtz down
as he entered the postage-stamp reception area. "Your brother,
sir. He would like you to call him as soon as possible."

Not a hint that the man thought otherwise, and yet Kurtz
couldn't help wondering. Four years he'd kept a room here,
since he'd first left the Agency and gone to work for Janson
and Morrow. Four years of odd hours and midnight depar-
tures, and always that same jester's grin to greet him. As if the
presence of a beefy blond American selling funeral supplies
out of a Brick Street hovel was the most natural thing in the
world.

*Hello, Mr. Kurtz. Welcome back, Mr. Kurtz. Business again,
Mr. Kurtz? That's the way it is with the dead: there are more of
them every day.*

"Thank you, Hamidur." Kurtz nodded, then started up the
impossibly narrow stairs to his room.

The funerary salesman was an old cliché from the Farm, a
guaranteed conversation stopper for use in waiting rooms or
on long flights, anywhere questions were best kept to a mini-

mum. By the time Kurtz joined the Agency it was more joke than anything, a good laugh for the new recruits, but Kurtz hadn't forgotten about it, and before leaving for his first posting he'd ordered an Edison Funeral Supply catalog to take with him.

He'd used it immediately, on his flight from Dulles to Amsterdam, leafing through the pages of cavity fluid and Eterna-Cribs, until the nervously talkative Dutch woman beside him fled to an empty seat.

What the creaky old OSS retiree at the Farm had failed to tell them, and most likely had not known, was that the farther east one traveled the less effective the ruse became. Once you breached the boundaries and safety of the Western world, death became less remarkable, and the accoutrements of death nothing more than a curiosity. This was something Kurtz had discovered on his own, though by the time he did, he'd been playing his part too long to give it up.

Kurtz slipped off his shoes and set them just outside the door, then undid the lock and let himself into his room. There was a smell to the space that he found immediately comforting. Dust and cheap disinfectant, the slivers of sandalwood-scented soap the maid left each week. And the sharp odor of cooking that lingered in the linens and drapes. Old grease and heavy spices from the kitchen two floors below.

On the desk was the newest version of the Edison catalog and Kurtz's black sample case. On the luggage stand sat a single small suitcase, neatly packed. Four years in this room, and this was all Kurtz had brought of himself. Even his Dopp kit was zippered and stowed.

He sat down on the bed and picked up the phone, glancing at his watch as he did so, noting the time back in the States before dialing Janson's number.

"Yes?" Janson answered on the second ring.

"You wanted me to call?" Kurtz asked.

"Yes. I need you to take a trip."

"You've found our Iranian friend?"

"No. It's the boy. He's gone."

Kurtz thought for a moment, letting the implications of the boy's disappearance sink in. "I thought we had a team in Madrid."

Janson didn't answer.

"Gone on his own or taken?" Kurtz asked finally.

"On his own, I presume."

"Any guesses where he's heading?"

"My money's on Casablanca. It's where he came from."

"And where he ran from once already," Kurtz reminded the man.

"Still," Janson countered. "It's home."

"Where do you want me first?" Kurtz asked.

"There's an overnight train that will get you to Madrid in the morning."

"And from there?"

Janson cleared his throat—a sign, Kurtz had learned long before, that the news to come was something he would doubtless prefer not to hear. "There's someone from army intel meeting you there."

Kurtz was silent.

"Special circumstances," Janson said, sensing Kurtz's unease. "It's the interrogator from Bagram. She's the one who turned the boy in the end. They were quite close, as I understand it. It will help to have someone he trusts."

She, Kurtz thought, *Kat,* but he didn't say anything.

"Any reason this is going to be a problem?" Janson asked.

He already knows how this is going to end, Kurtz thought, hearing the hesitation in the other man's voice, the gravity of the question.

"No," he said. "No problem at all."

MAJOR?

Kat looked up from the papers she was grading to see the dean of faculty at her office door.

"General," she answered, rising from her chair.

Still playing army? she could hear Colin say, and suddenly she was embarrassed by the pretensions of the place. Her rank a lie, even. The rank of an officer.

The man shifted from one foot to the other, glanced down at his fingers. Nervous, Kat had always thought, uncomfortable with his own authority.

"How's the new crop of cadets treating you?" he asked, with the forced joviality of someone who's about to break a particularly bad bit of news.

"Fine," Kat answered.

"There's someone coming to see you this afternoon," the dean said. "From Arlington."

Kat motioned to the papers on her desk. "I have class."

"It's been taken care of."

No explanation other than this.

Out in the hall a pair of cadets passed, walking with the strained posture that was required of all first-year students: chins up, backs straight, hands at sides.

Arlington, Kat thought. The Pentagon. "Am I being called up, sir?"

The General hesitated. "I don't know," he said guiltily.

But Kat could tell that he did, and that she was.

SEVEN

"You don't like us very much, do you?" Colin had asked.

It was Kat's last night in Oman, and she'd taken a taxi to the sprawling, American-style mall in Muscat. She'd been hoping for a change of scenery, a respite from the constant sea of army drab, but the mall's one bar, an American chain, was packed with coalition soldiers.

She didn't recognize Colin at first. He was wearing real civilian clothes. Without his M-16 and his entourage, he looked like any other off-duty soldier or civilian contractor.

"Bagram to K-2," he reminded Kat, climbing onto the empty stool beside her. "I was the green-looking one sitting across from you, trying not to sick-up my last MRE."

Kat took a long pull off her Budweiser, then set the bottle down on the bar. A group of marines had commandeered the jukebox, and it was belting out "Sweet Home Alabama" for the third time in a row. "I thought you SAS guys weren't afraid of anything."

"SBS." Colin grinned. "Special *Boat* Service. No mention of airplanes."

He'd shaved since she'd seen him on the C-130, and the

skin on his jaw was pale where his beard had been. He was slight of build, not much taller than she was, with the body of an acrobat, all finesse.

"And you?" he asked. "What brings you to our little corner of paradise?"

"Army intel," Kat said. "I've been at Kandahar." She didn't mention her transfer to Bagram. She had already made up her mind to sleep with him if things worked out that way, and she didn't want to complicate the situation with the possibility that they might see each other again.

Colin laughed. "No wonder you hate us so much. I'd be jealous, too, with the leash they keep you on."

"It's called the law," Kat countered defensively. "Without it we're no better than they are."

"Don't tell me you actually believe that bullshit."

"Don't tell me you don't."

Colin tilted his beer to his lips and finished off the bottle. "As far as I can tell," he said, "we're already no better than they are."

She half expected him to leave then, and was relieved when he signaled the bartender for another drink.

"So why are you here?" she asked.

He shrugged. "My friends are here, my team. We watch out for each other—it's what we do. And you? God and country, I suppose, setting the score straight like your compatriots over there?" He nodded at the marines.

"My brother died on September eleventh," Kat said.

Colin colored slightly. "I'm sorry."

There was nothing trite about the remark, no expectation of anything in return, just the truth of it, and Kat immediately regretted having said anything, as if she'd hit him below the belt.

"I didn't love him," she said after a moment, surprising herself with the confession. "I didn't even like him." It was the first time she had admitted this to anyone, but it seemed necessary, a reciprocation of his honesty.

THE KIND OF TOWN Susan had always wanted them to end up in, Morrow thought as he surveyed the hilltop campus and the neighborhood beyond. He had been here before, not this town, exactly, but ones just like it. Green hills and narrow streets, brick colonials looming importantly over garden club lawns. Carriage rides for the weekenders from D.C. Main Street storefronts selling overpriced antiques and useless knickknacks. The reek of history and horse shit. The past and all its idols like a cudgel.

A place to which old spies retired. Wives finally getting their due after a lifetime of reheating dinners and going alone to dance recitals and high-school football games. On the drive in, Morrow had seen more than one of the discreet bumper stickers people like him used to quietly announce themselves as members of the club. It was the kind of thing you wouldn't see unless you knew to look.

It was early afternoon, but the sky was dark as dusk, the horizon bruised and black by the fist of a thunderstorm moving across the valley. Down on the green plain of the campus, a handful of figures hurried to beat the rain, while the first-year cadets kept their slow and painful stride.

On the far side of the parade ground, a solitary figure in faculty green emerged from behind one of the barracks and darted forward, her heels sinking into the soft turf as she ran, her stride shortened by the hem of her skirt.

"Here comes Major Caldwell now," the General said solicitously. He raised his arm over Morrow's shoulder and pointed out the window.

She was smaller than Morrow had expected, with a soldier's precision of appearance, her brown hair cropped short against her neck, her shirtsleeves holding their creases in the damp September heat. Though even from a distance Morrow's practiced eye told him her meticulousness did not come naturally. Fifteen years in the military and she still walked with the cautious carriage of someone who had worked hard to learn her part. Precision and something else. Anger, perhaps. Years of resentments. What she'd had to fight for and what others had been given.

Caldwell, Katherine. Morrow reminded himself of the details of the woman's file as he watched her cross the parade ground. *Date of Birth: 7/2/1971. Place of Birth: Boise, Idaho.* A childhood patched together from nearly a dozen addresses. Spokane. Billings. Denver. Tucson. Las Vegas. Mother's various boyfriends. Father nowhere to be found.

And the ROTC. Not a ticket in, Morrow thought, but a way out. She'd been a mediocre student at best through high school, but the army must have seen promise in her, enough to funnel her into the intelligence corps. And then on to the Defense Language Institute in Monterey, where someone must have seen more than just promise. For at the DLI she'd been assigned to the Arabic course, which, at the time, was not only one of the smallest programs but the most difficult as well. A matter of chance, someone else's idea of where she belonged, and yet the assignment must have fit.

The first fat drops of rain spattered the window and the woman picked up her pace, sprinting the last few yards before disappearing into the building below.

"What did she do her doctoral work in?" Morrow asked.

"Islamic soteriology," the General answered. "I'm afraid the details are a bit over my head."

Salvation theory, Morrow thought, not what he would have guessed at all. But, at the same time, her choice made a kind of sense to him.

"I assume you know about her brother," the General offered.

Morrow shook his head. There had been nothing about a brother in her official army file.

The man glanced hastily over his shoulder as if to confirm that they were alone, then lowered his voice a notch. "He was killed in the September eleventh attacks," he said reverently. "Twin Towers."

Kᴀᴛ sᴍᴏᴏᴛʜᴇᴅ ʜᴇʀ sʜɪʀᴛ with the side of her hand and started down the second-floor corridor toward the Dean's Office, her reflection wavering in the floor's mirror polish. She knocked once and waited, heard the General's voice telling her to come in.

There was a man at the window, a civilian by his dress. Wash-and-wear khakis and a blue cotton shirt. Expensive and decidedly unstylish brown walking shoes. A grandfather's Saturday-afternoon outfit, though there was nothing grandfatherly about him.

He turned and looked directly at Kat. "Sergeant Caldwell," he said, using Kat's army rank, her proper rank. And then, with a dismissive nod to the General, "You may go now."

The General hesitated before glancing sheepishly at Kat and turning for the door.

"Sergeant," the man mused, once they were alone. "I must admit, I'm rather baffled. Most people in your shoes wouldn't have chosen to enlist. You didn't want to be an officer?"

Kat shook her head. "I don't like giving orders, sir."

"And yet here you are—Major."

"It's a job, sir."

"Fair enough." The man smiled slightly, mockingly, as if her answer confirmed something he'd known all along. "The General tells me you're a salvation specialist."

"Yes, sir."

"And what about you?"

"What about me, sir?"

"Do you believe in God and heaven and all that?"

It was a question people often felt compelled to ask when they found out what Kat's particular area of study was. She answered as she always did. "No, sir."

The man's expression changed slightly. From curiosity to admiration, Kat thought. "Your brother's death must have been hard for you."

"Yes, sir."

"You were with the interrogation unit at Bagram in the spring of 2002?" he asked.

"Yes, sir."

"I understand you were part of the team that handled a young Moroccan boy."

Kat nodded, wary of whatever game the man was playing. "Jamal, sir. His name was Jamal."

The man turned his back to Kat and looked out the window at the rain sheeting down on the parade grounds. Seventy, Kat thought, seventy-five, fighting the physical signs of his age but showing them nonetheless.

"Am I being called up for duty, sir?" she asked, though she was fairly certain by now that this wasn't the case. She couldn't imagine the army sending someone three hours just to deliver mobilization orders. Especially someone on a civilian's salary.

"You were close, then? You and the boy."

"I'm not sure I would use the term 'close,' sir," Kat said.

"But you spent quite a bit of time together. He must have come to trust you."

Kat shrugged. "No more than the others, sir."

"Must have been a bit more," the man countered, turning back to face her. "After all, I understand it was you who turned him in the end."

"It would have happened no matter what, sir."

"Have you heard from him since he left Bagram?"

"No, sir. I was told he would be going to Spain. To Madrid. That was all."

Silence then, and the rain, the sound like the rush of incoming surf.

"Has something happened to him, sir?"

Lightning flickered in the window and Kat started a slow count, waiting for the thunder to reach them. One mile for each second, a childhood rumor she had never been able to shake.

"You understand, Sergeant Caldwell, what Jamal was doing in Madrid?"

Kat nodded. "More or less, sir."

Eyes and ears, she had told the boy. *All you have to do is watch and listen. And when they come to you with questions you tell them what you know.* Jamal had nodded with the eagerness of someone whose entire existence was predicated on his ability to please. *They'll take care of you, Jamal.*

And America? The boy had asked.

Yes, America.

"He's disappeared," the man said at last. "A few days ago. We believe he's in serious danger."

"I'll tell you what I can, but it's been a long time, sir. The information in my reports is probably a lot more accurate than anything I could give you now."

The man lifted his face slightly and his eyes caught the gray light of the storm. "You've misunderstood, Sergeant. We need you to find the boy."

Kat was confused. "The reports are straightforward, sir. You don't need me to read them." But she understood as she spoke that this wasn't what the man was saying, that he actually meant for her to go to Madrid.

"There's a flight from Dulles this evening," he said, glancing at his watch. "I'll take you home to collect your things."

Kat didn't move. "Is this an order, sir?"

The man looked at her. He was obviously not accustomed to having his requests second-guessed in this way, and found her question impertinent. "Yes, Sergeant," he said. "It is."

EIGHT

Harry Comfort crossed his arms over his chest and stared out the window of the Young Brothers' Freight office. Outside, the blue crescent of Hilo Bay was almost entirely obscured by the morning downpour. It had been raining since he'd left Kamuela and crossed the mystical line that separated the leeward side of the island from the windward side. Two blocks to the west, a desert. Two blocks to the east, a rain forest.

The door behind the counter opened and the clerk Harry had been dealing with for the past two weeks appeared with a shipping manifest in his hand. He was native Hawaiian, tall and broad-shouldered. Close to Harry's age, but still in possession of a nearly impossible shock of black hair.

"Nothing for Comfort," he said, in the maddeningly unhurried manner that Harry had come to understand was the hallmark of any island transaction, and that Harry found all the more irksome because he knew it was in fact a far superior method of encountering the world than his own.

The man handed Harry the manifest in order to prove his point. "See, no Comfort."

Harry scanned the list of names. The clerk was right; the Celestron had most definitely not come in on that morning's barge.

"I'll be back midweek," Harry said ridiculously, as if this piece of information somehow changed things.

The clerk shrugged. "Sure, man. Whatever."

Harry thought for a moment. "Is there a pay phone close by?"

"Just there." The man raised his arm and pointed out the glass doors of the freight office to an alcove on the other side of the rain-washed dock.

Two weeks, Harry thought, as he stepped out of the air-conditioned office and pulled his jacket up over his head. Two weeks since the Celestron should have arrived. Six times he'd made the drive to Hilo, and always the same answer. Huddling under his jacket, Harry dashed for the alcove the clerk had indicated.

The last man on earth without a cell phone, Char had jibed, and Harry had wanted to tell her what he knew—how many ways they could be used against a person, how easy it was to track someone with a cell phone.

He fished a handful of coins from his pocket, lifted the pay phone's grease-smeared receiver, and slid a quarter into the slot, half surprised to hear the dial tone in his ear. "Haoli girls blow," someone had scrawled on the wall. And in reply, "So does your sister." Harry fumbled the remaining coins into the slot and punched in the number he knew by heart.

Four rings. Five. Midafternoon at the old house. The TV on full blast and Irene's corgi napping on the couch. Either she hadn't heard the phone or she was pretending that she hadn't.

And then, suddenly, her voice out of the ether. "Hello?"

"It's Harry."

Nothing.

He could see it all so clearly, the yellow kitchen wallpaper and the garden through the window, the thick screen of vegetation at the back of the yard.

"I've been waiting for the Celestron."

"Yes, well, we're all waiting for something."

She hadn't shipped it, Harry thought. The one thing he wanted and she hadn't done it.

"What do you want?" he asked. Three minutes tops, and he had no more change in his pocket.

"I want our life, Harry. All of it. The same thing I've always wanted. You, without a goddamned destination. I deserve it, you know."

"Yes," Harry agreed, thinking, Anything—anything but this. "You do."

"I'm selling the house," she said after a moment. "There are some papers we need to take care of."

"I'll call Saul," he told her.

She sighed. "It's a signature, Harry. Do we really need the lawyers? I can overnight the papers this afternoon."

Harry hesitated.

"I'm not coming to find you, if that's what you think. I'll throw the goddamn address away when I'm done, if it'll make you feel better."

No, he thought, she deserves so much more than this. But he couldn't bring himself to speak.

The line hummed between them, the silence of her acquiescence as relentless as the thrum of the rain on the bay.

"Do you have a pen?" he asked at last, before rattling off the address of the Kona Pack and Mail, where he kept a box.

"And a phone number," she said. "You know FedEx won't deliver without a phone number."

"Is that it?" he asked, after giving her his number at the Tamarack Pines.

"I almost forgot. There was a call for you the other night. A boy, I think."

Harry lifted his head. "A boy?"

"Yes. Poor English. An Arabic speaker, I think. I thought it was a wrong number at first."

"Must have been," he told her.

"No." She laughed then, the laugh Harry had remembered and forgotten more times than he could count, and Harry felt his regret like the ache of an old wound. "He asked me if I was Kepler."

Regret and something else now, the ligature of panic tightening over his throat.

"Harry?"

Then a stranger's voice broke in, the operator asking for money he didn't have.

"I've got to go," he told Irene. "I'm sorry. I'm out of change."

The line was quiet, and for a moment Harry thought they'd been disconnected, then he heard Irene's voice again.

"It's okay, Harry. Really. It's okay."

ALGECIRAS WAS EXACTLY as Jamal remembered it. Not so much a city as an ugly sprawl of gray buildings fringing an even uglier port. A place, it seemed to Jamal, under constant construction. Everyone and every thing on their way to somewhere else. In the distance, the great monolith of Gibraltar loomed like a boxer's fist. Above it all lingered a brown scrim of industrial haze, the collective fumes of the countless lorries and ships that passed through the town each day. And fear. The *guardia civil* on every corner. The breath of the Ceuta and Melilla transit camps hot on his neck. Failure in the form of concrete and barbed wire. Two thousand people in a space built for a fourth that many. Everything Jamal had run from five years ago, and now he was going back.

Abdullah's shop on the Calle San Bernardo was unchanged

as well, the old storefront peering out from under its warped awning, fading signs in the window advertising imaginary services in some dozen languages. *Change. Cambio. Wechsel.* The obvious poverty of the place a deterrent to all but the most naïve travelers. And the boys on the street outside, not just as Jamal remembered them but as he had once been. Abdullah's sweepers, trolling for new arrivals; others who had been lucky enough to survive the trip across and who now possessed a willingness driven by fear and hunger. The real business of the shop.

Ducking the venomous glances of the older boys, Jamal crossed the Calle San Bernardo and made his way up the shop's crumbling front steps. It was a place where nothing good had happened, to which Jamal had never once wished to return, and he had to remind himself once again of why he'd come—of the horror of his first crossing, of how, too poor to bargain for a space on a boat, he'd nearly suffocated in an airless shipping container. It was an experience he did not want to repeat.

Jamal forced himself across the threshold and into the wanly lit interior of the shop. The same posters he recognized from five years earlier still hung on the walls. Advertisements scavenged from the back dumpster of a travel agency in an unsuccessful attempt to legitimize the place. Panoramas of Fès and Ouarzazate, the Roman ruins at Volubilis. The colors faded now from desert golds and reds to ghostly blues. A world at permanent twilight.

In the rear of the shop, above a long counter emblazoned with airline insignia, an ancient television blared the din of a football match. And behind the counter, his bulk perched on a low stool, facing the screen, sat Abdullah. The turtle, Jamal and the other boys had called him, the crude nickname a reference to more than just his wide body and pinched head.

Jamal took a tentative step forward, and Abdullah glanced

over his shoulder. "Get out," he said gruffly, assessing Jamal with a hasty but practiced glance. The merchandise too old or too worn for his purposes. And then, when Jamal didn't move, "What do you think this is? An employment agency?"

Jamal ducked his head slightly, acutely aware of just how much rested on this one gesture of acquiescence, on the perfection of it. A pantomime of fear and desire at the same time. *My child,* he could hear Abdullah say, *my favorite one.* Breath and lips hot on his neck. *I'm not hurting you, am I?*

For a moment Abdullah's face registered nothing and Jamal was convinced that the man had forgotten him, then the turtle shifted on his stool and leaned forward.

"Jamal?" he wheezed. His eyes were moist with greed.

NINE

The prisoners came in blind and confused, shackled, shuffling forward. Naked as newborns, some wailing, others soiling themselves. Not men but cattle to the slaughter.

Kat knew from experience that these first moments of confusion were her single best ally. Once the prisoners made it through the shock of in-processing, through the cavity searches and the haircuts and the delousings, and realized there was nothing worse that could be done to them, they became as uncooperative as two-year-olds. Of those who didn't break in the first twenty-four hours, most never would. The ones who did talk invariably had the least to give.

Kat and the others had been trained on the Cold War model of full-scale conflict between two superpowers. On the premise that most, if not all, of the prisoners they encountered would be happy to tell their captors whatever they knew for a pack of Marlboros and a can of Coke. Nothing had prepared them for the war they were now being asked to fight. None of them could even have imagined it.

At Kandahar, intake and interrogations went strictly by the book, using the standard timeworn approaches Kat and her colleagues had had drilled into them. Classics with names like Fear Up or Love of Comrades, which invariably worked like a charm in mock-up interviews, and which may in fact have been effective on disgruntled Soviet soldiers but were worse than useless in Afghanistan. The few deviations the interrogators eventually made from the manual, like the decision to keep prisoners awake while they themselves pulled all-nighters typing up situation reports, were slowly and painfully agreed upon.

It was Kat's second day at Bagram, her first live shift at the facility, and already she could see that it was a whole different world at the northern base. The prisoners were harder, for one thing, angrier and less cooperative than any of the detainees Kat had encountered at Kandahar. There was an undercurrent of hostility among the interrogators as well, a recklessness Kat had never seen before, a willingness not just to bend the rules but to break them.

"It's a whole different ball game up here," one of Kat's former team members from Kandahar had told her when they ran into each other in the mess the night before. "It takes some getting used to, but once you do it feels good to be in charge."

This shift in attitude wasn't the only difference Kat noticed at Bagram. There had been only a handful of non-military personnel at Kandahar, civilian intelligence men who went by the collective moniker of Other Government Agencies, and who, for the most part, kept to their cramped and makeshift offices in the old terminal building. At the Bagram base the OGAs were suddenly everywhere, including the in-processing facility.

Most of these civilians came from the alphabet soup of the intelligence world—the CIA, the FBI, or their foreign counterparts. But there were others whose loyalties were less easily identifiable, and for whose services the military had clearly paid.

Such arrangements were not unusual. A good portion of the army's support staff, including many mess and transportation workers, were civilian contractors. But the idea of intelligence contractors was something else altogether, and Kat wasn't quite sure what she thought of it. At the very least, it would take some getting used to.

In the world outside, it was frigid early morning, the bald half-moon glaring down on the dark and dusty expanse of the Shomali Plains, but the oversized watch on the wrist of the young MP who'd been assigned to Kat blinked a stubborn 6 PM. Mountain time, Kat observed, home time. Somewhere in Wyoming or Montana, the kid's family was sitting down to dinner without him.

Inside the facility, under the stuttering glow of the perpetually failing fluorescents, it might as well have been high noon. Two Special Forces teams had just returned from the mountains, and the old Soviet machine shop that served as the facility's in-processing center was crowded and chaotic, the air thick with stale sweat and urine—the stench of hundreds of unbathed bodies in an airless space.

Kat's post, at the far end of the cavernous room, was the detainees' final stop before the mammoth cages in the main prison, the last in a series of humiliations in which they'd been stripped of their original clothes and repackaged in bright-orange jumpsuits and rubber slippers, and the men's final hope at a chance for freedom before they were caught permanently and inextricably in the web of military bureaucracy.

The Special Forces raids had been routine at Kandahar, and Kat was familiar with their results. The ostensible purpose of the sweeps was to ferret out the last of the holdouts. But the raids, conducted under the cover of darkness, were by definition indiscriminate, and more often than not the majority of prisoners were neither Taliban nor Al Qaeda but luckless peasants. Not good men, necessarily, but not bad men, either, fathers and grandfathers whose only loyalty was to their own survival. To Kat and the other interrogators fell the impossible task of separating the former from the latter. It was a job that was made all the more difficult by an insurmountable and nearly constant language barrier.

Kat was muddling through an intake interview in her halting Pashto, trying to calm the toothless old man across the table from her enough to get his name and age, when she saw Kurtz coming toward her through the crowd. She shouldn't have been surprised to see him. In the wake of September 11, Arabic speakers were a rare and precious commodity in the intelligence community, and she had thought of Kurtz more than once, but she had never given serious thought to the possibility that their paths might cross. Now here he was, just as she remembered him.

"Sergeant," he said, stopping in front of her and making a stiff demi-bow. It was a gesture Kat remembered clearly from Monterey, an aspect of Kurtz's awkward formality that had made him seem vulnerable at the time. "I believe you have an Arabic speaker in the medical line."

He still hated her, Kat thought. Nearly a decade had passed, and he still hadn't forgiven her for rejecting him.

"Hello, David," she said. And then, because it seemed ridiculous to say nothing, "You look good."

Kurtz nodded. "I was sorry to hear about your brother."

So he knew, had already known she was on the base. "I didn't realize I was a celebrity."

"I was at Major Greeley's press briefing this morning," Kurtz explained. "He's quite honored to have you here."

Kat had heard about the Major's daily briefings from some of the other interrogators, how he started each session with a canned obit of one of the September 11 victims.

Kat rose from her chair and glanced at the young MP. "See if you can find him something to drink," she said, gesturing to the old man. And then, to Kurtz, "Your Arabic speaker?"

The medical line was the prisoners' first stop after the initial trauma of having their clothes cut off. It was touted as a safety measure, a way of ensuring that no weapons or harmful diseases made their way into the facility. But both the prisoners and the interrogators understood that the real purpose of the examination was to establish exactly where and with whom all control lay, to cement the contract of power and powerlessness between prisoner and jailer.

Normally, Kat made it a point to stay away from this part of the intake process. There was a vulnerability about the male body that she found disturbing, and she didn't want her feelings to get in the way later, during interrogations. As she and Kurtz approached, the few prisoners who didn't already have their hands over their genitals moved quickly to cover themselves.

"There," Kurtz said, pointing to a young boy near the back of the line.

Kat's first thought was that Kurtz was obviously mistaken. She had seen her share of foreign fighters, but they were all grown men. This prisoner was barely more than a child, his face smooth and unshaved, his thin body that of an adolescent. Though anyone under sixteen was strictly off limits, a few underage locals were often swept up in the raids. Standard protocol was to release them back to their villages with a consolation bag of chocolate bars and hot tamales from the PX. No doubt that's what would happen to this boy.

"He's just a kid," Kat said dismissively.

The two burly MPs at the front of the line yelled for the next prisoner to step forward, then grabbed the man by his neck and forced his head down for the cavity search. Kat saw the boy's stomach convulse.

"I'm telling you," Kurtz insisted. "He's not local."

Kat moved to turn away, then stopped herself. The last

thing she wanted was to prove Kurtz right, but she wasn't altogether convinced that he was wrong. "Step forward, please," she said in Arabic, and to her surprise the boy did.

"What's your name?" she asked. For a moment, when he didn't say anything, she thought she had been mistaken, that the previous response had been just a coincidence.

Then he blinked up at her. "Jamal," he said through chattering teeth. He was shivering wildly, from fear or cold or both, and his upper lip was glazed with snot.

Kat turned to Kurtz. "Get me a blanket." And then, to the boy, "It's okay, you're going to be okay."

The boy nodded, clearly unconvinced, and wiped his nose with the back of his hand.

"How old are you, Jamal?"

He paused before answering, aware, Kat thought, as she was, of just how much rested on this one piece of information. A year in either direction the difference between a one-way ticket to Guantánamo and the rest of his life.

"Fifteen," he said at last, and Kat thought, Good boy, right answer.

She scanned the room, searching for Kurtz among the tsunami of bodies. A blanket, she told herself, glancing at the boy, at the wings of his collarbones protruding from the top of his gaunt torso. How long does it take to find a goddamn blanket?

But when she looked up again her eyes caught not Kurtz's but Colin's. He was watching her, as he obviously had been for some time.

THE RIGHT ANSWER or the wrong one, Kat thought as the plane touched down on the runway at Barajas and taxied toward the terminal.

I suggest you take a look at that, she could hear the man say.

Morrow, he'd finally told her his name was, the same name as the signature on her orders. And, on the floor in front of the car's passenger seat, Jamal's file, Kat's own words oddly unfamiliar to her after three years.

I suggest you take a look at that. And she had understood, correctly, that the three-hour drive to Dulles would be her only chance to do so.

The plane braked to a stop and the passengers leaped from their seats, smoothing the creases from their clothes, jockeying for position, taking what few extra inches they could get. Kat squeezed into the aisle and slid her bag from the overhead bin. After a long, sleepless night, she'd made the mistake of dozing for an hour at the tail end of the flight. Now she felt as if someone had rubbed a handful of sand into her eyes.

You will find someone waiting for you at the hotel in Madrid, Morrow had told her on the curb at Dulles before handing her a small brown envelope. Plane tickets and a hotel reservation. Five hundred euros in medium-sized bills. *Put the money in your billfold, please. It looks better that way.* Better to whom? Kat had wondered.

Someone jostled Kat from behind and she felt herself being swept forward, down the aisle, out through the narrow abattoir of the ramp, and into the terminal.

Pleasure, she reminded herself, sliding her passport from her purse, repeating her lines in her head one last time. *A Spanish vacation. Tapas and dancing. The obligatory afternoon at the Prado.*

Nothing to worry about. But, as she handed her passport to the young man at immigration, she had to fight to keep her hands from shaking.

WELCOME TO PARADISE. Kurtz's roommate, a fellow Agency recruit whose real name was Jonathon Pope, but who went by the unfortunate nickname of Digger, had remarked on their first night at Monterey.

Kurtz had heard plenty of stories about the Defense Language Institute, about the after-class beach parties and the women, but he hadn't really believed any of them. With the exception of a handful of older students, State Department civilians like Kurtz and Pope, most of whom were actually destined for intelligence careers of one form or another, the majority of the students appeared to have come straight from boot camp. It was an odd mix, the military's brightest, kids who hadn't necessarily shown promise in the civilian world but who had been handpicked from the sea of recruits. They were all young and tan, their bodies military lean.

"You gotta feel sorry for those assholes in Spanish," Kurtz observed, taking a swig of his beer. Spanish was one of the shortest courses at the institute, while Arabic, to which both Kurtz and Pope had been assigned, was notoriously long. From where Kurtz stood, a year's stint at the institute didn't look so bad.

"You think if we screw up badly enough they'll make us repeat the course?" Pope asked hopefully.

"I have a feeling these girls are just a bit out of our league," Kurtz said, realizing too late that Pope was the kind of man who undoubtedly had never felt such a thing in his life. "Age-wise, I mean."

Pope shook his head and squinted, showing his Kennedyesque wrinkles — a sign, in his world, not of age but of luxury: summers on the water and winters at Stowe or Chamonix. The well-earned ravages of a perpetual tan.

Kurtz let his eyes drift with Pope's toward the far end of the beach, where a group of female students were playing volleyball.

"That one, for instance," Pope announced, pointing to a

brunette in an orange bikini who had just stepped up to the service line.

She couldn't have been more than eighteen, Kurtz thought, tall and lanky, with the lingering awkwardness of a teenager, her hair pulled back into a long dark braid. When she tossed the ball into the air and jumped to meet it, her body arced perfectly, legs and chest and arm in one fluid and graceful motion of power.

It was Kurtz's first glimpse of Kat, and he would never forget it. He had an undeniable urge to possess her, as if by doing so he could claim a portion of her self-assurance.

"I'll bet she likes older men," Pope mused.

Kurtz was suddenly defensive. "Don't be an asshole," he snapped.

"YOUR KEY, SIR," the front-desk clerk said, patronizing Kurtz one final time with her impeccable English before sliding his key card across the narrow counter. She was attractive in a decidedly Iberian way, with a long neck and a slim nose, dark eyes set beneath carefully arched brows.

Kurtz turned gratefully from her gaze and made his way across the glass-and-steel lobby, toward the hallway that the woman had indicated led to his room. Spare and soulless, the hotel Janson had chosen was an homage to European modernity, part of a movement of designer bullying that Kurtz found especially unfortunate.

It was a style not unlike the architecture of the Gulf States, though there, against the sparse backdrop of sea and sand, such masculine simplicity, perfectly and richly executed, made a kind of sense, while here on the Continent it seemed merely gratuitous. A reaction, Kurtz thought, to centuries of culture.

Kurtz found his door off the first-floor hallway and let

himself inside, surveying the space as he turned the lock behind him. There was a shabbiness to the room that sheer force of size had camouflaged in the hotel's common areas. The white walls were scuffed, the cheap veneer on the bed and dresser curling away at the edges. Time, Kurtz thought, had already been unkind to the establishment.

Setting his sample case on the bed, Kurtz opened the leather flap and emptied the contents. Tiny bottles of orifice guard. Miniature sample urns and autopsy gloves. A stack of prayer cards addressing the various gods. Deterrent for even the most ambitious customs officer.

Any reason this is going to be a problem? he could hear Janson say as he lifted the false bottom from the case. And for the briefest of moments, looking down at the Beretta nestled there, he wasn't sure.

Almost as if to reassure himself, he picked up the gun and set it against his palm, slipped the spare clip into the stock.

TEN

Mother and child, Harry Comfort thought as he settled into his deck chair and scanned the horizon, contemplating the unobscured terror of the universe. The moon was not yet up, the sky as clear as Harry had seen it for some time. In the distance, Mauna Kea's humped back rose from the dark plain of ranch land. Above her, Cetus the whale slipped westward through the krill swirl of stars like a calf surfacing for air.

Harry took a sip of his vodka, then balanced the tumbler on his stomach and scanned the sky, letting his eyes come to rest on the green planet cradled just below Aquarius. Harry had been tracking Uranus for several weeks now, sketching the planet's slow progress with the diligence of a schoolboy, using his old Leica binoculars while he waited for his Celestron to arrive.

It wasn't glamorous work, but it was the kind of repetitive task Harry needed. His first months on the island, the night sky had been so overwhelming to him that he'd been unable to look at it for more than a few moments at a time, and Uranus had given him something to which he could tether his mind. He'd always had a soft spot for the crater-pocked planet, the sort of sentimental attachment one might feel for an old boxer who had once been great but had hung on too long and taken one too many beatings at the end.

Down in the pasture that abutted the Tamarack Pines, one of the steers lowed a mournful protest and the rest of the herd shifted gracelessly in reply, their hooves scuffling the soft earth.

Hawaii, is it? Heinz, the new European DO had remarked as they'd cleared up the last of Harry's paperwork. *Lots of retired Agency men there. I'll have Karen get you a list. Can't hurt to have some contacts. Show you around the island, treat you to a game of golf.*

Harry had agreed, smiling his usual accommodating smile. But in truth he hadn't been able to imagine anything worse. For a moment he'd even thought about changing his plans. But then he'd realized just what such a step would mean, how much he'd sacrificed for them already, and how he wouldn't be able to forgive himself if he gave them the rest of his life as well.

Harry finished his drink and set the empty glass on the lanai, then reached for his sketchbook and flashlight. How slow it all seemed from here, the progress of the planet across millions of miles of space nearly imperceptible. A few lines on paper, the relation of a handful of dim points of light. And yet this was the only way the mind could even begin to make sense of it all.

From somewhere inside the apartment came the muted sound of the phone ringing, but Harry didn't move to answer it. Char was the only person whose calls he cared to take, and she was asleep inside. It was too late for solicitors, which left only the possibility of a wrong number, or worse, one of those long, vacant calls filled with satellite chatter which Harry knew were not wrong numbers at all but vulgar reminders of everything he could not leave behind.

The kitchen light switched on, obliterating the sky, and Harry saw Char's shadow skate across the lanai. He had told her several times not to bother with the phone, but she was the kind of person for whom such a concept was entirely impossible to grasp. In Char's world, Harry was learning, a ringing phone was meant to be answered, even at one o'clock in the morning. Especially at one in the morning, for the likelihood of disaster was so much greater then, the prospect that the caller might need help.

It was this same impulse that had drawn Char to him, her innate desire to be of use in some way, to fix things that were broken—something, Harry couldn't help observing, that she appeared to be unable to accomplish in her own life. One day she was cleaning his house and the next she was in bed with him, as if his need for intimacy were as easily fulfilled as his desire for a clean bathroom.

In their interactions with each other Harry and Char observed the unwritten etiquette of exiles, which meant asking as few questions as possible about the past, but Harry had managed to glean the basics of what Char had left behind on the mainland. At least one ex-husband and two kids. A house and a car. A job that, most likely, had not required cleaning other people's toilets.

Harry turned in his chair and craned his neck, watching her through the patio doors. She had thrown on one of his shirts, but it was unbuttoned, and Harry could see her body and all its failings in the glare of the overhead lights. Her thighs were heavy and thick, her pubic hair a dark and unruly triangle, her stomach sagging, silvered with stretch marks. Two kids, Harry thought, possibly three.

Char picked up the phone and cradled it against her shoulder, then looked quizzically out at Harry.

"Hello?" he heard her say through the door.

Harry shook his head vigorously, trying to signal his desire not to be interrupted, but it was no use.

"Yes," she told the caller, motioning to the phone, as if Harry simply hadn't understood that it was for him. "He's right here. May I ask who's calling?"

A title searcher, Harry thought, watching this odd bit of professionalism revealed. Or an insurance adjuster, one of those necessary jobs that seem, to outsiders at least, completely unnecessary. That's what Char would have done. For a moment he could see her in a cheap suit and sensible pumps, eating a fast-food lunch in the front seat of her car.

"Hang on," she said into the phone, then she put her hand over the receiver and slid the patio door open.

Harry reached desperately for his drink and tilted the last of the dregs from the glass. Not a soul out there, he thought, whom he'd rather talk to sober.

Char leaned out toward him, her breasts slouching forward as she did, the nipples big and dark against Harry's shirt. "It's Dick Morrow," she whispered, shrugging slightly, as if even she was dubious of what the name meant. Then she thrust the phone into his hand.

Harry put the phone to his ear and waved her away. Not back to bed, for he knew better than to expect privacy, but his dignity required at least the illusion of it. He waited for her to move inside, then reached over and pulled the lanai door closed.

"Harry?" Dick Morrow's voice came through on the line. "Harry, it's Dick."

Six thousand miles between them and still the words were like a hammer in Harry's gut. "Yes?" he said quietly.

Morrow cleared his throat as Harry had heard him do so many times before. "Hawaii, is it?" he said, his tone carefully offhand. "Got your stargazing after all. I remember how beautiful it can be out—"

But Harry didn't let him finish. "What do you want?" he asked.

Another throat-clearing and then a moment of dramatic silence. "It's about Madrid, Harry."

He was supposed to ask now, but didn't, refused to be Morrow's accomplice. Instead, he watched Char pad across the kitchen and take her stash box, an old Lion Coffee can, from the cabinet above the sink.

"It's the boy," Morrow told him at last. "He's disappeared."

"I'd think that would be an Agency problem," Harry said, knowing full well the reach of Morrow's hand since his "retirement" to the Pentagon. "Aren't you supposed to be playing golf somewhere? I've heard Florida's great for that."

Morrow ignored the remark. "Any idea where he might have gone?"

"None whatsoever," Harry replied. This, at least, was the truth.

"He's in real trouble, Harry. I shouldn't have to tell you that. It's a matter now of who finds him first."

Yes, Harry thought, and God help him if it's you. "Maybe you should ask my replacement," he told Morrow. "He struck me as a real go-getter. Flynn, I think his name is."

Morrow cleared his throat yet again, and decades of practice and intuition told Harry that Justin Flynn was no longer available for questioning.

"I don't know anything. Surely they told you that. It's why they pulled me out in the end."

"They told me you had weekly meetings with the boy. You must have talked about something."

Not even an attempt to deny that he'd been poking around, Harry thought. And why should there be? They both knew each other's secrets.

"We played cards," Harry said, watching Char light a joint and take a long, satisfied drag.

Morrow was silent for a moment, contemplating Harry's unabashed incompetence. "You'll call me personally if you remember anything," he said. "You still have my number, don't you?"

"Yes," Harry said. And then, before Morrow had time to hang up, "How's Susan?"

It was a stupid thing to ask, suicidally so, and Harry detested himself immediately. But the question was out there now and couldn't be taken back.

"She's sick," Morrow said flatly. "Thyroid cancer. She's going to die soon."

"Oh," Harry blurted.

"Goodbye, Harry."

Harry set the phone down on the arm of his deck chair and looked up at the sky, searching for Uranus again. He felt as if he'd been knocked suddenly off balance, as if the sky had been thrown from its axis and into the dark smear of the sea. But the green planet was still there, like an anchor among the million scattered stars.

The glass door slid open and Harry heard Char step out onto the lanai, her bare feet rough against the wooden planks.

"I was beginning to think you didn't have any," she said, putting her hands on Harry's shoulders, bending down so that her breasts lay against his back.

"Any what?" Harry asked.

"Friends," she answered.

"You were right," he said, feeling suddenly old. "I don't."

She slid her arm around his neck and climbed into his lap, and Harry felt his groin stir with a kind of desperation he hadn't known in decades. He shifted slightly so that his hips were under hers, then set his hands on her waist and pulled her toward him. Her hair, long and thick, smelled of marijuana smoke, and of the faint jasmine perfume of her shampoo.

She leaned over and kissed him, then pulled back, a bemused smile on her face. "Perhaps your Mr. Morrow should call more often," she said playfully.

ELEVEN

"Lies!" The voice in the corridor outside Manar's room was loud and indignant, the words punctuated by the rhythmic shushing of a scrub brush on the terra-cotta floor. "All lies. How can he possibly claim he didn't know?"

Then a second voice, that of the family's elder housekeeper, Jamila. "He is our king. May God protect him." Whispered, as Manar knew her mother had instructed, as all conversation in the house was to be. As if Manar were sick and noise was the cause.

When she'd first come home, Manar had been grateful for the quiet. In the silence of the prison, her hearing had become as acute as that of a blind person, her ears attuned to the slightest variation. She had learned to recognize the shift in tone of the desert sand caressing her cell's single airshaft when the wind changed direction, or the subtle difference in the sound of another prisoner's voice through the wall when she was close to death.

During those first months at home, the barrage upon her senses—the colors, smells, tastes, and sounds—had been almost unbearable, and the indifference of those around her to the sensory bounty had enraged Manar. But now it was the whispering that bothered her more than anything, the hushed tones of her mother's staff a constant reminder of Manar's years in the desert and of everything she had lost.

"He is no better than his father." It was the first voice again.

The speaker, Manar guessed, was the woman she had seen earlier that morning in the courtyard with her mother, the newest member of the household staff. No one else would have been so brazen in her condemnation of the monarch.

The two women were talking about the recent scandal at the Ain Chock Charity House, and the king's professed ignorance. Though Manar purposefully avoided both the newspaper and the television, the story had not escaped her attention. She had overheard a similar conversation among the kitchen staff earlier that week, in which they had recounted the suffering of the orphans at the home, and the greed of the managers, who for years had been pocketing the home's operating budget.

The story hadn't surprised Manar: corruption never did. It shouldn't have surprised anyone, but there was something about the gruesome details of what had transpired, the squalid conditions in which the children had been living, and the humiliations they had been forced to endure, that had captured the imaginations of everyone in the city, especially the poor, who were barely one step removed from Ain Chock and places like it.

"My mother worked at Ain Chock during the years of lead," the younger woman said, using the popular term for the decades of brutal repression that characterized the reign of Hassan II, the father of the current king. "That's where they took the children of the disappeared, you know."

The women had progressed down the hallway, taking the sound of their brushes with them, but Manar heard Jamila click her tongue reproachfully, and the rustle of her scarf as she moved her head to look at the door of Manar's room. "The madame," she warned, her voice barely audible. "We musn't talk about these things."

Manar crept quietly to the door and pressed her ear against the wood, hoping to hear the younger woman's response, but none came. She had a sudden desire to see the woman; she had glimpsed her only briefly that morning, and she was curious now to put a face to the voice. But there was something besides mere curiosity behind Manar's urge, a need to be seen and acknowledged, for both women to know that she had heard them. Putting her hand on the knob, she pushed the door open and stepped out into the hallway.

Jamila looked up at the sound of the door opening. Her eyes caught Manar's briefly, long enough for Manar to read the look of absolute terror in them, then she returned hastily to her work, her arms moving frantically across the floor.

The younger woman looked up as well, and kept looking. She had just drawn her brush from the bucket of soapy water at her side, and her dark and muscular forearms were covered in a film of fine bubbles. She was Manar's age, though like Manar she looked a good deal older. Her face was that of a peasant, rough and unapologetic, her teeth broken and black.

"Good afternoon, Madame," she said.

"Good afternoon," Manar answered. "Jamila is looking after you?"

The woman nodded.

"I believe you know my name," Manar said. "And yours is . . . ?"

"Asiya."

The healer, Manar thought.

"I was sorry to hear about your child, Madame," Asiya offered.

It was the first time since her return from the desert that anyone had mentioned the child to Manar, and she had not been prepared for it. She felt her knees buckle under her, and struggled to stay upright.

"It was a boy or a girl?"

"A boy," Manar answered.

"I lost a son as well. To typhus. He was three."

Manar nodded. What was she to say? "He is in a better place now, *insh'Allah.*" What people offered at times like this.

"Yes," Asiya replied. "*Insh'Allah.*"

But it was clear from the tone of her voice that she put as little stock in God's will as Manar did.

I'm FINISHED." Abdullah declared, licking the last of the chocolate from his fingers and motioning lazily to the breakfast tray beside him on the bed. "You can take it now."

There was plenty of food left—yogurt and dates and churros enough to feed Jamal and at least a half dozen of the other boys, who, Jamal knew from past experience, lived in a state of constant hunger. But Jamal knew better than to ask.

He took the tray and backed away, gesticulating slightly, ingratiating himself, like a weaker dog confronting a stronger one.

Abdullah watched him go. "You may take a churro for yourself, if you'd like."

Jamal nodded, trying to convey a child's guileless gratitude. "Thank you, Papa."

But once he was out in the hall, with the door closed behind him, he could no longer control himself. Ravenous and shaking, he stuffed the pastries into his mouth one after another. He finished the churros, then moved on to the dates and the yogurt, licking the bowl clean before returning the tray to the kitchen.

Abdullah was still in bed when Jamal got back to the room. He had not bothered to dress, and appeared to have no intention of doing so. His fleshy body was fully on display, his genitals dwarfed by the enormous roll of fat that hung down from his abdomen. He patted the sheets beside him, and Jamal forced himself forward.

"You will talk to the captain today?" Jamal asked gingerly, not wanting to ruin all he'd accomplished the night before but needing to know.

Abdullah snorted. "Tomorrow," he said. "Tomorrow I will see the captain. In any case, you wouldn't want to go tonight. There are storms predicted."

Jamal glanced out the window at the flawlessly blue sky. What harm would it do the man to ask? he wondered, suddenly angry at being so blatantly lied to. Not money, for no one made the crossing heading south, and Jamal was certain that someone would take him on in exchange for labor and the company. If not, he still had the remnants of the American's hundred euros.

No, he thought, Abdullah was determined to punish him for leaving the first time. He had no intention of helping him find passage across the strait.

"I must leave as soon as possible," Jamal pleaded. And then, hoping to appeal to Abdullah's love of power. "I am in trouble, Papa. I need your help."

Abdullah smiled. The expression was not one of sympathy but one of self-interest, the look of someone suddenly recognizing his opportunities. "Of course I will help you," he crooned. "But you must give me time. These things are not easy to arrange."

"Yes," Jamal agreed. "Of course."

TWELVE

"How does a fifteen-year-old Moroccan boy end up on the Afghan jihadi circuit?" the provost marshal had wondered aloud, leaning back in his chair, rubbing his eyes with the heels of his hands. Like Kat and everyone else, he'd been up for nearly two days, and the exhaustion was plain on his face.

On the wall behind his desk was a poster of the World Trade Center in flames, with the words NYFD: WE WILL NEVER FORGET. The same poster was on the door of Kat's tent, and there was another one at the entrance to the mess hall. They were for sale in the PX, along with Operation Enduring Freedom key chains, Special Forces T-shirts, and handmade Afghan carpets. Along with Soldier of Fortune video games, shelves of American junk food and diaper wipes.

"We're still trying to figure that out, sir," Kat confessed. "He was traveling with two older men. He claims he met up with them at a guesthouse in Islamabad. He didn't come right out and say it, sir, but it sounds like he was a having a"—Kat stopped herself, searching for the right word—"a relationship with the owner. When these two offered to take him with them, he jumped at the chance."

The provost marshal looked down at Kat's leg. She realized that the heel of her boot was tapping impatiently on the linoleum floor.

"You in a hurry to get somewhere, Sergeant?"

"Just my bunk, sir," Kat lied. "I've got four hours before I have to be back in the booths."

The truth was that she'd already made up her mind that she wouldn't be getting any sleep. She hadn't had a chance to talk to Colin at the facility, but she'd heard from one of the other interrogators that his SBS team would be sticking around the base for the next two days. She was planning to head back to her tent in Viper City for a quick shower and a change of clothes, then over to the British compound.

"Have you gotten anything out of his traveling companions?"

"No, sir. They've been appropriated, sir."

The provost marshal nodded sympathetically. There was nothing to be done once civilian intelligence decided a prisoner was of interest. The men had disappeared from intake early that morning and most likely would not be coming back. "And before Pakistan?"

"He claims he left Morocco on his own about a year ago, stowed away in a container truck making the crossing from Tangier to Spain. It's quite a dangerous trip, sir." Kat paused, remembering her own trip across the strait and her brief stay in Tangier.

"He was in Algeciras for a couple of months. Another relationship. Same situation as the one in Islamabad. He eventually hooked up with some older Moroccans there. Pseudo-jihadis, from the sound of it. They're the ones who brought him to Pakistan in the first place."

"And you believe him?"

Kat shrugged. "Everything he's told us about the guest-house checks out with what we've heard before. It's a pretty popular stop on the jihadi railroad. I don't have much reason not to believe the rest of it. But he's not a jihadi, sir, if that's what you're thinking."

"Any family?"

"No, sir. He says he grew up in an orphanage in Casablanca. He told me some story about his mother being taken to live with the king. It's probably a lot less painful than the truth." Another pause as Kat contemplated the grimness of the boy's life. "He's been taking care of himself for a long time, sir. In whatever way he can."

She saw the provost marshal glance instinctively at the picture of his young daughter that was propped on his desk. She couldn't help feeling sorry for the man. Somewhere, she thought, in some other place, he was a good person, a good husband and father. But here even the most well-intentioned decisions were fraught with unforeseen consequences.

International laws required that they release any prisoner under the age of sixteen. If the boy had been Afghani, they would have taken him back to the village where they had found him, but they both knew that releasing him was not an option in this case. With no money and nowhere to go, the chances of his surviving in the perilous mountains were slim to none. If he did survive, he would face a grim future.

"Sir?" Kat prompted. A decision needed to be made, and it wasn't her place to make it. "I believe we have an obligation to him, sir."

"Does he have a number yet?" the provost marshal asked.

"We put him in the PUC system, sir."

The PUC system was a limbo of sorts, a way of cheating the military bureaucracy machine. Detainees declared "persons under U.S. control" were allowed to remain in the facility for up to two weeks without being entered into the official system.

"Good, that'll buy us some time. You can go now, Sergeant."

Kat got up to leave, saluting as she did so and receiving only a halfhearted gesture in return.

"And for God's sake," the man added. "Get him out of the cages."

An obligation. Kat thought as she took the key from the receptionist and started across the hotel's vast lobby. And Colin, laughing when she'd told him this: *Our only obligations in this place are to ourselves and our friends.* The callousness of the remark had angered her at the time, and she still believed Colin was wrong.

She was not naïve enough to think Jamal's interests were the only ones at stake here; clearly, Morrow's reasons for wanting to find him were not purely altruistic. But neither did she doubt that the boy was in trouble. Despite the assurances she herself had made to the contrary, Jamal's situation in Madrid would have been a perilous one. If his connection to the Americans had been found out, as Morrow had intimated, Jamal's life would certainly be in danger.

Yes, she had had an obligation to Jamal then, and she still did. After all, she was the one who had gotten him into this mess. It seemed only right that it fall to her to get him out. If she did find him, she might even arrange for him to go to America, as she had promised she would. Clearly, Morrow could make such a thing happen.

Besides, she reminded herself as she made her way down the long first-floor corridor, scanning the room numbers as she went, the decision was not hers to make. Her orders had been clear.

Kurtz had been off by a year; Kat was nineteen, not eighteen, as he'd guessed that first night on the beach. When he saw her in his Arabic class the morning after the welcome party, he made a point of sitting next to her.

The odd amalgam of gawkiness and grace that had drawn Kurtz to Kat on the volleyball court was nowhere evident in the classroom, where Kat was entirely without contradictions. Besides being notoriously difficult, the Arabic track at DLI at the time had the smallest enrollment of any of the courses the institute offered. Only the most gifted students were funneled into Arabic, and, among them, Kat still managed to stand out.

The late-in-life child of a German war bride and an American GI, Kurtz had been raised in a bilingual household, and he had a talent for languages. But he quickly recognized that Kat's ability was not merely talent but a gift. There was uncorrupted confidence to her voice, as if she had been born to the language, her speech in class like the sound of her hand on the ball that first night. Kurtz had been both captivated and covetous.

It had taken him nearly the full year to approach her on his own. Eleven months of group outings and late-night study sessions. Hundreds of shared meals in the mess. And when, drunk off cheap beer, he'd finally leaned toward her in the doorway of her dorm one evening, she had laughed at him.

SHE HAD LAUGHED. Kurtz thought bitterly, remembering the moment, the look on Kat's face as she'd moved instinctively away from him, part pity and part disgust. Amused at his presumption, at the fact that he would even think she could want such a thing. And then, recovering herself too late, she had mumbled something about friendship.

The door opened and Kurtz watched Kat step into the room's narrow foyer, pausing to let her eyes adjust. Wanting to give himself the advantage, Kurtz had purposefully drawn the curtains and turned off the lights in the main room. It would take a few moments for Kat to pick him out of the darkness, but he had a clear view of her.

Physically, she had not changed in the two years since Kurtz last saw her at Bagram. She was cleaner, of course, lacking the high-altitude tan that had been an inevitable side effect of life on the Shomali Plains. But the rest of her was the same, her body neat and trim, her hair cut just above her neck in a military style. She was dressed simply, in a cotton shirt and a pair of jeans, with a small canvas bag at her side.

A soldier at heart, Kurtz thought, with a soldier's sense of the world, that same antiquated notion of duty she had always possessed. But then she owed everything to the army, her sense of self even, so such loyalty was to be expected.

She blinked, then scanned the room, her gaze coming to rest on Kurtz.

"Hello, Kat." Kurtz leaned forward in his chair, watching her face change. "Weren't you expecting me?"

"No," she conceded, closing the door behind her, failing to hide her obvious discomfort.

"How was your flight?"

"Fine."

"The red-eye," Kurtz observed. "I never can get any sleep on a plane."

"I managed."

"I can call room service if you'd like." Kurtz reached over and switched the desk lamp on, illuminating the room's sharp angles, the distance between them. "You must be hungry."

"I'm fine, actually."

"Coffee, at least."

"I'm fine," she repeated.

Kurtz motioned to the chair opposite his. Did she know about Colin? he wondered. "I assume you've had a chance to reacquaint yourself with Jamal's file?"

Kat set her bag down but remained standing. She was not going to make this pleasant for him. "Yes, briefly."

"And? Do you have any thoughts on where he might be headed?"

"It would help if I knew who he was running from."

Did she really expect him to tell her this? Kurtz wondered, ignoring the comment. "The consensus seems to be that he's going home. Is this your opinion as well?"

Kat shrugged. "He has nowhere else to go."

"He'd have to get across the strait first. Do you really think he'd risk that again?"

"I guess it would depend on how desperate he is. But it might not be so dangerous going back. There's a lot more supply than demand heading south. If he knew who to ask, he could probably find a boat willing to take him on."

"And?"

"There was a man in Algeciras he mentioned a few times. A Moroccan. His name is Abdullah. He runs a rooming house of sorts for newcomers. Jamal stayed there when he first got to Spain. Not exactly a charitable enterprise, if you know what I mean. If I were Jamal, that would be my first stop."

Kurtz glanced at his watch. It was midmorning already, but if they caught the fast train they could be in Algeciras by that afternoon.

It had been an especially bad night for Susan, the worst in an increasingly grim series. She'd woken up five times in seven hours, her hoarse and anguished cries carrying up through the floorboards to Morrow's room. Each time, Morrow had heard the Russian go to her, stumbling wearily down the dark first-floor corridor like a nursing mother to a child.

The beginning of the end, Morrow thought as he lay in bed

and listened to Marina struggling yet again to calm Susan. He had seen many people die, but never like this.

Promise me you'll do what needs to be done, Susan had said, rolling toward him in the same bed the night after they had first found out about the cancer. Morrow had thought she was already asleep, and her voice in the darkness had startled him. *You can't let your weakness get the best of you. Not about this, Richard.* But he had not been able to answer her.

The following week she'd called the nursing agency. A week later, Marina had moved into the little guest room. Susan's very own angel of mercy and death, and a constant reminder of how Morrow had failed her.

He often wondered just what kind of contract the two women had, for he knew Susan well enough to be certain there was one. Unwritten, perhaps, but a contract nonetheless: the terms of her suffering, of just how much she was willing to bear. Surely, not much more than this.

The phone on Morrow's bedside table rang, jolting him from his sleepless meditation. Not quite seven, he thought, as he turned and fumbled with the receiver. An hour reserved exclusively for bad news.

"Sorry to wake you, Dick." Peter Janson was immediately apologetic on the other end of the line. "But I thought you'd want to know. We've had some news from Madrid."

"Go ahead."

"It turns out some friends of ours in Spain had a line on the phone at the butcher shop where the boy was staying. They've been listening in since the train bombings." Janson paused dramatically. "The boy made a phone call the night after the meeting in Malasaña. You won't believe who to."

Morrow didn't say anything. It was too early, and he was too tired to indulge Janson.

"Harry Comfort!" Janson revealed finally, sounding just slightly deflated by Morrow's apparent lack of enthusiasm.

"Well, not Harry but his ex-wife. Evidently Harry's gone and retired to Hawaii, of all places. I have to admit, I never would have expected that from him."

Harry and his goddamned card games, Morrow thought, remembering what Comfort had said when they spoke the night before. His last posting as a field man and he'd committed the number-one sin: he'd given the boy his number.

"In any case," Janson continued, "they didn't talk for long. She seemed to think it was a wrong number at first. But the kid said something about an S. Kepler. It's probably nothing, but I've got some people looking into it."

"Not S. Kepler," Morrow corrected him. "Johannes Kepler. The astronomer. You remember Harry and his ridiculous telescope. It's nothing."

"Still," Janson persisted, "the kid might try to contact him some other way. Should we put someone on him?"

The prospect seemed unlikely to Morrow. Even if Jamal did manage to track down his old handler, there was nothing Harry could do. He'd been half-drunk when Morrow called the night before, as he no doubt was most of the time. Hardly a threat. But still, if the boy did call again they would know exactly where he was.

"Yes," Morrow agreed. "And put a line on the ex-wife's phone, too, in case he tries there again."

THIRTEEN

"I thought the war was over," Harry had remarked, looking dubiously out over the dark countryside to which he was to be stationed.

It was July of 1973, six months after the signing of the Paris Peace Accords, four full months after the last American troops had left Vietnam, and from the roof of the Caravelle Hotel the flash of artillery was clearly visible in the distance.

"Tell that to the Vietnamese," somebody quipped, and everyone at the table laughed.

It was Harry's first night in Saigon after five years on what was commonly and gruesomely referred to as the night-soil circuit, for the Third World custom of draining septic tanks at night. Sweating it out with a permanent case of the runs in the worst of the backwater bases in Asia. And somehow he'd expected something different from Vietnam.

The usual welcoming committee had turned out for the free meal in Harry's honor: Jack McLeod and Steve Robinson, both case officers at the Saigon base; Peter Janson, the deputy chief of station; Dick Morrow, who was chief of base at the time. Plus two pretty secretaries to round out the crowd.

"You won't be up there for long," Jack McLeod remarked. "The ARVN are losing a good thousand troops a month to the Vietcong."

Pete Janson skewered an escargot with his tiny silver trident and stuffed it into his mouth. "Jack's got money on next December," he said, winking. "But I think we'll be here at least through spring. It's going to be a fight getting into Saigon." He shrugged in the direction of one of the secretaries, who was seated to Harry's right. "Susan's in charge of the pool, if you'd like to contribute."

"It's fifty dollars to buy in," Susan said, smiling condescendingly, issuing the information as if it were a warning.

She was thin and impossibly pretty, with the kind of nose the girls in his Ridgewood, New Jersey, high school often paid large sums of money to acquire. Though it was not her looks Harry had fallen in love with at that moment but her obvious and concrete sense of herself, something that Harry had never seen in a woman before.

"So what are we supposed to be doing here in the meantime?" he asked, taking a sip of his Côtes du Rhône, ducking Susan's gaze.

"Standard wine and dine," Steve Robinson said. "We've been focusing on the ICCS. The Poles, mainly. The Hungarians, as I'm sure you know, won't give us shit."

"No defections!" Janson interjected. "We'd have the whole Polish delegation in a matter of days."

The same old dance, Harry thought, only here instead of the consular staff it was the fruits of peace they were reaping, the very people the Paris Accords had sent in to make sure everyone got along.

The Vietnamese waiter appeared with their dinners. Harry, watching the man's calm face as he distributed the plates, thought naïvely, Well, he's not afraid.

"Nha Trang's not so bad, actually," Robinson offered,

tucking into his steaming coq au vin, seemingly oblivious to the tropical heat. "I was up there for a while this past winter. Your quarters come with a doll of a housekeeper. Pretty Vietnamese girl. Keep her in French chocolates and she'll do just about anything you ask. I'll get you the name of a good shop in Saigon before you leave."

Harry felt himself flush. He glanced over at Susan, who seemed unfazed by Robinson's remarks.

"Harry's quite the amateur astronomer," Morrow announced in a tone that verged on mockery. "Am I right?"

"Yes," Harry answered. "That's right."

"And what's your weapon of choice? Unitron? Zeiss?"

"I use a Celestron C-8, actually."

Morrow nodded. "There will be plenty of stars in Nha Trang."

Harry cut into his steak. He had ordered it medium-well, but it was still bloody, and the sight of the undercooked meat made him nauseous.

Susan leaned toward him. "You can send it back, you know."

Harry shook his head. "It's fine." He took a bite and chewed, washed the steak down with more red wine.

Susan watched him dubiously. "For chrissakes!" she said, waving to get the waiter's attention. "How did you want it cooked?"

"Really," Harry told her, blushing again. "I guess I'm just not all that hungry. Must be the heat."

But the waiter was already on his way over.

Susan pointed to Harry's plate. "Take it back," she commanded in perfect French.

Harry smiled at the waiter. "It's fine," he insisted. "It's really fine."

The waiter looked down at him, and Harry could tell by the look on the man's face that even he thought the steak should go back. But the entire table was watching by now and Harry, for reasons entirely beyond his control, could not back down.

"It's fine," he repeated, grinning crazily. "It's absolutely fine."

Then another flash lit up the countryside, this one bigger than the last, capturing the attention of everyone at the table, and Harry was mercifully rescued from himself.

After dinner, as they all stood on the steps of the Caravelle waiting for their cars, Pete Janson had nudged Harry. "Don't even think about it."

"Think about what?"

Janson snorted. "You think I'm some kind of asshole?"

Morrow's Mercedes pulled up, and Harry watched Susan climb into the passenger seat. "She have a thing with him?"

"She doesn't have 'a thing' with anyone. Believe me, we've all tried. Besides, Morrow's married."

"So?"

"So, nothing. Just trying to save you some trouble."

Harry nodded. He could see Susan through the car's window, her face dark, half hidden by the reflection of the hotel's façade. She turned to Morrow and said something, her bare shoulders curving intimately toward him. Then she reached over and rolled down her window.

"Welcome to Vietnam," she called out, still laughing at whatever joke she and Morrow had just shared.

THE FIRST OF HOW MANY HUMILIATIONS. Harry wondered as he rolled over in bed, dragging his insufficient allotment of covers with him. In the grainy, predawn light, he could just make out Char's shape beside him: hips and shoulders and shadowed face, mouth parted slightly like a child's in sleep. He should have seen everything coming that night at the Caravelle, he told himself, should have taken Janson's advice for the gift it was, but of course he hadn't. For a moment, the part of himself he dared not acknowledge was wretchedly gleeful at the thought of Susan's death.

Down in the pasture, the cattle were voicing their complaints. Life in paradise, Harry thought, and what more could they want? Another day of balmy sunshine? Yet more of that plush grass? If only they knew how bad most beasts had it.

Moving carefully so as not to disturb Char, Harry pushed the covers aside, swung his legs slowly off the bed, and reached for his worn copy of *Harmonies of the World* on the nightstand. *My Koran,* he could hear himself tell Jamal. It had been a foolish thing to say, as foolish as his final gesture had been. The torn page not just the sum of all his regrets but the worst of them as well. The final triumph of nostalgia over reason. Though even now Harry could think of no better vehicle for his failure than the work of Kepler, who had sacrificed so much in the futile service of longing, who had spent his entire life trying to reconcile the irreconcilable, who had believed he could somehow resolve science and God.

If you're ever in real trouble. He winced now, remembering the words. And what he should have said: *If you're ever in real trouble, for God's sake, don't call me.*

"Can't sleep?" Char reached out and touched Harry's back.

He shook his head, then turned to look at her. She had pulled the sheets aside, revealing her nakedness. Not Susan's body, he thought, looking at her, and not Irene's, but a body scarred by everything it had ever nurtured. Breasts and belly and thighs irrevocably changed.

She patted the bed in a gesture of invitation, not to sex but to sleep, and Harry thought, Yes, here is the sweet forgetting, absolution for the taking.

"Come back to bed," she said impatiently, reaching out for

him, pulling him down beside her, until there was nothing left for Harry to do but acquiesce.

TWO HOURS. Manar thought as she climbed down from the back of the bus and watched the housekeeper cross the street. That's how long it had taken to get from her mother's house in the leafy northern suburbs to this rambling slum on the southern edge of the city. Two hours each way and another eight scrubbing shit from their toilets. And for what? Manar didn't know exactly what her mother paid these women, but she was certain it wasn't enough.

She paused and glanced over her shoulder before trailing Asiya down into the sewer of the bidonville. The chances of her having been followed were slim; she'd been careful leaving the house. But still, the last thing she wanted was for anyone to know she had come. She had not yet invented a story to explain her disappearance, but there would be time for that on the ride home. For now, all her energy was focused on keeping track of Asiya's saffron-colored djellaba and matching scarf.

The sun had just set, turning the smog-choked sky a wild magenta. From the crest of the hill there was an unearthly beauty to the slum, the tin roofs flashing like pink sails across the hillside.

Two decades earlier, during her student days, Manar had frequented the city's bidonvilles, working with Yusuf and the others to organize strikes and protests, spreading the gospel of revolution, and she was struck now by just how little had changed. Except for the satellite dishes, which rose like so many alien moons from the tops of the more prosperous shanties, the slum was exactly as Manar remembered all slums to be.

Down in the narrow alleyways it was night already, the sun

long since vanished behind the quarter's shanty walls, the sky, where it was visible, crisscrossed by a chaotic web of pirated electrical wires. Cooking smells wafted from makeshift kitchens, the odors of rancid oil and spices mingling with those of the open sewer. And, here and there, the unmistakable stench of death. The smell of poverty, Manar thought, stumbling after Asiya, and of prison.

It's not your fight, she could hear her father say that last afternoon before her arrest. She had sneaked out then as well, after he had forbidden her to go to the strike. And the last thing she'd said to him, the last thing she would ever say to him: *It's everybody's fight.*

Such arrogance, she thought now, such utter naïveté. She was embarrassed by who she had been, by the shamefulness with which she had forced herself into these people's homes, the hubris with which she had assumed their suffering.

A group of pale figures appeared out of the darkness, four boys huddled hungrily around a can of butane, eyes wide from the fumes. Manar paused briefly to examine their faces, half hoping for a glimpse of the familiar and half dreading the possibility.

One of the first things Manar had learned in prison was that the least of her hopes—for her child, for a blanket in the winter, for a cell in which she could stand without crouching or a voice on the other side of the wall—were her worst enemies. If she was to continue to live, she had realized early on, she would have to do so entirely without expectation. To live, in essence, as if she were dead, and as if the child were dead as well. Anything else was too painful to bear.

This was the first time in many years that Manar had allowed herself such thoughts, that she had even dared to imagine that the boy might be alive, and she felt oddly fearless, even determined.

Asiya stopped at the door to one of the shanties and turned to look back at Manar. Waiting for her, Manar thought. And how long had the housekeeper known that she was being followed? Or had she guessed from the beginning, from their exchange in the hall that morning, that Manar would come?

"My home," she said, swinging the door open and gesturing for Manar to enter.

Manar moved forward and peered hesitantly inside. The house was just one small room. Dirt floor, four walls, and a roof. A curtain, for privacy, hung in one corner, and a few scavenged furnishings. An old woman squatted over a gas burner, stirring a large pot of stewed peas, her attention fixed on a small television.

"Come." Asiya nodded her encouragement, and Manar stepped slowly across the threshold.

"My mother," the housekeeper said, pointing to the old woman. "You have come to ask her about Ain Chock, yes?"

"Yes." There was an Egyptian soap opera on the television, the same one Manar's mother followed; she would be watching it now. Like most soap operas, it was the story of two families, one rich and one poor, and the intersections of their lives over the course of many years.

"You will eat with us," Asiya informed Manar. "And then she will tell you what you want to know."

The old woman ladled a helping of stew into a dish, and Manar squatted to receive it, offering her thanks. But when she lifted the bowl to her lips she felt suddenly sick. It wasn't the food; there were many years when she would have been grateful for such a feast. It was shame that stopped her.

She choked the meal down, forcing herself to finish, then accepted a second helping and finished that as well. The women would likely go hungry the next day because of their generosity. Manar knew this, but she also knew that to deny their hospitality would have been the worst insult; that they would rather starve than have their visitor leave with an empty stomach.

When they had finished eating, Asiya cleared their plates and put a kettle of water on the gas, then set out three chipped glasses for mint tea.

Yet another ritual, Manar thought, impatiently watching the housekeeper spoon dried mint and precious sugar into a pot.

Asiya finished serving the tea, then turned to her mother. "This is the one I told you about," she said, speaking loudly. "She has come to ask you about the child."

The old crone turned from the television and looked at Manar. "A boy or a girl?" she asked, revealing a mouthful of black teeth.

"A boy," Manar answered. "He would be nineteen now." She did a quick calculation in her mind. Yes, nineteen was right.

A cockroach crawled across the lip of the stew pot and the old woman flicked it away. Her fingernails were cracked and yellow. "There were boys like this at Ain Chock. I could have known him. What was his name?"

Manar opened her mouth to answer, then stopped herself. Yusuf, she thought, had always thought, for this was what they had agreed on—that if the child was a boy it would have his father's name. "I don't know," she admitted.

The old woman nodded, then reached out and took Manar's hand in her own. "It is for the best, sister, I assure you," she said. Her grip was surprisingly strong, her bony fingers clutching Manar's. "If your son was at Ain Chock, it is better not to know."

FOURTEEN

Barely three hours now, Kat had told herself as she started across Camp Viper, conscious of the fast-dwindling time left to her before she had to be back at the facility. If she hurried, she could still squeeze in a shower before heading to the British camp. After a night in intake and a day in the booths, she would have to.

In the real world, Kat was someone who took pride in the careful detachment with which she approached her relationships with men. When she'd slept with Colin in Oman, she'd told herself it would just be the one time, that the hazards here were too real and too many, the risk of her succumbing to her own vulnerability too high. She'd been right, she thought, and now she could not help herself.

As she turned down the narrow, rock-strewn alley that led to her tent, Kat saw her roommate, a nurse at the Combat Support Hospital, coming toward her. Sleep was as scarce a commodity for the nurses as it was for the interrogators, and the woman looked as if she'd just been roused prematurely from a much-needed nap.

"You've got company," she called out as she passed, her expression and tone showing no small amount of irritation.

Colin, Kat thought, hurrying the last few yards to the tent. But when she pulled the canvas flap aside and ducked through the low doorway she saw Kurtz sitting in the camp chair next to her cot, his bulky frame spread out over a large portion of her few square feet of precious private space.

"Expecting someone else?" he asked.

"I haven't slept in two days," Kat warned him, stopping just inside the door. "And I have to be back in the booths tonight. So whatever you have to say, say it fast and get out."

Kurtz reached down and produced two frosty bottles of beer from the floor beside him. It was Murree, not the usual Uzbek swill, and Kat was tempted, but she shook her head. "What do you want?"

Kurtz shrugged, popped the cap off one of the bottles, and took a long swig. "I heard you spent the whole day in with the boy."

"His name is Jamal," Kat corrected him.

"You learn anything?"

"Only that he prefers chicken tetrazzini to grilled beefsteak. But then, doesn't everyone?" Kat said, referring to the notoriously bad selection of MREs. "And he's a Yankees fan. But who isn't?"

"He was friendly, then?"

"Scared shitless is more like it. He's a smart kid. He knows exactly what we want to hear, and so far he's saying it."

Kurtz drained the remainder of his beer in one long swallow, tossed the empty bottle onto Kat's bunk, and opened the second Murree. "I've been talking to some of the Agency guys. They think they might be able to use him."

They, Kat thought, taking note of Kurtz's choice of words. When she'd first seen him in intake she'd assumed he was still with the Agency. Apparently, he wasn't.

"He's fifteen," she balked. "He's not even legal. We can't keep him once his PUC status runs out. You know that."

"Right," Kurtz said contemptuously. "So what, you're going to send him back where you found him? I read his file. He's got nowhere to go." Kurtz stood up.

It was a simple point and he had made it, but Kat couldn't help wondering what Kurtz's stake in the boy's future was.

He set the barely touched second beer on the wooden crate that served as Kat's bedside table. It was a calculated gesture of excess, a reminder of the resources that were available to him, and of what little regard he gave to wasting them. "They could help him, Kat," he said. "Get him a small stipend and a place to live. He could go back to Europe, or even to the U.S., if he works out."

Kat shook her head. "You saw him last night. He's just a kid."

"They're not talking about James Bond stuff. He'd just be part of the community. Best case, they'd never even need to use him. Worst case, he hears something interesting, he shares it."

"He won't do it," Kat insisted, though she knew that he would, and gladly.

"Bullshit." Kurtz called her bluff. "You said it yourself: he's a smart kid, he knows his odds."

"I won't do it."

"Sure you will."

"Get out of my tent," Kat snapped, motioning to the empty beer bottle on her cot. "And take your garbage with you."

Kurt stood up and stepped past her, blatantly ignoring her last request. "You don't have to give me an answer now," he sneered. "Go talk it over with your boyfriend, if you want. I'll see you back at the facility." Then he lifted the flap and disappeared into the afternoon glare.

ANYONE, KAT THOUGHT, as she watched Kurtz cross the sunny expanse of the Atocha Station's atrium and disappear behind the lush indoor forest of palm and banana trees. If it could have been anyone other than Kurtz. But it wasn't, and here they were.

Kat glanced around the terminal, trying to get her bearings. She'd told Kurtz that she needed to use the restroom while he saw about tickets to Algeciras. Technically, this was true, but she also wanted to check her answering machine in case Stuart had called again. She could have told the truth, but that would have meant explaining herself, and she didn't want to have to tell Kurtz about Colin.

Spotting a newspaper kiosk at the far end of the terminal and a bank of pay phones just beyond it, Kat started across the crowded hall. She had no small change on her, only the euros Morrow had given her at the airport, which meant she'd need a phone card, or at least some coins.

A group of backpackers had arrived at the kiosk before Kat and were stocking up on cigarettes and candy. Twenty-year-olds who'd been everywhere and seen everything, Kat thought, remembering how painfully naïve she'd felt on that earlier trip, how limited her own experiences had seemed to her.

Trying to mask her self-consciousness, she glanced down at the rows of newspapers on display. The selection was typical of a big-city train station: a preponderance of sports-related publications with a handful of highbrow selections thrown in, including the more popular foreign-language papers. A small headline at the very bottom of the front page of the London *Times* caught Kat's eye.

"Another Glitch in Prisoner Death Court-Martial," Kat read, reaching quickly for a copy. On the heels of the revelations of detainee abuse in Iraq, Stuart's case had gotten a fair amount of attention in the press, in the United States as well as in Britain, and Kat was not particularly surprised to see that Colin's death was news.

Unfolding the paper, she quickly skimmed the article:

Sources in Portsmouth confirm that the trial of a sailor accused of murdering a detainee in his custody in Afghanistan in the early summer of 2002 will take place as scheduled, despite the recent death of a key prosecution witness.

Former Special Boat Service member Colin Mitchell was found dead in London three days ago from an apparent intentional overdose. Mitchell's death is the second major setback for the prosecution in recent months.

It was revealed earlier this year that another potential witness had escaped while in U.S. custody at Bagram Air Base and was unavailable to testify. The witness in question, Hamid Bagheri, who is known to have ties to several terrorist organizations, is still at large.

"Anything interesting?"

Kat spun around to see Kurtz behind her. "Just catching up on the news," she said hastily, refolding the paper and setting it back on the rack so as to conceal the headline. Her hands were shaking. "You get the tickets?"

Kurtz glanced at the discarded newspaper. "You don't want to bring it along? We've got a long trip ahead of us."

Goading her, Kat thought, though she couldn't be sure. She shook her head. "I thought I'd try and get some sleep."

Kurtz smiled. It was an expression Kat had seen before, a mixture of condescension and contempt. "Suit yourself," he said.

And Kat thought, He knows.

THE LIGHT WAS FAST FADING by the time Kat finally left her tent and headed up Disney Drive, Bagram's main drag, toward the British camp at the far end of the airstrip. On the eastern side of the valley the moon was rising, while out in the west the sun cast its last rays up over the mountains. The sky was a deep and lucid blue that is possible only at very high altitudes, the mountains clear in the thin air, the winter's snows still lingering on the otherwise barren peaks.

Unlike most of the other soldiers at Bagram, Kat felt strangely at home in the lunar landscape of the Shomali Plains. The emptiness of it reminded her of the land along the Rocky Mountain Front, and of her childhood, which came back to her mostly as one long drive across the American West.

The Norwegian mine clearers had finished sweeping space for a playing field in the no-man's-land along the runway, and a few shirtless marines were playing a game of touch football in the fading twilight. Out on the airstrip, helicopters perched, menacing silhouettes, massive Chinooks and Black Hawks, and smaller and more agile Apaches, with their banks of Hellfire missiles cradled under each wing. In the distance, the listing corpses of abandoned MIGs and Hinds served as grim reminders of the Soviets' ignominious defeat.

In war there is little concern for housekeeping. This was especially true in Afghanistan, where the inhospitable terrain made it impractical for retreating armies to take any more than their own skins with them. Relics of the previous conflict, and of the base's original occupants, were everywhere at Bagram. The main prison floor, where the cages now stood, had once been a vast aircraft shop. Abandoned Soviet machinery lined the walls, the pieces formless and hulking beneath black tarps. Virtually every surface was marked with Russian graffiti. Reminders of a grand and bloody failure, Kat thought, the voices of young men who had not made it home. But more than that: warnings of what could go wrong this time around.

Kat passed the Special Forces camp, with its barbed-wire fence and mammoth barbecue pit, then turned into the front gate of the British compound. The British camp, or Camp Gibraltar, as it was commonly known, was the subject of constant speculation and no small amount of jealousy among the base's non-British personnel. In the brief time Kat had been at Bagram, she'd heard all sorts of rumors about the superiority of the British compound, ranging from the cleanliness of the showers to the quality of the food.

From the outside, at least, the rumors appeared to be true. The camp was stereotypical in its orderliness, more like a Hollywood version of a military base than the reality Kat was used to. The tents were laid out in strict rows, the ground leveled and cleared. Bright Union Jacks and Scottish Saltires fluttered in the evening breeze.

An MP stopped Kat at the front gate and asked to see her credentials. Understandably, the Brits were fiercely protective of the small patch of colonial comforts they had managed to scrape out of the arid Afghan earth, and the compound was normally off limits to Americans. Kat was hoping her civilian clothes would provide the illusion of clout necessary to talk her way inside.

"I'm here to see the soldiers from C Squadron," she said confidently, providing as little information as possible. If the MP was going to take her for a civilian OGA, he would have to be properly confused. "We've got some questions about the prisoners they brought into the facility last night."

The man eyed Kat warily, but she could tell it was all show, that he already knew he had to let her in. "They're in the mess," he grumbled, indicating a large tent toward the rear of the compound.

Fear and its perks, Kat thought as she headed back along

the dirt drive, feeling good about her new role. And suddenly she understood the allure of the Agency, the benefits of being able to go wherever, whenever.

Inside the mess it was fish-and-chips night, the air rich with the smells of real food and real cooking. Unlike the Americans' meals, which were flown in from Germany and then reheated, the food here was prepared by actual human beings.

Kat scanned the crowded tent, her eyes falling on a group of soldiers in the far corner, some of whom she recognized from the flight up to K-2. This was Colin's squadron, but Colin wasn't among them.

Adopting her best OGA swagger, Kat made her way across the mess. "Where's Lieutenant Mitchell?" she snapped.

Several of the men looked up from their dinners, but none of them said anything.

"U.S. intel," Kat said imperiously. "I've got some questions about one of the detainees he brought in last night."

"He and Kelso are still out at the salt pit," one of the troopers sneered.

The salt pit, Kat knew, was the old brickmaking factory on the way to Kabul that civilian intelligence had recently coopted as their own private interrogation facility. Kat had heard plenty of complaints about it from other interrogators since she arrived. In Kat's experience, it wouldn't have been unusual for the Special Forces guys to accompany detainees out to the OGA facility; at Kandahar, special ops and civilian intel had worked hand in hand, going on raids together and even conducting battlefield interrogations. But the trooper's tone told her there was something more going on here.

Kat opened her mouth to ask when Colin was expected back, then thought better of it.

"We'll be sure to pass your message along," another trooper said, and uneasy laughter erupted from the group.

Yes, Kat thought, there was definitely something wrong.

It was no longer dusk when she reached the main gate and turned back down Disney Drive. The sky was black and cloudless, illuminated by the bare-bulb glare of a thin wedge of moon. There was a live-fire exercise going on across the valley. Large puffs of dust and smoke rose from the distant hills, followed a few seconds later by the delayed thunderclaps of the marines' 155-mm M198 howitzers.

There was no point in going back to her tent now, Kat thought. She could never fall asleep with the howitzers firing. And, even if she did manage it, she was due back in the booths in less than two hours. A catnap would only leave her groggy and pissed off. No, she decided, heading back to the prison facility, she may as well get some work done.

After the nonstop activity of the previous two days, all of Kat's colleagues who could were taking advantage of the lull in detainee arrivals to sleep, and Kat, suddenly exhausted, kicked herself now for not having done the same.

Except for one other interrogator, a Lebanese-American kid from Brooklyn, who, like Kat, was one of the unit's few Arabic speakers, the Interrogation Control Element, or ICE, as Kat and the other interrogators referred to it, was deserted.

"Can't sleep?" the kid, who went by his last name, Hariri, asked, looking up from the interrogation report he was working on.

"Those goddamn howitzers," Kat complained, pouring herself a cup of coffee and slumping into a chair.

Hariri smiled. "You get used to it, believe me."

"So what are you doing here, then?"

"Just getting a jump on things."

A New Yorker and an Arab, Kat thought, looking at the kid, two awfully big burdens to carry in this war. She took a sip of the coffee and winced. She liked the high-octane variety, but this stuff was so thick she had to chew it.

"You hear about the Iranians?" Hariri asked.

"The pair who came in last night?" As far as Kat knew, Jamal's traveling companions were the only Iranians in custody.

Hariri nodded gravely. "One of them's dead."

"What happened?" The well-being of their prisoners was something all the interrogators took very seriously, and from the look on Hariri's face Kat could tell that he took it personally as well.

"I don't know all the details. Apparently the guy suffocated." He lowered his voice and glanced quickly around the room. "It was out at the civilian facility. You know what kind of stuff goes on out there."

The salt pit, Kat thought, nodding to reassure Hariri that she did in fact know what went on with the civilian interrogators. Now she understood why the SBS guys had been so testy with her in the British mess: the Iranians had been their prisoners.

Surely, brother," the man who called himself Ahmed said, resting his hand on Abdullah's shoulder and glancing pointedly at Jamal. "Your good works will not go unnoticed by Allah."

Ahmed, dressed in an imam's traditional brown robe and skullcap, was like so many others Jamal had known. Dutiful men, men of the mosque, pious in their declarations, if not always in their actions. Like Bagheri, or the two men with whom Jamal had left Abdullah's the first time.

Those two, also Moroccans, had approached Jamal one day near the ferry docks, promising a way out where Jamal had imagined none. Three good meals and a safe place to sleep, little brother. And Jamal, weighing the demands of piety against those of Abdullah, had hesitated only briefly before making his decision. After three months of Abdullah's late-night gropings and the shame and pain that inevitably followed, Jamal had been more than willing to sacrifice his soul to whatever god those men believed in for the preservation of his body. Though if he had known the extent of that sacrifice at the time, his choice might have been a different one.

Abdullah nodded beatifically. "It is true. I am like a father to these boys. By the will of Allah."

It was a hollow invocation, God's name spoken not out of piety but in the pursuit of whatever business opportunity Ahmed had to offer. There were people, mostly those who had never had to suffer the depredations of the flesh, who believed in the integrity of the soul above all else. But Jamal was not one of them, and neither, he knew, was Abdullah.

Abdullah turned to Jamal. "You will bring us tea," he commanded. And then, softening his tone for the benefit of the other man. "Brother."

Bowing slightly, Jamal turned and let himself out into the hall. Body or soul, he thought, as he made his way down the stairs to Abdullah's kitchen. So little was left of both, and yet it was clear to Jamal that if he stayed he would have to make the same choice again, that Abdullah had no intention of helping him leave Algeciras.

He reached the first-floor landing and stopped, contemplating the door to the kitchen, and at the opposite end of the hall, the one that led out onto the street. Body or soul, he reminded himself. His alone to squander or save.

If he was going to run, now was the time.

FIFTEEN

Stuart Kelso paused in front of a kebab shop on Albert Road and watched the tall figure skate behind him in the window's reflection. He was fairly confident the man was following him, but it was always hard to be sure about these things and, with the costs of misjudgment what they were, it was better to be absolutely certain before making even the slightest gesture of acknowledgment. Especially in a place like Portsmouth, where practically every third person was a sailor, and where rumor could travel quickly to the wrong ears.

Stuart waited, watching the man duck into a Boots pharmacy on the next block without so much as a single glance back. Wrong then, he told himself, feeling a twinge of disappointment as he started off down the street again. The man had been just his type, clean-cut and athletic, as Stuart himself was. But not a sailor from the looks of him. A student more likely, as was nearly everyone in this part of the city.

Over the course of the past year, with the trial looming, Stuart had made the trip south more times than he would have liked, and he'd gotten to know Portsmouth in the process. He had discovered the university neighborhood of Southsea and

Albert Road while trying to clear his head after one of his first
meetings with his lawyers, and the cluster of head shops and
curry restaurants had quickly become his favorite escape.

As Stuart passed the Boots, the man emerged again and fell
in step behind him. Stuart felt a surge of adrenaline. It was not
unlike the feeling he got on patrol when he knew something
bad was about to happen. A mixture of fear and excitement—
the relief, finally, of action, after hours or days of anticipation.

Stuart stopped again and the man moved on ahead, this
time looking quickly back to confirm that Stuart had understood before turning off Albert Road and onto a smaller, resi-
dential street. There was no mistaking the message now, and
Stuart felt his pulse rise as he strode along after the man, then
followed him up a small flight of steps and through the door of
a slightly ramshackle walk-up.

"I love you navy boys," the man said when Stuart stepped
into the building's narrow foyer. He was wearing a leather
jacket, new evidently, for the close space was heavy with the
musty smell of it and with the fainter, slightly spicy odor of
cologne. "All that hiding and seeking. Brings back some of the
romance of the old days, doesn't it?"

Stuart didn't answer. He was mainly ashamed of the sub-
terfuge with which he was forced to conduct his private life,
embarrassed that he allowed himself to be made to hide these
things.

"Shall we go up, then?" the man said, nodding at the stairwell.

There was something about the man's manner, something
beyond just the purpose of their meeting, that made Stuart
suddenly and uncharacteristically afraid. His hands were large
and powerful, the hands of someone who used them regularly.
Not a student, after all, Stuart thought, his fear turning into excitement.

The stranger led him to a small room off the third-floor

landing. Not so much a flat as a place kept specifically for this purpose, with a key left above the door. Inside there was one small bed and a single chair, a sink in the corner with a half-used bar of soap on the rim.

Special Forces, Stuart realized, watching the man walk to the only window and pull the shade, recognizing the guarded physicality with which he carried himself. One of his own, though neither of them could acknowledge the kinship.

Stuart took his own jacket off, then turned and laid it on the chair. "I'm meeting a friend in twenty minutes," he said, wanting to make it clear that this would not be a prolonged affair.

"You might be a bit late," the man said. He crossed from the window and pressed himself against Stuart, putting his mouth to Stuart's ear.

Then Stuart felt the man's rough hand on his arm and something else. A flush of pain, entirely unexpected. A knife like fire in his gut.

"Sorry about that," the man whispered, releasing his grip.

Stuart stumbled backward, his arms windmilling frantically, his legs buckling beneath him. It took him a moment to notice the bloody gash, another to understand that it was in fact his body that had been wounded. By then there was nothing to be done.

SHE KNEW, Kurtz thought, glancing over at Kat as they emerged from the Algeciras train station onto the Calle San Bernardo. Kat knew about Colin's death, yet she did not want him to know. The thought gave Kurtz no small amount of satisfaction.

"It shouldn't be far," she said. The four words were almost as much as she'd spoken on the train ride down. "According to Jamal's description, the shop is right on the main tourist corridor, between the train station and the ferry."

"That is, if it's still here," Kurtz cautioned, already wondering what they would do if they couldn't find the place. Establishments like this weren't exactly known for their longevity. The boy's information was at least three years old.

Kat looked up, scanning the buildings on either side of the street. "I'm assuming you have some cash to work with?"

Kurtz nodded. Money was not a problem.

"Good." Kat slowed her pace. "There," she said.

Ahead of them, a handful of dirty Moroccan boys were spread out along the sidewalk, hawking their services to passersby.

"Money change!" a boy of about fifteen in a faded Harvard T-shirt called out, making a beeline for two young British backpackers Kurtz recognized from their train. "Moroccan dirham here. Ferry tickets."

Reluctantly, the women slowed and then stopped, listening while the boy gestured to the storefront behind him. One of the women, the savvier of the two, glanced around, then made a move to continue on, but it was too late; the boy had the other one hooked already, and Kurtz knew it was only a matter of time before he had them both.

As he and Kat approached, the pair were already turning to follow the boy, but Kat stopped them.

"Keep moving," she said. Her voice was flat, pitched with authority. The women gaped, then hurried away. When the boy tried to do the same, Kat caught him by the arm. "We're looking for Abdullah," she told him in Arabic.

The boy shrugged, but Kat wasn't having it. She glanced over her shoulder at Kurtz and spoke in rapid Spanish. "Here's one for Melilla."

The boy's eyes widened into two pools of fear at the mention of the immigrant detention center. "There," he said, pointing to the same grimy storefront he'd indicated while talking to the women. "Mr. Abdullah is inside."

Kat released the boy and looked pointedly at Kurtz, as if to say, "That's how it's done," then turned and started for the open door.

"I'll handle the man," Kurtz told her as they stepped inside.

Deep and narrow and completely empty except for a scuffed counter at the rear, the shop had all the ambience of a long-neglected aquarium. Filthy fluorescents, swarmed by clouds of frantic moths, their shades mottled by the carcasses of the dead, stuttered overhead. The walls, once a common variant of institutional green, had been rendered an even more depressing algal shade by years of nicotine stains. Badly faded travel posters, the pigments dulled entirely to blues and grays, enhanced the aquatic nightmarescape. In the corner, a dead roach lay belly-up. Behind the counter, a television flickered soundlessly, the only sign of possible human presence.

Kat strode to the counter and rang the tarnished service bell. Almost immediately, like an octopus emerging from its lair, a man appeared from the back of the shop.

"May I help you?" he asked, taking the spit-darkened stub of a cigar from his mouth and eyeing the two visitors with no small amount of suspicion. He was grossly, almost perversely fat, his tiny head bobbing on his huge body.

"Are you Abdullah?" Kat asked before Kurtz had a chance to say anything.

The man nodded.

"We're looking for a Moroccan boy," Kat went on. "His name is Jamal."

Abdullah looked at Kurtz, and Kurtz could see only contempt in the man's eyes, scorn for Kat's brazenness. For an instant the two men understood each other completely.

"I'm afraid you've come to the wrong place," Abdullah answered, addressing Kurtz. "As you can see, there is no such person here."

"We're prepared to compensate you fairly for your time," Kat said, adding, "We know the boy has been here."

His eyes still on Kurtz, Abdullah nodded toward Kat. "Tell the woman to wait outside."

Kat started to protest, but Kurtz cut her off. "Leave us."

For a moment she didn't move. "Go," Kurtz repeated without looking at her, and this time she turned and made her way out of the shop.

"What the woman said was true," he told Abdullah once they were alone. "You are a businessman. I understand that your time is valuable."

Abdullah smiled, satisfied, Kurtz thought, with both the current proposition and the fact that his earlier request had been so swiftly fulfilled. "Ten thousand," he said calmly.

Kurtz laughed. "Five hundred euros," he countered, applying the tenfold inflation rule of thumb he always employed when bargaining with Arabs.

"Five thousand," Abdullah replied.

"Seven-fifty."

Abdullah looked pained. "One thousand," he agreed at last. "And you'll pay me first. That's not negotiable."

Kurtz opened his sample bag and counted out ten hundred-euro notes. Janson wouldn't be happy, but then he never was. There was a price to be paid for everything; Janson should have learned that by now.

Abdullah took the money, checking to make sure it was all there, before secreting it behind the counter. "The boy ran off this morning," he said then, folding his arms across his massive chest in a gesture of pure defensiveness. "He came to me looking for someone to take him across the strait, but of course I know nothing about those things."

"Of course," Kurtz said, understanding that he'd been cheated, and that there was nothing to be done about it. "He's trying to get to Morocco, then?" he asked, as if he could still salvage something from their exchange.

But Abdullah only shrugged. "If that's what you say, brother." Then he smiled at Kurtz, showing a mouthful of rotten teeth.

I⊤ WAS KURTZ ALL OVER. Kat fumed as she stood on the sidewalk outside the shop. She had learned long ago not to let men like Abdullah bother her, had even figured out how to use their prejudice to her advantage, but she refused to tolerate that kind of treatment from Kurtz. Besides, experience told her that the other man would be the one to benefit from the divide-and-conquer routine; that Kurtz, having shown his willingness to be complicit, would almost certainly get nowhere with Abdullah now.

Kat glanced down the sidewalk. With the exception of a few stragglers, the passengers from her train had passed by already on their way to the docks, and most of the boys had deserted their posts for more lucrative ventures. Kat knew from her interviews with Jamal at Bagram that a good part of Abdullah's income came from the pickpocketing the boys did in the tourist bars and the crowded ferry terminal, and this was no doubt where they had gone. But the boy in the Harvard T-shirt was still working the street.

A textbook candidate for intimidation, Kat thought, watching him dart into a doorway at the sight of two Spanish cops on the other side of the street. It was almost unfair how easy it had been the first time she approached him, and Kat felt a pang of guilt as she started toward him once again.

She moved to the doorway, blocking him in. "There has been a new boy here, yes? An older boy, looking for Abdullah?"

She gave him a moment to answer and, when he didn't,

glanced over her shoulder at the pair of *guardia civil* officers. "I've been to the camps," she said, raising her voice just slightly. "Believe me, you are better off out here."

The boy swallowed, hard enough for Kat to hear it.

Kat pushed all pity from her mind, as she'd been taught to do, and pressed on. "Where is he?"

Nothing.

"*Aquí!*" she yelled, and this time the boy's hand flew to hers.

"Please," he begged. "Please. I saw him. He was here."

Kat looked back over her shoulder and watched the cops slow, then move on again. "When?" she asked.

"He came last night. He stayed in Abdullah's room."

"He's still here?"

The boy shook his head. "I saw him at the docks this afternoon."

"The ferry docks?" Kat asked, thinking, The trucks. He was heading back as he'd come.

The boy nodded. His hand was still on hers, his grip desperate.

Kat eased her arm away, reached into the pocket of her jacket, and pulled out her billfold. "Here," she said, fishing out twenty euros for the boy.

He snatched the money from her, but the look on his face was accusatory, as if he knew how little the money meant to her, and that it was merely a salve for her own conscience.

Jamal hunkered down behind a stack of Gauloises boxes and watched the milky aureole of the Spanish customs inspector's flashlight play across the ceiling and walls. There was a part of him that wanted more than anything to be found, and he had to fight the urge to cry out.

The beam paused for a moment and Jamal caught a glimpse

of shaky Arabic on the far wall, the writing of someone who had come before him. The beginning of a prayer for those near death, the letters fading toward a crooked scrawl, the request verging on heretical, for no good Muslim was supposed to ask for the end: "O Allah, keep me alive so long as it is in my best interest and give me death when it is in my best interest."

Then the light was gone, and the inspector with it. Jamal felt the container's massive door slam shut and heard the sound of the long steel bolt sliding into place.

He drew his knees to his chest and closed his eyes against the darkness, trying not to think about the prayer or the fate of the boy who had written it there, trying not to judge the odds of his own survival. He had been lucky on his first crossing, had emerged from his carbon dioxide–induced haze with nothing worse than an unrelenting headache and brutal nausea. But he couldn't help worrying that he'd spent all of his good fortune and that this time things would be very different.

When the truck started up Jamal smelled the diesel fumes almost instantly, the saccharine odor mingling with the to-bacco in the boxes. Two, three hours if he was lucky, he told himself. And if he wasn't, it could be days before the door opened again. He switched on the small flashlight he'd brought and surveyed his provisions: a thin blanket and a gallon jug of water, a box of biscuits and a plastic bucket for a toilet. He had prepared himself as best he could.

The truck lurched forward and the floor swayed beneath him. Yes, he thought, forcing himself to turn the flashlight off and tamping down the welling panic in his throat, what happened from here was beyond his control.

SIXTEEN

"I see you got your French chocolates," Susan had remarked, glancing at the shopping bag in Harry's hand.

It was nearly a month since they'd met at the Caravelle, and Harry hadn't recognized her at first. In the daytime ex-pat squalor of the Duc Hotel's bar, Susan had seemed like another person altogether, younger and more vulnerable than the woman he remembered. She was wearing a white sundress made of eyelet cotton. Her hair was drawn back in a school-girl's ponytail.

She extended her hand. "Susan Maxwell. We met at that awful dinner."

"Yes, of course. Harry Comfort." Harry returned the gesture. Her grip was surprisingly strong, a man's handshake. Harry looked self-consciously at the shopping bag. "It's not what you think. I mean, it's a thank-you is all, for my house-keeper."

Susan looked amused. "How are you liking Nha Trang? Getting plenty of stargazing done with that Celestron of yours?"

The Vietnamese bartender came over before Harry could answer, and Harry ordered a vodka martini. The man paused and, when Harry didn't say anything, gestured to Susan. "And for the mademoiselle?" His tone was polite yet condescending, his contempt for Harry's coarseness barely restrained.

Harry could hear his father, some drunken counsel on manhood: *Always order for the lady, son.* "She'll have the same," he blurted, glancing at the empty martini glass in front of Susan.

The bartender looked at her for confirmation.

"A Gibson, please," she told the man.

"Sorry," Harry apologized.

But Susan waved her hand dismissively. "To tell you the truth, I'd rather order for myself. Sometimes I feel like a goddamn child with all that chivalry."

She was drunk, Harry realized. And, what's more, she looked as if she might have been crying. The Duc was the Agency's transient facility in Saigon, and there were any number of reasons that she might be there, but Harry had the distinct impression that she was waiting for someone. Morrow, he thought.

She fumbled a cigarette from her pack on the bar and Harry rushed to light it.

"So Nha Trang," she said. "You never answered my question."

Harry smiled, trying to lighten the mood. "I've been sworn to secrecy," he said, "so don't repeat this, but it's a nonstop party up there. Shuffleboard at the Czech consulate on Friday. Bridge with the Poles on Saturday. Lately the Soviets have been hosting a potluck Sunday. They don't call it the Schenectady of the East for nothing."

Susan tipped her head back and laughed. Just a bit too enthusiastically, Harry knew, but he felt triumphant nonetheless. "You should come up sometime," he continued. "We don't

normally let the Saigon riffraff in, but I could vouch for you."
The invitation was made without any serious expectation, but
he could see something click in Susan's face, the recognition of
an opportunity.

"You'll show me the stars?" she asked.

"If you'd like."

The bartender came with their drinks, and Susan took a
long, grateful sip. Yes, Harry thought, she had definitely been
crying. There was a faint smear on each cheek where her
makeup had run. And how long, he wondered, had she been
waiting? Two drinks? Three? More? She seemed like a woman
who could hold her liquor, so it must have been quite a while.

"You don't find it disconcerting?" she asked. "I mean the
universe and infinity and all that."

Harry shrugged. "Not really. Do you?"

"Honestly?" She turned on her stool so that her leg was
just touching Harry's. "The idea of all that space has always
scared me. It's something I try not to think about."

Harry could feel the warmth of her skin through his pant
leg. He knew he should move, but he couldn't bring himself
to. "Actually," he said, "it's kind of comforting to me, knowing my place. None of us are ever as important as we think we
are."

She set her glass down and looked intently at him, as if pon-
dering something. "Do you have a room?" she asked at last.

Harry nodded.

Susan moved her leg closer to his, then put her hand on his
knee. "Can I see it?"

Harry was confused. "See what?" he murmured stupidly.

"Your room, Harry. I want to see your room."

HIS CHOICE. Harry thought, as he turned into the parking lot of
the Kona Pack and Mail. He had seen the consequences clearly

that afternoon at the Duc, had understood from the beginning what his role in Susan and Morrow's affair would be, just what she wanted from him, and yet he had not been able to stop himself.

Their sex had been hurried and disappointing, begun and ended in a matter of fumbling seconds. An act to be endured, Harry had thought, watching Susan's grim face beneath him, her small breasts jerking up and back as he moved into her with the sloppy eagerness of a schoolboy.

Afterward, watching her sleep, he had felt ashamed. In the untempered afternoon light, the shoddiness of their surroundings was in full view. The room's scuffed walls and mildewed curtains. The ancient stains on the frayed sheets, relics of prior trysts.

Harry had left a note on the bedside table, something about a meeting at the Saigon station, which he'd meant as a merciful out for both of them. Then he'd taken a trishaw to a bar in Pham Ngu Lao and spent the rest of the evening wondering how they would avoid each other in the future. When he finally went back to his room early that morning, he was relieved to find Susan gone.

Harry turned off the engine and glanced in his rearview mirror, watching the same white Escort he'd noticed on the drive down pull into a parking space across the street. There were two men in the car. Too burly to be Agency and certainly not discreet enough. Though it occurred to Harry that being noticed was probably what they wanted, that they had been sent more as a warning than anything. Morrow's way of letting Harry know that it would be in everyone's best interest for him to share whatever he knew about Jamal.

He's in real trouble, Harry could hear Morrow say. He wondered if it wasn't Dick who was in over his head here. The boy was disposable, after all, and would not have merited even the Escort's rental price, much less the monkeys in the front seat.

Harry climbed out of the car and waved pleasantly to the two men. No harm, he thought, in letting them know they were doing their job. Then he crossed the breezeway and slipped into the Pack and Mail, where, he knew, Irene's papers would be waiting for him.

LIKE A KID AT CHRISTMAS. Kat had thought, watching Jamal hesitate, unable to make up his mind where to begin. On the table between them was a scavenged bounty of junk food. Beef jerky, a can of Pringles potato chips, various candy bars, blueberry Pop-Tarts, and a can of Mountain Dew. It wasn't exactly what the Red Cross would have considered a balanced meal, and Kat couldn't help wondering if she hadn't crossed some kind of ethical line.

Jamal opened the red Pringles tube and shook out a handful of potato chips. "So perfect!" he exclaimed, marveling at the uniformity of the chips. His command of English was a skill he was determined to show off, despite Kat's persistent efforts to communicate with him in Arabic.

Kat gave him a moment to absorb the miracle of modern food preparation. "Were you able to get some sleep?" she asked.

Jamal nodded enthusiastically. "It's very good here."

Kat had managed to find a spot for him on the upper deck of the prison facility, in one of the makeshift cells the interrogators had created and set aside for prisoners who were deemed either too fragile or too important to be mixed in with the others. With its pallet bed and bare overhead bulb it was the most basic of accommodations, but it was paradise compared with the cages. Jamal had been made well aware of how lucky he was.

"I want you to tell me about your parents," Kat said.

Jamal set down the Pringles and picked up the Pop-Tarts, examining the box carefully. "It is sweet?" he asked.

"Yes." Kat pressed on. "Your parents, Jamal. Your mother died when you were a baby?"

He looked up from the box. "I told you already. She is not dead."

"Of course. She lives with the king."

"It's true," Jamal insisted, reading her skepticism. "The cook told me."

Kat nodded benignly. "And your father?"

The boy set down the unopened Pop-Tarts box and picked up a Snickers bar instead. "I think this is better."

"Sweeter," Kat observed.

"It's chocolate, yes?"

"Yes."

Jamal smiled. "I like chocolate. Do you like chocolate, Mrs. Kat?"

"Yes," Kat told him. "Very much. And it's just Kat, okay? Not Mrs."

"Why not?" It was a scholarly question.

"Because Mrs. is only for married women."

"And you are not married?"

"No."

"Your husband is dead?"

Kat shook her head. "I don't have a husband."

"Oh." Jamal said, his eyes widening in a look of sudden comprehension. "You are a soldier, yes? Like the women at the camp. Mr. Hamid told me about the women soldiers."

"Yes," Kat agreed. "We are all soldiers here."

"And at the camp in Herat as well. Mr. Hamid said so."

Kat was puzzled. "Herat? Was that where you were heading?"

Jamal nodded. "He said the women were in charge there, that I would have to get used to it being this way."

"In charge, how?" Kat asked, thinking surely this was Bagheri's version of a joke, his comment on the men there.

"In charge of everything," the boy answered. "He said they were soldiers, like you are, that they carried weapons and even killed people."

"American women?" Kat asked.

"No," Jamal told her. "Muslim women."

Kat shook her head, smiling at the boy's gullibility. "No, Jamal. I don't think so. Not Muslim women."

Jamal shrugged, unwrapped the candy bar, and took a bite.

"Jamal?" she asked cautiously, watching him eat. "What would you think about helping us?" There, she had said it.

The boy stopped chewing and looked at her. "You mean like a spy?"

So he knew the word. "No. Like a friend. You could help us, and we could help you."

"How?"

"I don't know yet." She stopped, choosing her words carefully. "There are people who want to do bad things to other people."

"Like the towers?"

He was smart, Kat thought. Perhaps too smart for Kurtz's purposes. "Yes, exactly. Like the towers. You could listen for us, and if you heard something, someone planning something bad, you could let us know."

He took another bite of the Snickers bar and contemplated Kat's proposal. "And you would help me?"

"Yes. We would give you money. And other things. Chocolate." God, she couldn't believe she was saying this. Would they give him money? she wondered. Surely they would. They would have to. She thought back to those two brief days in

Tangier, the urchins at the ferry dock. Yes, she told herself, it was all for the best. "You would be taken care of."

"And where would I live?" Jamal asked, already starting to come around to the idea.

"I'm not sure. You might go back to Spain, I suppose."

His eyes lit up. "Or to America?"

"I don't know." It was possible, wasn't it? "Maybe."

And, just like that, the worst was done.

The blanket that served as the cell's door opened then and Hariri ducked his head inside. "There's a man here to see you," he said. "In the ICE."

Kurtz, Kat thought. Like a shark to the kill.

"I'll be back later," she told Jamal, rising from her chair and following Hariri out into the corridor.

"How's the prince?" Hariri asked.

"Who?"

"The prince," Hariri repeated, motioning toward Jamal's cell. "That's what the MPs are calling your boy."

Kat shrugged, smiling slightly at the nickname. "As good as can be expected. He just told me some crazy story about a camp in Herat with Muslim women soldiers. He claims that's where he and his buddies were headed."

"MEK?" Hariri suggested.

Kat shook her head. She was hardly an expert on the MEK, but she knew Afghanistan was well outside its territory. The group had traditionally conducted its military operations from within Iraq.

Originally founded by students at Tehran University, the Mojahedin-e Khalq had been serious players in the Iranian revolution years earlier, but they had since transformed themselves into a kind of bizarre military cult, combining Marxist ideology and Islamic theology with strident feminism.

Not long after the overthrow of the shah, the ayatollahs, threatened by the MEK's burgeoning power, had turned on the group, waging a fierce and bloody campaign against it. Its leadership all but obliterated, the few remaining members of the MEK had fled into exile in France, where, under the influence of a charismatic leader and his iron-willed wife, and with the help of friends with extremely deep pockets, they had refashioned themselves entirely.

"In Herat?" Kat asked skeptically.

"I guess not," Hariri agreed.

"It sounds to me like his friends were having him on."

They had reached the ICE, and Hariri stepped hurriedly forward, opening the door.

She had done it, Kat thought, steeling herself for the imminent encounter with Kurtz. She had done what he asked, and she did not feel good about it.

But when she stepped into the ICE she saw that it wasn't Kurtz who was waiting for her but Colin. He was filthy, his face and clothes covered with grease and dirt. There was dried blood beneath his right eye and the beginning of a bad bruise.

"I heard you were over at Camp Gibraltar," he said. "I came straightaway."

MITCHELL It was Stuart who woke them the next morning, his voice penetrating the darkness of the cargo container where they'd slept. The giant box was one of four that had been joined together to make the British interrogation facility. From what Kat could see, there was no indication that the structure had ever held prisoners. There was, however, ample evidence that Kat and Colin were not the first couple to have sought refuge there. "Hey, Mitchell, your friend's got a visitor at the gate. An American civilian named Kurtz."

Colin rolled over and switched on the camp lantern he'd brought, then glanced at his watch.

"What time is it?" Kat asked.

"Six-thirty."

"Shit!" They'd been asleep for nearly twelve hours, longer, it seemed, than the total number of hours Kat had slept since coming to Afghanistan. She sat up, scrambling to find her boots, feeling groggy and disoriented.

"Don't worry," Colin said. "The MPs won't let him into camp."

Colin leaned back on the makeshift bed he'd fashioned for them out of camp blankets and pulled Kat down toward him. "You'll come back tonight?"

Kat felt suddenly awkward. They had both been too exhausted for anything but sleep the night before, but the intimacy of it, here in this place where such unremarkable acts were taboo, seemed almost obscene, more so than if they had had sex. "If I can get away," she said, pulling back, finally locating her boots.

Colin touched her arm. "What's wrong?"

"Nothing." She slipped on her boots and pulled the laces tight, trying not to look at him.

He twisted around until he was in her line of sight. "What is it?"

"Nothing. Really. It's just this place, everything. Aren't you afraid?" She had not meant to say it, but now that she had there was no going back.

Colin shook his head. "Afraid of what?" he asked, as if he hadn't even considered the idea until now.

What wasn't there to be afraid of in this place, Kat thought. Death. Pain. The loss of all those things that kept one human. And now, despite her best attempts to hold her feelings for Colin to a minimum, there would be him to fear for as well. Kat stood up without answering him.

"I should go," she said. "He'll be wondering what's keeping me." She looked back at Colin. "Ten," she told him, softening just slightly. "I'll be here at ten if I can." Then she made her way out into the chill morning.

Kurtz was waiting for her outside the front gate with a look of stern impatience on his face.

"I hope you know what you're getting yourself into," he said as they started down Disney Drive together.

What a father would tell a child, Kat thought. "I can take care of myself," she snapped.

"Don't ever do that to me again," Kat said, tossing her bag aside and sloughing her jacket.

The hotel Kurtz had chosen was a dingy establishment, with tiny beds and claustrophobic rooms, greasy windows that looked out onto an industrial view of the Algeciras waterfront, and a shared cold-water shower down the hall. One star, Kat thought, only by the grace and muscle of a well-placed fifty-euro note. It was not unlike the hotel where she'd spent the night before making the crossing to Morocco three years earlier, only that establishment had been farther inland, in the squalid backpackers' quarter near the outdoor market.

"Do what?" Kurtz asked, feigning ignorance.

"I'm serious," Kat warned him. "Orders or no, you undermine me like that again and I'm on the first flight home. Understand?"

She stepped over to the window and looked across the ferry docks, from which the day's last boat to Tangier had departed some time earlier. Down on the pier's concrete apron, several dozen trucks were already massed for the morning crossing, their cabs dark. Across the bay, Gibraltar rose magnificently from the darkness, its scarred cliff face lit from below, solemn and intimidating.

A reckless choice, Kat told herself, thinking of Jamal, wondering just how much it would take to get her into one of those containers. Fear and desperation, degrees of which she could not even pretend to imagine. She knew for a fact that more died than lived on the trip across, many more. And to go this way, in the opposite direction of hope, back to the place from which one had run, from which one had already risked one's life to escape. To know how it would end even, in the untempered darkness, falling to final sleep.

Kurtz laughed mirthlessly. "How many people know you're here, Kat?"

Kat wheeled to face him. His eyes in the room's bald light were dull and impassive. "Is that a threat?"

"Just making an observation."

Despite everything, Kat had never feared Kurtz before. From the beginning, she had taken his anger as an expression of powerlessness. She had been alternately pitying and repulsed, but never afraid. Now, suddenly, she understood and she was.

SEVENTEEN

It was well into spring before Harry saw Susan again, nearly eight months since their meeting at the Hotel Duc, a stifling winter of interminable cocktail parties and elaborate dinners, of deflecting the none too discreet advances of languishing consular wives.

For the first few weeks after their indiscretion, Harry had worried that Morrow would find out. Saigon was not a city known for keeping its secrets, and Harry thought it more than possible that Susan would choose to tell Morrow herself. After all, revenge was effective only when both parties were aware of what had happened. But if Morrow did know he showed no indication of it, and eventually Harry gave the whole thing less and less thought. He even managed a sporadic affair with one of the wives from the Hungarian delegation, an unnatural blonde named Marta with a Teutonic ferocity in bed.

When Morrow called in April to say he'd be coming up to Nha Trang, Harry's first thought was that Susan had finally played her hand. He had not known quite what to expect—affairs like his and Susan's were not uncommon in the world in which they revolved, and these types of indiscretions were generally forgiven—but he prepared himself for the worst nonetheless, putting aside enough alcohol to dull himself against whatever pain—mental or physical—he might have to endure.

Harry wasn't sure whether to be relieved or not to see a figure in the passenger seat as he watched Morrow's Mercedes pull in through the gate from his second-floor office. He'd known people to bring backup to confrontations like this, either as witnesses or as extra muscle, though he couldn't see Morrow as someone who resolved his problems through physical means. Perhaps, he thought, the other person was there to make sure Harry went peacefully.

But when the door swung open it wasn't Janson or Robinson or any of the others from the Saigon station who stepped out onto the drive but Susan. She was wearing a lavender shirtwaist dress with a patterned chiffon scarf knotted at her throat, and she looked both ridiculously out of place and strikingly at ease against the tattered colonial backdrop of the villa.

She shaded her eyes with her hand and looked up, her gaze directed toward the exact spot where Harry stood. Harry ducked away from the open window.

"He's hiding from us," he heard her say to Morrow, laughing. "I saw him in the window."

Then Morrow, also amused. "I think he has a bit of a crush on you."

"We see you up there, Harry!" Susan called out. "You know, we won't bite!"

Harry flattened himself against the wall, desperately wishing he could replay the previous moments, knowing exactly how foolish he looked. "Just coming down," he called out as breezily as he could.

Susan and Morrow had let themselves inside and were already making themselves comfortable in the first-floor sitting room by the time Harry got downstairs. The villa wasn't Harry's, and he wasn't proprietary about the place, but the booze was his, and he was displeased to see Morrow helping himself to a bottle of twelve-year-old single malt from the liquor cabinet.

"I didn't realize you were bringing someone," Harry said testily.

Morrow set three cut-crystal glasses on the bar cart. "Susan's been bothering me for months about coming to see that telescope of yours. She said you invited her up."

Harry glanced over at Susan.

"You did invite me," she said, winking at him. "That afternoon at the Duc, or don't you remember?"

"I never thanked you for looking after her. I'm afraid I got hung up at the station. Susan speaks very highly of you, you know?" Morrow poured out two glasses of scotch, then gestured to Harry with the bottle. "You'll join us?"

Harry nodded eagerly. God, how he needed that drink. "Are you staying for dinner? I'll need to let An know."

"And breakfast, too. For Susan, that is." Morrow offered Harry a glass. "I'd stay the night as well, but I have to get back to Saigon. You won't mind showing her the ropes, will you?"

"No." Harry gulped the scotch. Over Morrow's shoulder, Susan winked at him again. "Not at all."

"Good. You can bring her back down tomorrow."

"Tomorrow?" Harry asked.

"Yes," Morrow replied. "I've scheduled a meeting for the afternoon. Is there a problem?"

"No," Harry mumbled. "Of course not."

"It's settled, then." Morrow raised his glass in a toast. "To Harry and his Celestron."

"Yes," Susan said. "To Harry."

"Don't think I don't know I'm being used," Harry told Susan later that night, after Morrow had left. They were sitting on the veranda waiting for An to finish her work and retire to her quarters. It was a futile pretense at propriety, for the house-keeper had already made it clear that she knew exactly what was going on, but by now they were all too committed to the deception to stop.

Susan took a long, satisfied drag off her cigarette, leaned her head back, and looked up at the sky. "It's clouding over," she remarked.

"Does he know?" Harry asked, still unsure of exactly how to interpret Morrow's earlier comments.

Susan laughed. "Of course not. He'd kill you if he did."

The way she spoke made Harry understand that the last comment was literal.

"You won't be a bore about this, will you?" she asked. "I mean, you of all people, getting bent out of shape."

"What's that supposed to mean?"

"You're not exactly a stranger to using people, are you? At least I've got my cards on the table."

She was right, of course.

She touched his hand. "I like you, Harry. Can't we just have a little fun?"

She had a smell to her, a rich smell, like that of a French de-partment store. The perpetual scent of expensive perfume and cosmetics and tissue paper. Like a gift that had been wrapped just for him.

He took her face in his hands and kissed her. It was reck-less, he knew, but he did it nonetheless.

And then, from inside the house, came An's voice. "Mr. Harry. I finish with the mademoiselle's room now. You need anything else?"

"No, An." He pulled away from Susan. "We're fine, thank you. Thank you for your help."

"Yes, Mr. Harry. Good night." As the woman turned to go, her eyes caught Susan's and a look of utter disapproval crossed her face.

Susan blinked then, and in that brief moment Harry could see that she was not all she claimed to be.

"You know he won't leave her," he said after An had finally gone. "His wife, I mean. They never do."

"I suppose you're right," Susan agreed, recovering herself, though it was obvious that she didn't believe what she said. She looked up at the overcast sky again. "No stars tonight."

"No," Harry said. "I guess you'll have to come back."

AND SHE HAD. Harry remembered now as he drove north out of Kailua into the charred landscape of the lava fields, keeping an eye on the white Escort in his rearview mirror, the two heads silhouetted behind the glass. Not as often as he would have liked, but she had come nonetheless, through the summer and into the next year, into that last long winter of collapse. Sometimes, as on that first visit, Morrow brought her himself. On those occasions Harry would be obligated to unsheathe the Celestron and put on a real show. But more often it was just the two of them, with An lurking reproachfully in the background, like the unacknowledged specter of Harry's own conscience.

Looking back on their affair from the cusp of old age, it was almost impossible for Harry to recall the frenzy of it, the urgency with which he had approached her, as if sex and ownership were one and the same, as if through mere possession he could be transformed.

He had wanted her physically, certainly, but it was the other, less tangible things that he had not been able to resist.

Like her ease with the servants, even An, who hated her. Those ephemeral marks of class which Harry did not possess.

In the distance, the prehistoric mass of Mauna Loa rose from its black skirts. Fourteen thousand feet, and another sixteen thousand to the ocean floor, nearly the height of Everest. Along the high, sloping crest, a row of observatories shimmered, miragelike, in the thin air.

Harry rolled down his window and let the hot breeze flood the car, the sulfur and asphalt smell of the volcanic plain. After so much time in the lush uplands, the starkness seemed like a modernist's vision of hell. Penance for what? Harry wondered. He glanced at the envelope on the passenger seat, Irene's familiar scrawl on the shipping label. Gluttony? Greed? The sin of self-deception?

Along the highway, island graffiti, written in white coral, studded the black berms of lava rock: MARRY ME KAIPO. The message was inscribed inside a large heart. Here and there a delicate tuft of pili grass or the scorched and gnarled skeleton of a kiawe bush fought its way up out of the rocks. But apart from these small concessions to life the plain seemed utterly uninhabited.

Of course, Morrow had known all along. *If it hadn't been you, it would have been someone else,* he had said. This, years after it was all over. *You didn't really think she'd pick you?*

The sign for the old Kona airport loomed out of the wasteland and Harry tapped the brakes, the old anger getting the better of him, the old shame. Dodging oncoming traffic, he veered sharply to the left and started down the long dirt road that led to the water, slowing just slightly to make sure the Escort followed behind.

The old airport, perched at the edge of the Pacific, had been out of commission for several decades, since a larger facility was built farther north, but the state had wisely taken advantage of the property's proximity to one of the island's nicer beaches and turned it into a state park, using the runway as a parking lot and the old terminal buildings as administration facilities.

Harry wasn't much for the beach, but Char had dragged him here a couple of times, and he clearly remembered seeing a pay phone. They would take care of this now, he told himself, glancing back at the Escort. They would finish things once and for all.

It was a weekday, early still, and the beach parking lot was nearly deserted, only a handful of spaces claimed by salt-eaten island vehicles. Harry pulled up in front of the old terminal building and climbed out of his car, trying to conjure Morrow's home number. He'd had an impeccable recall for numbers at one time, photographic even, but his mind was not what it used to be and he was unsure as he strode to the pay phone on the breezeway. Behind him, the Escort pulled into a space on the far side of the lot, close to the beach.

Harry pushed a pocketful of change into the slot and waited for the dial tone, then punched in the number.

Two rings. Four. Six. Perhaps he had gotten it wrong.

Eight rings and then a click. "Hello?" It was Susan.

He fumbled for something to say.

"Hello?"

"I'm calling for Dick Morrow." Harry swallowed hard, tasting panic in the back of his throat.

She paused. "Harry? Is that you?" Her voice on the line was exactly as he remembered it.

"I'm sorry?" What was he afraid of? he wondered. Why did he feel the need to lie?

"Never mind." She sounded almost disappointed. "I thought you were someone else. I'll see if I can find him."

There was a rustling as she set the phone down, then her voice, distant. "Marina! Marina, is my husband home?"

Another female voice, this one foreign. Footsteps and the sound of a door slamming. The click of a second line.

"Yes?" Morrow.

"Call your dogs off, Dick." Harry said.

He could hear Morrow's hand cover the receiver and a muffled shout. "Marina! Hang up the line." Then Morrow was back. "Calm down, Harry."

"I am calm." And he was, surprisingly so. "I don't know anything about the boy or where he's run off to, and I'd appreciate being left alone. I've got your goons right here. You can talk to them now if you'd like." He waved to the men in the Escort, motioning for them to join him. "Hey! Starsky! Hutch! Over here!"

The pair glanced awkwardly at each other, then looked out toward the beach.

"Calm down," Morrow repeated. "We know about the phone call, Harry. We know he tried to contact you. You gave him your number, didn't you?"

"A minor lapse in judgment," Harry said. Then, in an effort to deflect the question, "What could you possibly want with the boy, anyway? He was a dead end."

"No, Harry, you were the dead end."

"He didn't even go to the mosque," Harry protested. "He spent his Fridays cruising for johns in the Rosaleda, for God's sake."

"That's not what he told your replacement."

"I don't believe it."

"Believe what you like," Morrow told him. "But I'm afraid I can't turn you loose just yet. What if the boy were to call you again? What if Irene were to somehow pass him on to you this time?"

"Leave her out of this," Harry said, though he knew the protest was futile.

"I wish we could trust you, Harry, I really do. But what's to say you won't have another one of your minor lapses in judgment? No, I'm afraid the goons, as you refer to them, will have to stay."

"Fuck you."

"You, too," Morrow said cheerily. "You'll call me if you hear anything."

EIGHTEEN

Where had this woman come from? Manar wondered as she stepped out onto the street and pulled the gate shut behind her, hearing the iron latch click firmly into place. Who was she, this other self who was afraid of nothing, who needed, suddenly and without question, to know?

Manar had told no one of her visit to Asiya's house, or of what had taken her there: the fragile hope she had allowed herself to nurture. To her mother, Manar knew, any thoughts of the child were merely reminders of the shame they had all been forced to endure because of Manar's choices, like the scar on their household that Manar herself had become—the thing about which one spoke only in whispers, and never to those outside the immediate family.

Manar had tried hard to put the idea of the boy aside. She knew the kind of lives for which the children of the charity houses were destined, knew desperation and its consequences intimately. She understood what the old woman had meant when she said Manar was better off not knowing. But she had not been able to let her thoughts of the child go.

After her visit to the housekeeper she'd lain awake remembering those few moments in the prison hospital, his smell when she'd held him to her. And for the first time since they'd taken him from her all those years ago, she had begun to hope, not for his death but for his survival.

From the dark city came the mournful call of the muezzin, the first of the day's five reminders. Not of God, for Manar had long since ceased to believe in God, but of his betrayal.

Manar reached up and adjusted her head scarf, pulling the fabric down around her face not out of modesty but to ensure that she was not recognized. Then, without knowing it, she turned east, toward Mecca, and started down the street.

"They hate you because you are not one of them," Rachida, the old widow who ran the kitchen at Ain Chock, had told Jamal once, after he'd come to her seeking solace for a particularly bad beating he'd suffered at the hands of some of the other boys. "Their mothers were whores," she had hissed. "But yours was one of the disappeared."

Disappeared. Jamal had heard the word whispered uneasily by some of the older residents of the orphanage, and from this he had been able to glean that it was a punishment of sorts, something much worse than the narrow stick the director kept in his office. "Disappeared to where?" he asked.

The old woman touched a swab of iodine to the cut on his cheek, and Jamal tried not to flinch at the pain.

"To the desert," she said, conjuring in Jamal's mind a cartoon image of a palm-shaded oasis and a pack of lazy camels.

"Could I visit her sometime?"

Rachida laughed mirthlessly. "Where she has gone, you would not want to visit."

"Yes, I would," Jamal insisted.

But the old woman was firm. "No one goes to the desert who wishes to come back," she said, moving away and busying herself with a large pot of lentils that was cooking on the stove.

"But what did she do wrong?" Jamal asked. "Who took her there?"

Rachida clucked her tongue disapprovingly. "You ask too many questions," she said, brandishing her wooden spoon. "It was the king who took her. Now shoo."

The king. Later that night, lying awake in the fetid darkness of the dormitory, Jamal had not been able to keep himself from repeating to his friend Nordine what Rachida had told him.

But Nordine, one year older and ten years wiser, had only laughed. "Why would the king take your mother to the desert?"

It was a fair question, and one that Jamal could not answer. He shook his head. "I don't know."

"Disappeared or dead," Nordine said. "What is the difference? You are still here like the rest of us."

To Jamal there was a great difference, a confirmation of what he had suspected all along: that he was different from the others, that he did not belong in this place, after all.

He did not say this to Nordine, but when he closed his eyes he saw his mother in splendid wedding attire, her bride's caftan and headdress heavy with gold-thread embroidery, her hands elaborately hennaed. Not a whore, then, but pure as a virgin, as he'd always known she was. Her eyes were downcast to preserve her modesty, her feet delicate in white leather slippers. Beneath her, carpets of the finest wool had been spread out over the sand.

In his new dream, Jamal's mother put her hand up to beckon him forward. There were intricate patterns on her fingers and palms, whorls and eddies like the design of moving water or the twisted branches of a tree, the stain of the henna still fresh on her skin. Her hair was dark and uncovered, falling loose around her shoulders, over her white marriage dress. All around them stretched a vast plain, red sand and blue sky. The sun was a pure white fire overhead.

Jamal climbed down and started toward her, walking with difficulty over the shifting ground. He would have to get used to this, he told himself, if he was going to live in the desert. His progress now was slow, and she was moving quickly ahead of him, intent on something in the distance.

"Wait!" Jamal called out.

Her dress was white linen, like the *ihram* of a pilgrim, made from two pieces of seamless cloth. She turned and looked briefly back at him, smiling.

"Stop!" Jamal called again.

"Hurry!" she replied, motioning once more for him to follow. She smelled like lotus and rainwater, like the earth of the grave. Her linen shroud was tight against her body, the cloth wound five times, as the hadith said it should be for burial, her feet and head covered.

"Hurry!" Not his mother's voice now but that of a man. Then a second voice and a third, each in rapid Arabic.

"He lives?"

"Hurry! *Zid! Zid!*"

Jamal felt himself being lifted up and carried forward. He could smell the ocean, the brine stink of it mingling with the coppery odor of burned phosphate. It was the unmistakable smell of home. In the distance, the muezzin was singing the first call to prayers.

"Brother!" one of the men said. "Wake up, brother!"

Slowly, Jamal opened his eyes. "Where am I?"

The man grinned, showing rotten teeth, then clamped his hand on Jamal's shoulder. "Casa," he said. "Where else?"

Driving was one of many skills Manar had forgotten during her time away. She knew the city transit system well, had spent many hours since her return riding the crowded buses, often with no destination in mind. But today she knew exactly where she was going. She had made her plans meticulously the night before, tracing and retracing the route she would take, setting aside her fare in exact change.

Anfa was not a neighborhood from which people commuted by public transport. Those who were able to live here could afford not just cars but drivers as well. At this early hour, no one was leaving. Instead, the influx was of workers from the city's poorer quarters—cooks and maids, gardeners and chauffeurs—and the bus stop on the Boulevard d'Anfa was accordingly deserted. The boulevard itself was empty as well, the storefronts all dark. All except for the French bakery on the far corner, in whose light-flooded interior Manar could make out opulent rows of *pains au chocolat* and *apricotines*.

Manar glanced at her watch as she sat down on the bench to wait. Her nerves had pressed her out of the house earlier than necessary. Now it would be a good ten minutes before she could expect the bus. She took a deep breath and exhaled, trying to calm herself for what lay ahead.

It was here, she could not help recalling, that she had waited for the bus that would take her to meet Yusuf and the others so many years ago. Here, that last afternoon, on the same bench, with the same perfume of butter and sugar in the air. Only then the smell, rich as it was, had made her sick.

It had been two weeks since she'd first known for certain that she was pregnant, since she and her sister had huddled anxiously around the contraband home test in her sister's bathroom. Two weeks and she had still not found the courage to tell Yusuf, though she knew that he would be overjoyed.

They had already spoken of marriage. Now there would be no question about the matter. And Manar should have been happy as well, though as much as she loved him, she had not been ready to compromise the person she was.

She had planned to tell him that evening, after the demonstration. But by the time she arrived the strike had turned violent, and she was unable to find him before being swept up in the chaos herself.

It would be years before she knew what happened to him. On her first day home, her mother told her. *That boy you were seeing. They killed him, you know. Shot him in the street like a dog.* As simple as that. And Manar had felt a flood of relief, knowing he had not been made to suffer, knowing her worst fears, all those dreams of his ransacked body, were only that.

NINETEEN

From the street, the Ain Chock Charity House looked no different from the rest of Casablanca's state-built apartment blocks, looming, soulless structures that had been built to replace the squalor of the bidonvilles, but which had managed only to reduce poverty to its basest level. Whatever small redemptions the slums offered—the community of others, the culture of place, the simple gift of individuality—were all but negated by the architectural fascism of the government buildings, the relentless repetition of gray cement and soot-darkened windows, the surrounding aprons of hard-beaten earth.

It was midmorning by the time Manar descended from the last of three buses that had carried her from the privileged world of Anfa to this dismal industrial neighborhood on the outskirts of the city. She should have been nervous as she walked the last few blocks to the orphanage and approached the building's imposing front gate. Should have been, but wasn't. Beneath her loose djellaba and dark scarf, her body buzzed with an almost ecstatic sense of calm. It was something, she imagined, like what a Sufi dancer must feel, or someone standing in the eye of a scouring sandstorm. The kind of peace that came from being at the very nadir of the world, with everything else in revolution.

Inside the front gate, in what had once been a courtyard, a squatters' village had sprung up, more miserable than any slum Manar had ever seen. Not just children but the old and sick and lame had congregated within the walls of the orphanage. In the doorway of the shanty closest to the gate, an old woman, blind and legless, sat tending a pitiful fire. Farther inside, a young girl with the moon face of Down syndrome held a screaming baby. Beside her, a boy was skinning a rat.

The settlement itself had the runaway look of an organic being, some kind of wild cantilevered fungus that had grown forever out and up, the new obliterating the old, until the entire organism appeared ready to collapse beneath the weight of its own ambition.

Manar had not gone more than a few meters before she found herself surrounded by some dozen boys. "Dinars," one of them pleaded. He was the oldest of the bunch, though he couldn't have been more than nine or ten. He lifted his shirt and pointed to his sunken stomach, then made the universal sign for food. He was a seasoned beggar, the gestures, Manar thought, pure theater. But the look on his face said there was nothing contrived about his hunger.

Manar reached into her robe and pulled out a single tendinar coin. She would have fed them all if she could have, but as it was she could allow herself neither pity nor compassion. She would accomplish nothing if she did. "Take me to the director," she told the oldest boy, holding the coin just out of his reach.

He turned and hissed at the others, who disappeared almost as quickly as they had come, scattering into the series of narrow alleyways that branched chaotically off the settlement's main artery.

The boy glanced at Manar, then started off ahead of her. Sizing her up, she thought, for maximum profit. And how many times had she done the same? Trying to gauge each new guard, trying to guess just what it would take, just how much more of her waning self could be pared off and sacrificed, just what could be gotten in return. An extra piece of bread. A single wedge of an orange. The comfort, just once, of having her name spoken aloud by another human being.

The boy was fast, his bare feet deft at navigating the piles of rotting garbage and smeared feces, and Manar was out of breath by the time they reached the building's front portal.

"Here, sister. This way." The boy stopped in the open doorway and beckoned her forward.

Manar crossed the threshold and stepped inside, then shrank back, gagging at the unmistakable stench of death. The nose, she knew from experience, can acclimate to almost any smell: urine, feces, rot, the tang of the unwashed body. But never the stink of a human corpse. Never. No wonder the residents had moved outside.

Covering her nose and mouth with a corner of her djellaba and moving slowly, Manar forced herself to step into the darkness of the building's foyer. There appeared to be no electricity. Most of the light fixtures and wire had been ripped from the walls and ceilings for sale in the junk bazaar, leaving only rough holes. The more tenacious fixtures had merely been stripped of their bulbs.

Through the open doors of the rooms off the corridor, Manar could make out rows of moldy mattresses and mounds of filthy bedding, the skeletal remains of a few sad toys. It seemed utterly impossible that any child could live in such squalor, and yet here and there huddled figures showed themselves—a single boy or a group of boys. Not children but the ragged ghosts of children.

Undeterred by the squalor, Manar's guide darted forward,

pausing frequently to allow her to catch up. The floor beneath his bare feet was littered with broken glass and cracked tiles.

"Be careful!" Manar called out ridiculously.

He glanced back at her with a look of exasperated patience before ducking into a small alcove at the very end of the main hallway.

"Here!" he declared triumphantly, once Manar had joined him. He beamed up at her, his smile all teeth in the gloom, then indicated a peeling door marked "Director."

The door was half ajar. Manar stepped forward and nudged it with her foot, revealing a broken desk and two steel cabinets adrift amid a sea of scattered papers and dusty files.

The boy reached for the ten-dinar coin in Manar's hand. "Where is the director?" she asked, holding the money just out of his reach, needing him still.

A shrug. "He has not been here for many months now."

"And the staff? The other adults?"

Another shrug.

"You are on your own, then?"

"The king has sent you?" the boy asked hopefully. "You have come to help us?"

Manar shook her head. She could not lie to him. "How long have you lived here?"

"All my life."

"I'm looking for someone," she said. "A child who was sent here to live many years ago. You might know him."

The boy regarded her suspiciously. Surely no one with good intentions would need such information.

Manar reached into her robe once more and pulled out a second ten-dinar coin.

"How old is he?" the boy asked.

"He would be nineteen now."

"And his name?"

"I don't know his name."

"There are many boys here. Many who come and go. It will be difficult, I think. You can tell me how he looks?"

Manar shook her head. "I would know him if I saw him," she said, not certain whether she believed this.

There must have been other women like Manar who had come asking the same question, who had said this very same thing, for the boy suddenly seemed to understand. "Sister," he said, turning back toward the hallway and motioning for Manar to follow. "There is something you must see."

WE ARE BOTH SAFELY ACROSS and well cared for, thanks be to Allah and our new friends here in Spain, Jamal had written on a postcard sometime after his arrival in Algeciras. It was the only letter he had ever posted in his life, and he had needed the help of one of Abdullah's older boys. What he wrote was a lie, and he knew it. But he also knew it was what those he'd left behind were waiting to hear. Not only that their friends were safe but that the way out existed for them as well. Jamal did not want to be the one to tell them otherwise. Besides, the truth was too humiliating to convey.

In fact, he had not seen Nordine for over a month, since they'd separated from each other in Tangier. The journey north had taken them nearly a week, begging or stealing rides, walking a good portion of the way, and they were desperate and starving long before they arrived in Tangier. Jamal had wanted to turn back before they even reached the city, but Nordine had insisted that they continue on.

"You are always imagining the worst, little brother," he'd chided Jamal. "We are so close now. What could go wrong?"

A lifetime of hustling to survive at the orphanage had done little to prepare either of the boys for the bottleneck of desperate humanity they encountered in Tangier. All Africa appeared to have converged on the city, all with the same suicidal purpose in mind—that of crossing the narrow yet deadly strip of water that stood between them and the European continent.

On the spectrum of hunger, there is really only one moment that matters: the instant when one's loyalty shifts irrevocably from pride to survival. For Jamal, that moment came on his fifth night in Tangier, when, while hustling tourists on the street outside the CTM bus station, he and Nordine unknowingly infringed upon the territory of some older boys and were beaten almost unconscious for their mistake. Later, as they huddled in the doorway of a mosque in the *ville nouvelle*, Jamal realized that if he didn't eat soon he would lose all will to do so, and would eventually die.

The next morning, while Nordine slept, Jamal left his friend and walked up into the old city, to a café on the Petit Socco, where, he had noticed, a certain kind of European man liked to take his morning coffee. Two hours later, in a one-room flat overlooking the Church of the Immaculate Conception, in return for a fifty-dinar note, he had done with his body things that, just a few days earlier, he would have deemed unthinkable.

In this way he had survived.

THE MORNING WAS BRIGHT. the breeze cool, even here, miles from the sea, among the city's derelict factories and sprawling apartment blocks. It was a day Jamal had imagined many times. The hero's return. Money in his pocket and more on the way. Lambs for the slaughter. A feast in the courtyard. A flurry of candy and sweets. And now here he was, coming back not as a prince but as a beggar.

Encumbered by the weight of his shame, Jamal paused briefly in the shadow of the orphanage and contemplated the place from which he had fled so many years ago. There was the second-floor window, five from the front, from which he had seen the world for his first fifteen years. And there, beneath it, the director's office, where Jamal had had his first lessons in humiliation. He told himself that it should not have been this way. But it was.

In his gut he wanted to run, and for a moment he considered doing so. Then the image of the dead American sprawled across the bed at the hotel in Lavapiés came back to him. He heard the man's voice once again from the bottom of the stairs, that awkward Arabic that he would never be able to forget. *We're your friends, Jamal.*

No, he thought, moving forward toward the gate, with its weathered inscription—"Ain Chock Charity House"—it should not have been this way. But surely if there was one place the Americans would not think to look it was here.

The courtyard of Ain Chock had always been home to a rambling squatters' camp. The home was not officially allowed to keep boys after they reached the age of sixteen, but prospects were few and many boys chose to stay on nonetheless, living off the scraps of the orphanage's scraps, squeezing what little they could out of the younger boys in exchange for certain protections. But the settlement had grown considerably in the years since Jamal had left. It now had the look of something permanent, more like the city's larger bidonvilles than the haphazard collection of tarps and boxes it had once been.

Just inside the gate, Jamal was greeted by an old woman in a stained cotton djellaba. "Brother," she rasped, holding out her withered hand and rocking forward on mere stumps of legs.

Not just lame but blind, he thought, watching the gray orbs of her eyes. He reached into his pocket, letting the coins he carried jangle against each other.

"*Teta,*" he crooned affectionately. *Grandma.* "What has happened here? Where have all these people come from?"

"Where else would you have us go?"

"But the director," Jamal asked. "He allows you to stay?"

"Haven't you heard, brother? There is no director now."

"And the boys?" In coming back to the orphanage, Jamal had foolishly assumed that he would take up the thread of his old life. He could see now that this would be impossible. And yet he knew that he would not survive on his own.

The woman shrugged. "Some are here still, but many have gone. Many are dead."

"There was a widow who worked in the kitchen," Jamal said, remembering the small kindnesses the cook had shown him. "Her name was Rachida."

Another shrug, this gesture more final than the last. She had told him everything she knew.

Jamal took a euro coin from his pocket and slipped it into her outstretched palm. "*As-salamu alaykum,*" he told her. *Peace be upon you.*

She ran her weathered thumb across the strange money, then closed her fingers around it. "*As-saluma alaykum, wa rahmatullahi.*" *And mercy as well.*

"*Wa rahmatullahi,*" Jamal agreed, then started forward into the courtyard.

SHE SHOULD HAVE KNOWN, Manar thought, looking at the faces on the wall in front of her, feeling the suffocating grip of her own failure. She should have been certain, should have been able to point to each photograph and say with confidence: mine, not mine. A real mother would have been able to do this, but she could not.

In each boy, in each set of features, Manar could see both her own child and the impossibility of such an idea. If only she could smell them, she told herself. If only she could push each brown lock of hair aside until she found the single blessed mark. Then she would know.

"Who are they?" she asked her young guide.

"The ones who have gone," he said.

Manar was puzzled. "Gone where?"

The boy made a skyward gesture. For a moment Manar thought that this was his way of telling her they had died.

"To the North," he said at last.

"To Europe, you mean?"

The boy nodded with enthusiasm. "In a year or so, I will go, too."

"It's dangerous," Manar warned him. "You know that, don't you?"

But the boy only shrugged.

Manar took a deep breath and let her eyes wander back over the faded photographs. Many had messages scrawled on them, parting words of encouragement for those left behind, or inside jokes—the bravado of children whose sense of humor appeared miraculously, unfathomably intact.

And how many of them, Manar wondered as she took in the lopsided grins and unnaturally old eyes, had made it? A few, if they were lucky. A number, out of the wall full of photographs, so small that Manar could no doubt count it on her fingers.

"Do any of them ever come back?" she asked.

The boy laughed at the absurdity of this idea. "Why, sister? Why would they come back?"

Jamal stopped in the doorway and peered into the building's dark interior, letting his eyes adjust to the sudden change in light. The stench from inside was worse than he remembered, the smell utterly human in its depravity. He could not bring himself to go inside.

Five years of degradations, he thought, suddenly exhausted, unable to go on. Five years of whoring himself in one way or another, of allowing himself to be swept across three continents. And now here he was, a stranger in the place that had once been his home.

He felt as he had that night in Tangier, caught between despair and self-preservation, only this time he feared he would not have the strength to act. He put his hand in his pocket and felt what remained of the money the American had given him, calculating just how long it would last, how many more days of food and shelter he could buy. Three, maybe four, he decided. And then what? He did not think he would be able to bring himself to do what was necessary.

"Jamal?"

The voice, almost familiar, came from behind him. Jamal turned to see two young men, one in a soccer jersey and track pants, the other in blue jeans and a worn leather jacket.

The man in the soccer jersey motioned to his chest. "It's Adil."

"Adil?" Jamal squinted, trying to match the boyish features he remembered to the adult who now stood before him. "The professor!" he exclaimed. It was a nickname Adil had earned by being the smartest of the boys.

Adil came forward and put his arms around Jamal.

"What are you doing here?" Jamal asked after they had embraced.

"I could ask you the same thing."

"Yes," Jamal conceded. "But I asked you first."

Adil smiled warmly. "God willing, it is only temporary. I will finish university at the end of this year. But for now this place is cheaper than the dorms. And you? I thought we would not see you again." And then, in an aside to his companion, "Jamal made the crossing to Spain several years ago."

The young man in the leather jacket nodded. It was a gesture not of understanding but of scorn. "Did you get tired of the European women?" he sneered.

"Mahjoub is from Rabat," Adil said, as if this explained everything, and in a way it did.

Jamal nodded. He had known more than his share of Mahjoubs in his life, and he understood everything he needed to about the young man: namely, that he was not to be trusted.

They stood there awkwardly for a moment, exchanging wary glances, then Adil clamped his arm around Jamal's shoulder once again. "But you must be hungry," he said. "Come, we will find you something to eat."

MANAR SLIPPED THE TWO PROMISED COINS into the boy's hand and watched him scamper away down the long corridor. Past his retreating figure, three sun-smeared shapes, like figures on an Impressionist's canvas, were visible in the bright rectangle of the doorway.

Breathing through her mouth, picking her way around the rafts of debris, Manar moved forward toward the promise of daylight. *It is for the best, sister.* She could hear the old woman again. *If your son was at Ain Chock, it is better not to know.*

The boy reached the doorway and stopped briefly to look back at Manar before disappearing into the glare of the courtyard. A survivor, she told herself, wondering if the same was true of her son. If he was, his instincts would have had to come from someone other than her. She had known strong people, and she knew with certainty that she was not one of them.

Her guide slipped away and Manar saw the three figures turn as if to go, one slightly apart from the others. For an instant, just an instant, it was as if Manar's heart had been yanked violently from her body. He turned and the gesture did not belong to the figure before her in the courtyard but to Yusuf. And in this single, ordinary movement Manar was momentarily reconciled with everything from which she had been separated.

In that instant it was Yusuf's torso in the doorway, his shoulders slumping slightly forward as if burdened by some unseen load. Yusuf as he had been so many times in their tiny borrowed flat near the university. As he had been that last time, when she had wished to tell him about the child but hadn't.

"Wait!" she called out, but the figures were already gone.

She stumbled forward, moving as quickly as possible. By the time she managed to reach the doorway, the three had disappeared altogether and she was no longer certain of what she had seen.

Perhaps there had been nothing, she told herself as she stood there blinking in the light, scanning the chaos of the courtyard, the collapsing façades and the alleys twisting back into darkness. Perhaps, in her desperation to find something, she had imagined it all. In fact, she knew. There could be no other answer.

TWENTY

From his post in Xuan Loc, Harry had seen the end coming with a kind of absolute clarity he had never before imagined himself capable of. But then, by the autumn of 1974, only a fool, or the handful of lunatics in the ambassador's office, would have bargained otherwise. Even before December, when Congress took the final step of voting to cut off all military aid to South Vietnam, it was painfully obvious to Harry and his colleagues that the winter approaching would be their last in Vietnam.

Within the international community, those last few months there was an adrenaline- and alcohol-fueled frenzy that Harry would later come to recognize as typical of such times. It was an attitude possible only for those lucky few who knew they would be getting safely out and so could enjoy the thrills of war from a distance, knowing they would not have to cope with the aftermath. But for the Vietnamese, the end of the American presence in their country meant something else entirely.

He and An did not talk about what was happening. The Vietnamese were stoics to a degree that Harry had not yet encountered and never would again. But her fear was obvious. She was the only surviving child in her family, and her elderly parents relied on her for everything. Though An had taken her job not out of loyalty but out of necessity, they both knew that her motives would make no difference once the North Vietnamese arrived. Whether she would be allowed to live was not entirely clear; certainly the outcome would not be a happy one for her or for her parents.

In early March, several days after the People's Army launched its virtually unchallenged invasion of the Central Highlands, Harry went down to the kitchen to find An unmoving at the sink, staring out the window at the rain-drenched garden, her arms sunk to the elbows in cold dishwater.

"I can get you out, you know," he'd told her then. It was a reckless thing to say, for he did not in fact know whether such a thing would be possible. There had been talk of getting everyone out, of course, but a reasonable person could see that there was only so much room, only so many who could be accommodated. But Harry had not been able to stop himself. "Your parents as well," he continued rashly. "You'll all be taken care of."

But she did not move. It was almost as if she didn't believe him, and so Harry added, without thinking, "I promise."

She glanced up at him, not gratefully, but with a ferocious resignation, as if she already knew that he would betray her and could not stand the insult of his assurance.

And then, as if somehow able to sense the awkwardness of his predicament and the immediacy with which he needed rescuing, the phone rang, enabling Harry to turn away from her.

Even the staunchest optimists at the embassy were concerned by the situation in the North, and Harry's phone had been ringing regularly since the invasion as various reports made their way to Saigon and out into the wider world. So

Harry was surprised when, instead of one of the Saigon regulars calling with an update, it was Susan on the other end of the line.

He could tell immediately that something was wrong. She had planned to come up over the weekend but was no doubt thinking better of it.

"Probably best if you stay put for now," he offered hastily, trying to put her at ease. And then, when she didn't reply, "Maybe I can come down next week." Come down for good, more likely, he thought.

"We're getting married, Harry."

It took Harry a moment to hear what she had said, and even then he did not quite understand. "I'm sorry?"

"I wanted you to hear it from me." Her tone was magnanimous, with just a hint of pity, as if she were sparing him something. "Dick's wife has agreed to a divorce."

Harry said nothing.

"Don't be upset," Susan continued. "We all knew this was coming."

Her goddamned honesty, he thought. But she was right. She had told him herself that this was the way things would end, but he had not wanted to believe her.

"Dick says it's a matter of weeks before we all have to go. It would have been over between us in any case. You could see that much."

But he hadn't. Somehow he'd imagined a future for the two of them—Susan at his side, the remote possibility of children, all of it occurring in a place other than this one. It was an unfinished idea, but one that existed nonetheless, and the thought of surrendering it hurt him deeply.

"I'm sure we'll see each other before it's all over," Susan said then, as if it were the end of summer camp she was talking about and not the collapse of a nation.

"Yes," Harry replied. "I'm sure we will."

And, like that, it was over.

TRYING TO IGNORE the unforgiving pain in his back and knees, Harry lowered himself to the floor and reached under his bed, feeling for the safe he'd stowed there when he first moved in. There had been a time not long ago when such an action wouldn't have warranted so much as a second thought. But, now that he was already down, Harry realized too late that this time had passed, and that there was a very real possibility he might not be able to get back up again.

Here was the real misery of aging, he thought, the truth no one ever told you: when infirmity came, it did so with surprising speed. It was worse for men, he supposed. Women faced the disintegration of their bodies early on, beginning with the consequences of childbirth, while men were unmercifully allowed to continue believing in the fiction of their youthfulness.

Harry's right hand recognized the shape of the safe, pushed much farther under the box spring than he would have liked. What had he been thinking, he wondered, as he forced his belly onto the floor and twisted his torso, extending both arms beneath the bed. At the time, he knew that an arm's length wasn't far enough, but it was the best he'd been able to do. There were only so many places in a retirement condominium that a person could hide something.

Awkwardly, Harry pulled the safe toward him and out from under the bed frame. Then he rolled over onto his back and lay for a moment staring up at the ceiling before finally summoning the will to get up.

The safe itself was nondescript, a standard gray fireproof box Harry had bought for thirty dollars at the office-supply store in Kailua. It was a receptacle that even most burglars would have passed by—a place to keep birth certificates and living wills, items of limited value to anyone except the one or two persons to whom they were invaluable. Such was the case with most of the contents of Harry's safe.

The box, covered with a thick layer of dust, had obviously not been disturbed, but Harry could feel his heart leaping all the same as he dialed the combination and cracked the hinges. For most of his adult life Harry had had a contingency plan, an escape hatch through which he could disappear if things ever got too hairy. When he moved to the island he'd told himself he was through with such things, that to run at this point in his life would be the worst kind of capitulation. But he had not been able to let go of the idea entirely. Now he was grateful he hadn't.

Inside the safe were documents of various kinds: passports and driver's licenses, a handful of credit cards to match. And, at the bottom, a stack of hundred-dollar bills. A hundred in all. Ten thousand dollars for a rainy day.

Harry took out the money and fingered it, then set it aside and picked up one of the passports, a dark-blue booklet embossed with the elaborate Canadian seal. *No one bothers a Canadian,* Harry's old friend Eduardo Morais had remarked when Harry commissioned the document from him. That had been nearly five years ago. Now Morais, like so many of the others Harry had once called friends, no longer existed except in Harry's memory.

Harry opened the passport's front flap and looked down at his own face staring back at him, his old man's teeth and chin, the flesh gone soft from age and drink. It was a wonder Char would have him, a wonder any woman would.

As if on cue, Harry heard the sound of Char's key in the front lock. Hastily, he closed the passport and stuffed it and the money into the small overnight bag he'd packed for himself. Then he pushed the safe back under the bed.

"Hello, lover!" he heard Char call out, then two loud thumps as she kicked her clogs off.

Harry stepped out of the bedroom to meet her. "How was your class?"

She had come from a pottery class she was taking at the Kamuela community center, and her clothes were splattered and stained.

She stopped halfway across the living room. "What's wrong?"

"I'm going to have to go away for a while."

She looked at him for a moment, then came forward and put her arms around him. Harry could smell the studio on her, the pleasant odors of dried clay and kiln fire.

"There are things you should know," he began, "things I want you to understand."

She shook her head, then reached up and touched her finger to his lips. "You're a good person, Harry Comfort."

It was in no way a benediction. Her refusal to hear his confession made that clear. But there was a permission of sorts in what she said, an acknowledgment of the fact that he was capable, at least, of redemption. That they all were.

She rested her head on his chest and Harry was grateful, relieved not to have to look her in the eye.

TWENTY-ONE

After so much time spent living within the plodding works of military bureaucracy, Kat had assumed that whatever handover of Jamal was planned would take months to happen. At those not infrequent times when her guilt got the best of her, she took comfort in the myriad frustrations she'd dealt with since arriving in Afghanistan: the supply of tampons she'd requested dozens of times while at Kandahar that had never, to her knowledge, arrived; the space heaters they had so desperately needed for the booths that first winter which had sat in a warehouse in K-2 for six weeks, waiting for some supply sergeant's signature before they could make their way south.

Surely, she told herself, a living, breathing human being, with all the attendant complications, would require as much time and bureaucratic energy as a box of feminine-hygiene products or a piece of hardware. Surely something would happen in the meantime to change the boy's fate, some contingency for which they had not planned. They were in a war, after all, and there was no saying what might occur.

So when Kurtz appeared at her desk less than two weeks after their first encounter with the news that Jamal would be leaving the following morning, Kat was unnerved. Since Jamal's arrival, the boy had become Kat's major responsibility, and the two of them had developed a relationship. It was one of jailer to prisoner, to be sure, about this Kat had no illusions, but it was a relationship nonetheless, and Kat was not prepared for it to end.

She was still working at the in-processing facility and in the booths as needed, but the bulk of her downtime was spent with Jamal, preparing him as best she could for what lay ahead, working to cement whatever trust they had already established. He had not asked her any specific questions about his leaving, and Kat, not wanting to contemplate the subject, had been more than happy to remain silent.

"Have you told Jamal yet?" she asked, glancing up from the report she was working on.

Kurtz shook his head. "I thought you could tell him over dinner tonight. Give you a chance to say your goodbyes."

"He'll want to know where he's going."

"They need him in Madrid," Kurtz told her. *They,* as if he himself had no part in the matter. "I can arrange for something special to be brought over from the mess. Any requests?"

Kat thought for a minute, then shook her head. Asking for something felt too much like planning a condemned man's last meal.

But when she finally got to Jamal's cell later that evening, she was instantly sorry she had left the decision up to Kurtz. He'd brought them two trays of Salisbury steak. It was by far the least palatable of all the choices the mess offered, with accompanying powdered mashed potatoes, gray canned green beans, and Jell-O salad.

Trying to show enthusiasm for the dinners, Kat sat down at the wooden crate she'd salvaged for Jamal to use as a table.

"Private Boyd is bringing his PlayStation to the lounge tonight," Jamal announced excitedly. "I can go?"

Kat nodded. "Yes, but after we eat." Jamal had become a mascot of sorts around the facility, especially among some of the younger MPs, like Boyd, who saw Jamal as a kind of pliable younger sibling. Kurtz had encouraged the relationship, and the tactic seemed to have worked; Jamal was now completely enamored of the soldiers, and his English was improving daily.

Jamal picked up his knife and fork and contemplated his tray before digging into the pile of mashed potatoes. He and Kat had discussed American food at length, especially potatoes, for which Jamal had developed a deep appreciation.

"I have some news for you, Jamal," Kat said, leaving her own meal untouched, figuring she could make herself some instant soup in the lounge.

"You are sending me to America?" Jamal asked.

"Not yet," Kat told him. "You'll be going to Spain first, to Madrid."

Jamal set his fork down. This was not good news. "You said I would go to America."

"No, Jamal," Kat corrected him. "I said you might go to America. And you still might. It's just that Madrid is where you're needed now."

"I want to stay here," Jamal insisted. He looked as if he was about to cry.

"You can't stay here forever," Kat said. "You know that. None of us can. In another few months I'll be leaving myself."

Jamal brightened, though whether his change of mood was genuine or for her benefit Kat could not be sure. The latter, she thought, knowing his desperation to please her. "And later I will go to America?"

"Yes." What was she supposed to say? "Yes, later."

Kat had known that she was lying when she told Jamal she would be back in the morning to see him off, but she made the promise anyway. She convinced herself it wasn't cowardice that motivated her deception but concern, wanting the boy to get a good night's sleep before a long day of traveling. But the truth was that she couldn't bring herself to be there when Kurtz came for him, and neither could she find the courage to tell Jamal.

She'd taken up a collection in the ICE, netting nearly a hundred dollars in pocket money and a hefty supply of junk food. To this she added her own donation and, in a sacrifice that she knew was provoked entirely by guilt, her iPod. All of this she entrusted to one of the night-duty MPs, with the instructions that Jamal be given it in the morning.

It was late when Kat finally left the facility, nearly midnight, and she found herself heading down Disney Drive toward the British camp. She and Colin hadn't planned to meet, but she knew that she couldn't go back to her tent without some kind of consolation.

It was nearly a mile to the far end of the runway, and Kat was shivering by the time she reached the British camp, her toes numb in her boots, her cheeks pinched and red. June, Kat thought, and she could see her breath in the air, could feel the threat of snow in the knife's edge of wind that cut through her thin jacket. The sky was overcast, the clouds thick enough to mask any hint of moonlight or stars.

Kat knew the MPs at the British gate by now. Colin's team had been held on base for nearly two weeks, since the death of the Iranian, and Kat had become a regular visitor to the camp during that time. Normally, she tried to bring some small token graft with her—the British soldiers were especially fond of the packets of powdered-drink mix the Americans inexplicably received in all of their care packages—but tonight she was empty-handed.

The guard waved her over, and Kat shrugged her apologies. "I'll get you next time," she told him, cupping her hands to her mouth and savoring the warmth of her breath in her palms.

"Don't worry about it." He smiled, slightly embarrassed, as always, to be included in their charade. For by now it was clear that Kat's visits to the camp were anything but official. "They're next door," he said, motioning in the direction from which she had just come.

Kat glanced back down the empty road toward the barbed-wire enclosure that was the official home of Bagram's special-operations task force. The camp was strictly off limits to any non–Special Forces personnel. Kat had never once ventured inside its perimeter, and she was reluctant to do so now, but the thought of making the cold walk back to her tent with only her own accusatory thoughts for company was more than she could bear. Waving to the British MP, she trudged off down Disney Drive, then turned in through the unmanned entrance to the Special Forces camp.

Unlike the neighboring British camp, with its neat rows of tents and bright flags, the Special Forces facility was more post-apocalyptic fraternity house than colonial outpost. Just inside the front gate was a giant barbecue pit, over which some enterprising soldiers were roasting a whole goat on a large, mechanized spit. Like all the native Afghan creatures Kat had encountered, it was a scrawny, pitiful beast, its head lolling loose on its half-severed neck, its doleful eyes reflecting the flames.

The men, Rangers from the looks of them, glanced up with mild interest as Kat passed but made no move to stop her. Kids, Kat thought. Her brother's age and younger. Some of them not even old enough to grow a respectable beard. And certainly none of them were about to tell a woman in civilian clothes where she could or could not be. Instead, one of them reached forward with the barrel of his M4 carbine and prodded the carcass in an adolescent mimicry of anal sex. The others laughed crudely.

Kat stopped just inside the pit's smoky halo and addressed

the soldier who had made the gesture. "I'm looking for the British team," she said.

He shrugged—outsiders were not welcome here, that much was clear—then pursed his lips and spit into the fire. "They've got some tents back behind the mess," he said with palpable hostility, nodding toward a large, low structure.

Turning, Kat made her way along the trajectory of the Ranger's gaze toward the rear of the camp. Unlike the tents in Viper City, to which soldiers were quick to add their own creature comforts—mini refrigerators and laptops, photographs of family and friends—the accommodations here were basic at best, temporary shelter for the brief forays the Special Forces soldiers were occasionally forced to make back to Bagram for supplies or to drop off prisoners.

Provisional, just as Colin was, Kat thought, glancing at the squatters' tents and Porta Johns, chiding herself for having imagined otherwise, for having convinced herself the two of them could somehow overcome their surroundings. She reached the dark mess hall and paused, ready to turn back, her teeth chattering as she scanned the last few rows of tents. Out past the fence, the rotting hulk of an old MIG glinted in the perimeter lights.

There was a noise from behind her, a boot stuttering across the uneven ground, and Kat turned to see Colin emerging from around the corner of the mess.

"Kat?" The surprise in his voice was edged with irritation. "What are you doing here?"

"I'm sorry," she apologized. "I shouldn't have come."

Colin stopped where he was, offering her no argument.

"They're taking Jamal in the morning," she said.

"Oh." He nodded, distracted, then glanced past her toward the front gate.

Waiting for someone, Kat thought, and for a moment the thought that Colin was having an affair with someone other than her crossed her mind. "'Oh'?" she said angrily. "That's all you have to say?"

"What do you want me to say? You went into this with your eyes wide open. You made your choice, now it's time to live with it."

"It was the right thing to do," she shot back, suddenly defensive. "We couldn't very well send him back where he'd come from."

"No," Colin agreed, "you couldn't."

It was the same unsentimentality she'd fallen for that first night in Oman and it seemed unfair to hold it against him now, but she did. "At least I don't have his blood on my hands," she said. Though they hadn't spoken about the Iranian, Colin had been visibly shaken by the prisoner's death, and Kat knew full well the force of the barb.

He lunged forward, grabbing her. "You don't know anything about what happened out there, understand? Nothing." He was utterly, terrifyingly calm in his anger, his hand hard on her wrist, the force in the gesture just enough to inflict the maximum pain without breaking Kat's arm.

"You're hurting me," she told him, fighting to keep her voice steady.

"Lovers' quarrel?" The voice came from behind Kat.

Colin released his grip, and she spun around to see Kurtz coming toward them. He had a smug look on his face. Pleased, she thought, to see them like this.

Colin stepped away, distancing himself from her. "She was just leaving."

And suddenly Kat realized that it was Kurtz he'd been waiting for. "Yes," she agreed, trying but failing to make sense of the situation, to imagine what Kurtz was doing there. She looked over at Colin, but he refused to meet her gaze. "I think I'd better go."

"Looks like we'll be here for a while," Kat observed as Kurtz pulled their rented Peugeot off the highway and into the parking lot of a BP station.

Kurtz nudged the car into a slot next to the pumps, cut the engine, and looked at his watch. It was midafternoon, time for the *Asr*, and a crowd of men, most of them truck drivers from what Kurtz could tell, were gathered near two outside water spigots.

It had taken them more than five frustrating hours to get a rental car and get out of Tangier. Now this simple stop for gas would set them back another half hour, and that was if they were lucky.

"I don't think we're in Kansas anymore," Kurtz remarked.

Kat unbuckled her seat belt and opened the passenger door. "I'm going to find a bathroom," she announced, climbing out of the Peugeot.

Kurtz watched her disappear into the station, then turned his attention to the men. The pre-prayer ablutions was a ritual Kurtz had seen hundreds, perhaps even thousands of times, but it continued to fascinate him nonetheless. It was always a remarkable thing to watch grown men debasing themselves in public. For the cleansing, like the prayer itself, was performed in such a way as to humble, even humiliate, the worshipper.

As with the prayer itself, there were strict rules to be followed, a sequence in which everything was to be done. First the declaration of pious intent, then the washing itself. The hands three times, the mouth three times, the nose three times, and so on. The ears just once, in a fashion both graceful and ridiculous, the gestures like those of a baseball player signaling a teammate, the inner sides with the forefingers and the outer sides with the thumbs.

The true believers are those who feel a fear in their hearts when God is mentioned. Kurtz thought of the words of the Koran as he watched the men roll their socks down and set them carefully aside. It was this last step of the process that he found most disarming, the men's feet bare and vulnerable beneath the spigot.

Kurtz had crushed a man's foot once, using only his hands and a piece of wood, so he knew from experience just how easy it was to do, how delicate were the bones upon which men, even those of physical power, walked.

Not just once a day, he thought, but five times, and each time the same supplication. It was simply not possible for someone raised in the West to conceive of such a thing, to understand the sheer surrender required for faith on such a level.

For a moment, Kurtz felt a hot surge of jealousy toward the men. As they unrolled their prayer rugs and moved into the *qiyam*—hands to the ears, palms to the *qiblah*—he thought that this was what was needed. No questions, no moral equivocating, just the courage to know, to bow down and sublimate yourself entirely. To do what needed to be done.

Kat had forgotten what it meant to be a woman in an Islamic country. Even in a place like Morocco, swamped as it was with Western tourists, she was aware of just how much was forbidden her based on her sex. Much of Arab life is lived in public, in cafés and town squares, places from which women are effectively barred. And though Kat understood that there was a different life, rich in its own right, being lived in kitchens and behind *mashrabiyya,* she questioned the equality of that life. The fact that she could neither see it nor participate in it only added to her skepticism.

She had witnessed this kind of segregation to a much more terrifying degree in Afghanistan. The women there had been nothing more than ghosts, groups of huddled and silent figures begging along the roadsides or gliding to and from the market. She herself had faced the stares of the Afghan men in the booth, the cold looks of disdain and shame. Or, worse, the desperate attempts to keep from looking at her at all. But there she had been insulated by her uniform. There she had been the one with all the power. While here, she was quickly realizing, the opposite was true.

Kat tried not to look at the group of men performing their ablutions as she made her way across the parking lot and into the gas station. Her mere presence during their prayers, she knew, was not just distracting but forbidden, and she had no desire to impose herself on them. But she needed to find a bathroom and she figured it was better to do so now than to wait until they were engaged in prayer.

An old man, bent and palsied, had been left inside to watch the counter and the cash register. He glanced up at the sound of the door opening, his rheumy eyes taking Kat in with obvious skepticism.

Kat smiled her most non-threatening smile. "*As-salam alaykum,*" she said. The words felt good in her mouth, as they always did, the sounds rich and strong. If nothing else was true, she loved this language.

The man's face widened into a thin but appreciative grin. "*Wa alaykum as-salam,*" he replied. *And upon you, too.*

Kat asked him about the bathroom, and he motioned with a grunt toward the back of the building and a door, slightly ajar.

The facilities, it turned out, were located just off the rear of the station, in a small cinderblock outbuilding. Though primitive by Western standards, they were clean and functional, and Kat was grateful for them. As she made her way back inside, she noticed a weather-worn pay phone attached to the station's rear wall.

"Does the phone in the back work?" she asked the old man, and was surprised to get a vigorous nod in response.

All the currency she had on her was in euros, but she was hoping the gas station, situated as it was on the main road south from Tangier, would be willing to offer her some kind of exchange. She glanced around the cluttered shop, taking in the dusty merchandise: cans of motor oil and racks of plastic prayer beads, bright packages of Bamiball lollipops and Nestlé chocolate bars. And, on a shelf next to the cash register, a pile of colorful head scarves.

Glancing out the front window to confirm that Kurtz was still in the car, Kat pointed to the pile of scarves. "I'll take the blue one, please." In any case, it would not be a bad thing to have. She took a twenty-euro note from her pocket and offered it to the man. "I'm sorry. It's all I have."

"It's good, it's good," he replied, waving off her apology. He handed her the scarf and a seventy-unit phone card, happily taking the twenty euros. And then, in the same way one might encourage a child, he made a brief pantomime to show Kat that she should put the scarf on.

To the old man's immediate delight, she did as she was told. Then she headed out to the back courtyard.

Time was of the essence now, Kat reminded herself. There was only so much of it to be explained by a bathroom trip. Keeping one eye on the door, Kat slid her card into the phone's slot, lifted the receiver, and dialed the number at Colin's farm.

Two rings. Three. Four. The flat double tones of the British phone system.

"Hello?" The voice was unfamiliar. Male, with the timbre of late middle age.

"Hello. This is Kat Caldwell. I'm calling for Stuart Kelso." Silence.

"I was a friend of Colin's," she offered.

Another pause. Perhaps she'd dialed the wrong number. She was about to say so when the man spoke at last.

"This is Donald Mitchell, Kat." Colin's father.

Kat had not met him, but she had a picture in her mind: an older, more weathered version of Colin. *Old hippies,* Colin had said once, describing his parents. *They don't know quite what to make of me.* Kat couldn't help wondering what they made of her.

"Mr. Mitchell. I'm sorry . . ." She hesitated, trying to think of something to say, knowing from experience that anything she offered would sound trite at best. "I'm sorry to bother you. Stuart said I could reach him here."

"Stuart's dead, Kat." Just like that.

"Excuse me?"

"They found him last night in a communal flat down in Portsmouth. Appears he got in with some rough trade." He seemed grateful to have something, anything, to talk about besides his own son's death.

Kat's head was spinning. "I don't understand."

"Some bloke he picked up in town, they think. Apparently there's a lot of that down there."

He was, she realized at last, telling her that Stuart was gay, and that he'd been murdered by another man.

"Everyone will know now," he continued. "Of course he had to be careful about that, in his line of work. I can't say this kind of thing didn't cross our minds before. It's a dangerous business, all that secrecy."

"Yes," Kat agreed, "it's terrible." And then, wishing she could say more, but conscious of both Kurtz and her fast-dwindling phone card, "I was calling about Colin, Mr. Mitchell. About your plans."

At the mention of Colin, the man's voice shifted audibly. "We still haven't made any, what with everything that's happened. And there's the body to come back still. He would have liked to be in the mountains, so I suppose that's what we'll do. But nothing official." He paused then, collecting himself. "You're welcome to come over whenever you can. I'm sure Colin would appreciate it. He liked you very much. But then I'm sure you knew that."

The comment took Kat off guard. Suddenly, she was crying.

From inside the gas station came the sound of a door slamming and two voices. Kurtz's overbearing Arabic and the old man answering back. Kat pinched the bridge of her nose and took a deep breath. Kurtz would not see her like this. "I'm sorry," she told Colin's father, "I have to go."

"THERE ARE NOT MANY of us left," Adil said, dividing the last of the tea among their chipped cups, listing the names of the others who had chosen to brave the trip north.

Jamal looked down at his feet. Their meal had been a feast, and he felt ashamed for having taken the guest's portions offered him. His own greed sickened him.

From somewhere in the distance, outside the walls of Ain Chock, the call to prayer could be heard. *Asr*, Jamal thought, the day three-fifths gone already. There was a time when he would not have noticed the muezzin's call, but after so long away the day's division had become foreign to him. It would take some time to get used to it again.

Mahjoub downed the dregs of his tea and stood up from the vegetable crate that served as the abode's only table. "I'm going to the mosque," he announced, then eyed Jamal one last time before ducking through the shanty's low door.

"Don't worry about him," Adil remarked after Mahjoub had gone, sensing Jamal's discomfort with the young man.

"He's not so bad. And he can get us things. He knows people at the mosque."

Jamal nodded uneasily. He was familiar with this kind of charity.

"To our dear director," Adil said, smiling as he raised his teacup in a toast. It was a joke from the old days, an expression of what the boys had always been too afraid to voice.

"To the director," Jamal replied. Then, suddenly: "I'm in trouble, Adil."

Adil set his tea down. "You are home now," he said, his expression serious.

"No." Jamal shook his head. "I should not have come here."

"Shh," Adil scolded him gently. "You are tired. You will sleep here tonight and in the morning things will not seem so bad."

Jamal knew he should go, but the thought of leaving the relative comfort of Ain Chock was too much for him. In his exhaustion, he began to weep. "I will leave in the morning," he said. "I promise you."

Adil reached over and put his hand on Jamal's shoulder. "Brother," he said, "you will stay as long as you need to."

TWENTY-TWO

The morning of Jamal's departure, Kat stayed in her tent until she heard the early transport lumber down the runway on its way to K-2. By the time she finally reported for her shift, shortly after nine, the facility was in chaos. Climbing up to the ICE, Kat could see that the main cages were packed to capacity.

"Where the fuck have you been?" the day-shift officer in charge, an Iowa business-school grad named Kyle Hewson, snapped when Kat walked into the ICE.

Kat shrugged. "I'm here now."

"We could have used you five hours ago," Hewson grunted, then turned back to his computer, too busy to waste any more time on Kat. "Hariri needs help in seven. He'll bring you up to speed."

The choice to pair two of the unit's few Arabic speakers was an idiotic waste, but it was typical of Hewson, whose decisions were guided by some oblique management calculus, the reasoning behind which only a fellow MBA could have understood. But Kat was in no position to argue. Grateful for the reprieve, she headed out of the ICE and onto the catwalk that ringed the main prison floor, along which most of the interrogation booths were located.

The VIP cells, including the one where Jamal had been housed since his arrival, were off this same walkway, and Kat was conscious of a knot in her stomach as she approached the boy's quarters. Someone, perhaps even Jamal on his way out, had thrown the blanket that normally covered the doorway aside, and Kat could not keep herself from peering into the space as she passed, half expecting to see the boy's gawky face grinning back at her. He'd left behind his army-issue Koran and a pile of dog-eared comic books, but what little else he'd had in the way of possessions—a calendar of beach scenes that Kat had bought from a Hawaiian nurse for a ridiculous price, a Manchester United jersey Colin had won in a poker game at the British camp—were gone. Kat forced herself to keep moving.

Time in the booth is like dog years, in that one hour spent with a prisoner can easily feel like seven. Kat didn't know how long Hariri had been at it that morning, but when she ducked her head through the makeshift doorway of his booth she could see that he was already well past his limit.

"What's going on?" Kat asked when Hariri joined her outside the booth. "Hewson's in one of his moods."

Hariri stepped closer to Kat and lowered his voice to just above a whisper. "No one's confirming it, but the word from the MPs is that there was an escape last night."

Kat couldn't keep from laughing. She might have believed such a thing at Kandahar, where security at the hastily constructed facility was dodgy at times, but the idea of someone slipping out of the Bagram prison was utterly incredible.

The cages themselves were entirely transparent, lit from above and monitored by live MPs twenty-four hours a day. The only time the prisoners left was for interrogations, and then only under the strictest security, passing through one locked door and into a sally port before being shackled and led through a second locked door. At every step of the way, the men were accompanied by at least two MPs. And this was just the first line of defense. Anyone who managed to somehow outwit the cages would then have to negotiate a series of walls and electrified fences before encountering, just outside the prison, one of the most heavily mined strips of land in all Afghanistan.

"You've got to be shitting me," Kat said. "Spider-Man couldn't escape from this place."

But Hariri shook his head, serious. "I heard it was the second Iranian, the one whose friend died out at the civilian facility."

Kat was incredulous. "You're telling me he just strolled out of here?"

Hariri shrugged. "I'm telling you he's gone." He lowered his voice yet again, and glanced cautiously over his shoulder. "Everyone knows those Special Forces guys can walk through walls."

"What are you saying?" The implication was clear, but Kat wanted Hariri to say it to her face. It was no secret in the ICE that something was going on between her and Colin.

"I'm sorry, Kat, but I just can't imagine any of those guys are too broke up about this."

He was right, of course. If something out of bounds had happened at the salt pit, Colin's team had both motive and opportunity to see the Iranian gone; besides them, he was the only possible witness to the other prisoner's death. But Kat still wasn't buying it. "I know the guys on that team," she insisted. "They may not always play by the rules, but they wouldn't do something like this. I mean, come on, think about what you're saying."

Hariri nodded. "I'm sure you're right," he said without conviction.

Kat motioned to the booth. Better, she told herself, to let it go and concentrate on the demons they had at least a chance of slaying. "Hewson said you'd bring me up to speed."

COLIN AND NOW STUART. Kat thought, wrestling with the unsettling fact of Stuart's death as she and Kurtz hurtled south through the smog-drenched Casablanca suburbs. She had been prepared to accept Colin's suicide, had seen the gesture as yet another mark of just how little they really knew each other, an extension of whatever misunderstanding had passed between them that last night at Bagram. But the two deaths together seemed like an uncomfortable coincidence.

Kat looked over at Kurtz, at his face in hard profile, his hands on the wheel. Did he know? she wondered. Had he known about Colin all along?

Kurtz shifted his eyes from the road and glanced at her. "Something wrong?"

Kat shook her head. Just days before the court-martial was scheduled to begin, she thought, and Stuart and Colin were dead. They were dead and here she was with Kurtz, looking for the boy who had come in with the Iranians in the first place. No, there was more than mere coincidence at work.

"I was wondering about Jamal," she said, struggling to keep her voice steady. "What happens if we find him?"

Distracted, Kurtz glanced over his shoulder, then wheeled the Peugeot around a clot of merging cars. It was late afternoon, nearing rush hour, and the road was clogged with traffic, all of it moving at a near-suicidal pace. "How much farther?" he asked, nodding toward the map he'd given her after their last stop.

Other than what Kat had gleaned from Jamal's sketchy descriptions, she knew little about the Ain Chock Charity House. Jamal had mentioned several times that it was south of the city, but where, exactly, was not something Kat had had the time to pursue during their conversations at Bagram. But Kurtz knew. Clearly, he had been prepared to come this far.

Kat reached for the map and unfolded it, let her eyes move down the paper and come to rest on the *X* Kurtz had drawn in the city's southern suburbs. "Another mile or so," she guessed, looking around for landmarks, finding their position in relation to the map.

"Good," Kurtz remarked, glancing out the window toward where the sun hung low in the sky.

Conscious, as she was, of what little daylight was left to them, and of how utterly at a disadvantage they would be once darkness fell. It is one thing to be a stranger in a place like Casablanca during the daytime, quite another after the sun goes down. If they didn't find the orphanage soon, they would have no choice but to wait until morning.

"Jamal," she persisted. "What are we going to do with him?"

Kurtz's eyes focused back on the road. "I suppose that depends on what he tells us."

It was an odd thing, Kat thought, to say about someone in danger. "But there must be a plan. For getting him out of here, I mean. Will he be coming back with us?"

"Yes," he said distractedly. And then, making a point of turning and looking her directly in the eye, as only someone who is lying will, "It's all arranged. He'll be coming with us."

After all her years of training and all her hours in the booth, there were still times when Kat could not say with any certainty whether she was being lied to. But this was not one of those times. It was clear to her that Kurtz wasn't telling the truth. And though his dishonesty came as no surprise, she was taken aback by the recklessness of his lie. As always, he did not think her up to the task. It was, she thought, the worst kind of hubris.

"Is this it?" he asked, slowing the Peugeot.

Kat looked down at the map again. "Yes. Here. Turn here."

Kurtz turned the wheel sharply, taking them off the highway and into a neighborhood of industrial buildings and government-style slums. In the distance, a squat gray structure loomed before them. Five floors high and nearly as long as a football field. A prison, Kat thought immediately, for there was almost nothing else it could be. Then she remembered Jamal's description of Ain Chock, and realized this was it, the place where the boy had spent the first fifteen years of his life.

It was well past midnight when Kat and Hariri finished in the booth and made their way back along the catwalk to the ICE. Down in the cages, the prisoners were tucked in for the night, most of them sleeping soundly despite the unrelenting glare from the overhead lights and the semiautomatic weapons trained on them. It was a scene Kat had witnessed countless times, but which never failed to unnerve her: the men one to a pallet beneath their astronauts' Mylar blankets, knees and arms drawn in to protect themselves from the cold, spines almost universally curved in the classic fetal pose, as if each body were in the midst of some kind of organic transformation, on its way to becoming something else.

After the intimacy of the booth, the chaos of the ICE was an affront to Kat's senses. The regular night crew had all sorts of perverse tactics for keeping themselves awake, most of which would have been violations of international law had they been used on the prisoners. Tonight's strategy, which had the added benefit of making Kat feel impossibly old, involved blasting Green Day's "American Idiot" at decibels normally used to extract confessions from high-ranking Al Qaeda members.

A small but boisterous group of men—not just interroga-

tors but MPs and a couple of civilians as well, Kurtz included—
were huddled around one of the operations monitors. Intent
on something, Kat observed, most likely one of the seemingly
endless and infinitely complicated battlefield-simulating computer games the younger soldiers spent a good deal of their
downtime playing.

Trying to shake the booth-numbness from her head, Kat
helped herself to a cup of fuel-grade coffee and found a free
computer where she could type up her interrogation report.
For an instant, she allowed herself to think about Colin. Seeing Kurtz reminded her of what had happened at the Special
Forces compound the night before. The way she and Colin
had left things was sitting badly with her. She'd hoped to make
it back to the British compound that night to clear the air, but
it didn't look as if that was going to happen now. Green Day
or not, it was going to be a long shift.

A collective cry of triumph erupted from the group at the
monitor, and Kat glanced up from her work.

"They're in!" one of the MPs said excitedly. Then he and
the others exchanged testosterone-injected high fives.

When the men moved, Kat could make out a portion of the
monitor, a night-vision flickering of ghostlike shapes moving
in formation across the screen. Not a game, she realized then,
recognizing the grainy look of the footage from the few times
she'd seen it at Kandahar, during Operation Anaconda. What
the men were watching was real-time feed from the battlefield.
A Special Forces raid, from the looks of it. Some enterprising
soldier must have hacked into the central communications network, hoping for some late-night entertainment.

Kat stood up, craning her neck to get a better view. "Anyone know who that is?" she asked.

"British team," the MP who'd hand-slapped the others
said, and then, with fervent appreciation, "Those SAS guys are
real motherfuckers."

One of the interrogators looked over his shoulder at Kat. "It's SBS, actually. One of the teams from C Squadron."

Kat felt sick. She had no illusions about the danger inherent in these nighttime raids. So far, she had managed to avoid thinking of Colin in such a context. But now there was no getting around the possibility that he might be down there, one of those eerie figures on the screen. She glanced over to see Kurtz watching her.

Everything would be fine, she told herself, ducking Kurtz's gaze, not wanting to give him reason to gloat. The raids were standard practice, after all, and almost always went off smoothly. Besides, Colin had said nothing about leaving when she'd seen him the night before, and surely he would have. For all she knew he was still on base, getting fat and happy on meat pies and fish and chips over at Camp Gibraltar.

"There!" somebody shouted. "There!"

A single figure had stepped out of a structure in the upper right-hand corner of the screen and was heading straight for the soldiers.

"Get him!" someone else yelled, with the same enthusiasm he might have shown for his favorite linebacker. "Get the fucker!"

Something must have alerted the men on the ground to the interloper. They stopped in unison, then moved quickly to the outside, in an apparent attempt to flank the figure.

"Motherfuckers!" the appreciative MP repeated, flashing a touchdown smile to the rest of the group. "What did I tell you? Those guys are bad motherfuckers!"

"Not so fast," one of the civilians interjected. "Look at this."

Some two dozen figures had appeared on either side of the screen and were converging slowly and steadily on the British soldiers.

"Who the hell is that?" someone asked.

"It's an ambush," the civilian who'd first noticed the crisis said softly. "It's a goddamn ambush."

He was right. It didn't take a military mastermind to see that the whole thing was a setup, that the first solitary figure had been nothing more than bait. Someone had known the team was coming.

"We can't be the only ones watching this," one of the interrogators said. "There's got to be a chopper in the area."

There was an explosion then, the blast big and bright enough to fill almost the entire screen. When the glare subsided, Kat could see that several of the British soldiers had been thrown to the ground. The ones who were still able to had regrouped almost instantly and were exchanging heavy gunfire with the men flanking them.

"Where's that fucking chopper?" someone yelled. Despite the gunfire, the figures on the outer flanks had begun to advance again, moving slowly forward, forming a loose circle around the British team.

Kat scanned the figures on the ground. Two had rolled over and were firing their guns, but one lay motionless, his left knee cocked slightly, his arms sprawled at his sides. There was no way of knowing who he was.

"Look, here!" one of the MPs yelled. "I think someone's coming."

The figures in the outer circle had stopped advancing and were now rapidly moving back in the direction from which they'd come.

The chopper, Kat thought, please, God, let it be the chopper. And it was.

A tracer rocketed in from the left side of the screen. A Hydra, Kat guessed, from the explosion that followed, taking out a handful of the fast-retreating figures and sending the rest scattering across the hilly terrain. A second blast followed, and then a third.

The group in the ICE erupted in cheers.

"Die, you Taliban fuck!" the enthusiastic MP yelled, addressing a writhing figure on the monitor.

Kat looked away, suddenly embarrassed, not wanting to be a witness to the man's death. As she did so, her eyes caught Kurtz's. He was staring straight at her, his lips curved. He made no move to look away, but nodded instead, slightly, almost imperceptibly, as if confirming her worst fears.

He knew, Kat thought for an instant, just an instant. And then, realizing how ridiculous such an idea was, she felt suddenly guilty for having thought it.

She looked back at the monitor, and she could see the scorpion-like silhouette of the medevac helicopter and the British team scurrying toward it with their wounded. No, she told herself, these things happened. They were in a war, after all.

NOTHING, KAT REALIZED, stopping just inside the front gate, surveying the wasteland that was Ain Chock—the broken windows and tattered tarps, the garbage fires burning in the lanes. After everything Jamal had told her, she had understood nothing.

They beat us, Jamal had said once, talking about his childhood at the orphanage, and Kat had thought, Yes, they beat you. But the boy's words came back to her as she followed Kurtz into the putrid maze of the courtyard shantytown. They beat him, she thought, and the beatings themselves now seemed trivial in relation to the utter brutality of the actual place.

Third World slums can be dangerous for outsiders, especially those with obvious means, and Kat had prepared herself for a confrontation. But she could see now that there was no reason to be afraid. The inhabitants here were the castoffs of the castoffs, the ancient and the sick and the mentally faltering, those from whom life had been drained like the juice from an orange, and whose deflated faces followed Kat and Kurtz with dispassionate interest.

Someone somewhere was burning shit. The stench of it, rank and utterly familiar, reminded Kat of the months she'd spent at Kandahar, and of the lunar desolation of that place. She had not realized it at the time—none of them had—but looking back she could see a certain symmetry to their time there, a kind of perfection in the emptiness of those surroundings, the landscape scoured as they themselves had been. Scoured by rage and grief, stinking of revenge.

The orphanage itself appeared to Kat to be uninhabited, or, at least, uninhabitable. Through the broken first-floor windows Kat could see piles of garbage and upturned mattresses, walls flushed with black mold. As she and Kurtz approached the front door, two young men emerged from the dilapidated building carrying disordered bundles of electrical wire.

How much, Kat wondered, did they expect to get for their effort? A few dirham coins in the scrap market, if they were lucky. Not even enough to put a down payment on their next meal.

They were close to Jamal's age, one dressed like a soccer player in red track pants and a green-and-yellow shirt, the other playing the part of a New Jersey goodfella in blue jeans and a leather jacket. Kat was about to call to them when she heard Kurtz's stilted Arabic.

"Hey! You! What are you doing?"

The two scavengers looked up, their eyes flicking briefly from Kat to Kurtz and back again. Nonplussed, they shifted their burdens slightly and continued walking.

"Hey!" Kurtz called again, but this time Kat put her hand on his arm to silence him.

She nodded and smiled broadly, greeting the young men in the traditional manner. She was still wearing the head scarf she'd picked up at the gas station and she was glad of it, hoping it might buy her some small modicum of respectability.

The pair stopped where they were but did not return Kat's greeting.

"Brothers," she continued, trying to erase any hint of threat from her voice. "Perhaps you can help us. We are looking for a friend, a young man close to your age. His name is Jamal."

The sporting one fingered his bundle of wires. "There is no one by that name here," he said forcefully.

"Are you certain?" Kat asked, glancing at the second man, the one in the leather jacket. He was standing slightly back from his friend, his eyes hard on Kat, his expression suggestive, almost sexual. Was it the look, Kat wondered, of someone who wanted to speak but could not?

"We are prepared to show our gratitude," Kurtz interjected.

Yes, Kat thought, watching the man in the leather jacket, his eyes flaring at the suggestion of money: this one would tell them what they wanted to know. But not now, not here.

"We cannot help you," the sporting one insisted, turning to go.

The second man moved to follow, but as he did his eyes met Kat's one final time. What passed between them then was like the look of two lovers, two people drawn to congress with each other but unable at that moment to consummate their desires.

Then, in an instant, the pair was gone, swallowed by the shadowed mouth of one of the courtyard's many narrow alleyways, disappeared into the stinking bowels of the slum.

Kat looked up at the sky. "It's getting dark," she said.

"Yes," Kurtz agreed unhappily. "We should go."

TWENTY-THREE

"Is it 'in like a lion, out like a lamb,' or the other way around?" Janson had mused, trying to delay the inevitable, the real reason for his call: that the time had come to cut and run. "I never can get it straight."

"The first one, I think," Harry offered. "But from up here March looked a hell of a lot like a lion coming and going."

It was April Fools' Day, the Monday after Easter, and Da Nang, barely four hundred kilometers to the north, had fallen to the Vietcong the day before. It was a matter of days, possibly even hours, before the North Vietnamese reached Nha Trang.

"What's the word on friends?" Harry asked, thinking about his earlier promise to An. "Staff and such."

"Officially, everyone who needs a ride gets one."

"And unofficially?"

"What do you think, Harry?"

There was An's face again, her stony prediction of his failure.

"Tell me how many you've got," Janson relented, "and I'll get them on the transport list. It's the best I can do. We should have started moving people out weeks ago, but Martin's still convinced we can hold Saigon."

"Three altogether. My housekeeper and her parents."

"Names?"

Christ, Harry thought, he didn't even know. The woman who cooked his meals and kept his bathroom clean, and he had never bothered to learn her full name. "Nguyen," he said, taking a shot in the dark, naming a good portion of the population of Vietnam. "Nguyen, An. And family."

"You need to get them here yesterday, Harry. Sooner, if possible. People are starting to panic. You heard what happened with Ed Daley."

Janson was referring to Daley's flight into Da Nang two days earlier to rescue women and children. The World Airways jet had been commandeered by three hundred ARVN soldiers while it sat on the tarmac and had barely made it into the air. At least one unlucky stowaway was crushed to death in the wheel well when the landing gear retracted.

"Yesterday," Harry agreed. Then he hung up the phone and went downstairs.

Like any good servant, An had schooled herself in the culinary language of her masters. Using a dog-eared copy of the 1969 embassy wives' *Bloom Where You're Planted* cookbook and the small selection of canned goods imported from the Saigon commissary, An regularly attempted such American standards as tuna casserole, Swedish meatballs, and ambrosia salad.

She was in the midst of one of these concoctions, trying to make sense of a can of cream of mushroom soup, when Harry found her in the kitchen.

"Beef stroganoff for lunch today," she announced, dumping the contents of the can into a mixing bowl and regarding the gelatinous mass with consternation.

Harry shook his head. "No, An. No lunch today."

She looked up at him, dismayed. "You don't like?"

"Honestly? No. But that's beside the point. You've heard what happened in Da Nang?"

An nodded.

Of course, Harry thought. Death on the march, and here she was, making stroganoff for his lunch. "We need to leave for Saigon as soon as possible. You'll go get your parents."

"Now?"

"Yes, right now."

"But lunch?"

"I'll take care of it," Harry told her gently. "Go get your parents." He glanced at his watch. It was early still, barely eight. They would need to leave by noon in order to make sure they didn't run out of daylight. "You'll be back here by noon at the latest." He tapped his watch for emphasis. "Twelve o'clock."

An untied her apron and laid it on the counter. "Yes, Mr. Harry."

Harry watched her leave through the garden, then started back upstairs. There was a strict protocol to observe when abandoning a station, a long list of items that needed to be destroyed, files and papers, the capture of which could be devastating to the agents implicated therein. And there was the Celestron to think of as well. The telescope would need to be packed for the long car trip south. Harry would be hard-pressed to get it all done by noon.

He had just reached the second-floor landing and was making a mental list of his priorities when he heard the phone in his office ringing. Janson again, he thought, hurrying to answer. But when he lifted the receiver it was Susan on the other end.

"Harry!" She sounded upset, possibly drunk. "Harry, it's Susan. Is Dick there?"

"No," Harry replied coldly. It was the first time he'd spoken to Susan since she'd called to tell him she and Morrow were getting married. Her voice was like whiskey on a still-tender wound.

"He and Jack McLeod went up to the subbase in Cam Ranh three days ago," she said shakily. "They were supposed to be back last night. No one's heard anything."

"So it's good news."

"Don't be an idiot."

"Too late for that."

Silence, then the sound of muffled sobs.

That voice, Harry thought, that perfectly cultivated mixture of vulnerability and suggestion. "I'm sure everything's fine," he told her, hating himself for his capitulation.

"No," she insisted. "Something's happened. I know it." She took a deep breath, as if preparing to dive. "If you could just go down there. Just drive down and see."

Harry laughed. "You can't be serious."

But she was. "Please, Harry." She was crying again, sobbing in short, shuddering bursts.

An hour down and an hour back, Harry told himself, pretending to count, in a logical way, the time it would take him to make the round-trip to Cam Ranh, when what he was actually thinking about was Susan's mouth during sex, the way her lips parted at the very moment he entered her, as if she were about to speak. An hour up, a quick check of the Cam Ranh subbase, and then back again. As if the choice could be a rational one. As if there could be any choice at all. As if he could, for even one moment, consider refusing her.

"Please, Harry. I'm scared."

He glanced around his office at the metal filing cabinets, the stack of folders on his desk. Not as much to take care of as he'd first thought. Put a match to it and be done.

"Okay," he said. "I'll go."

THE PLANE CAME IN GENTLY. banking across the mine-lashed Alleghenies and the emerald cradle of the Shenandoah Valley. Over the battle-worn fields of Manassas and their moldering ghosts. Nearly five thousand dead in one day, Harry thought, trying to concentrate on anything other than his own imminent death. Almost twice as many Union as Confederate, but hardly a victory for the seventeen hundred southern boys who'd fallen along the banks of Bull Run, and whose sacrifice history would eventually prove worthless.

It was, as the captain had informed them at the beginning of the flight, a perfect day to fly. *Perfect as they come,* he'd announced as the 737 climbed into the desert-dry air over Phoenix for the second leg of Harry's journey. Yet Harry could taste the bitter bile of fear in his throat with each slight shift of the engines, each shudder of the wings. He did not like flying, never had, could not muster the faith needed to enter cheerfully into such a contract. As the ground loomed up beneath them, Harry closed his eyes and prayed to all the gods he didn't believe in that the end would at least come swiftly. Then the tires hit the runway and the giant craft bounced, defying the forces of gravity one last time, and Harry realized they were down.

It had been remarkably easy to give Morrow's men the slip the night before. Just after nine o'clock Harry had driven down to Kailua, parked his car in the guest lot at the King Kamehameha, and gone into the hotel bar to have a drink. Two overpriced and underpoured martinis later, having shed his dour outer layer of clothing in the lobby bathroom in exchange for a bright tourist's shirt and knee-length shorts, Harry was on his way to the airport to catch the mainland redeye, packed into the hotel's free shuttle with a dozen sunburned Germans and a pair of hostile honeymooners who managed to sit side by side for the entire trip without once touching.

And now, some fourteen jet-lagged hours later, nearly a full day with the time difference thrown in, here he was. Back in the place to which he'd sworn he would never return. Home to the cradle and grave of all his regrets. The plane rolled to a stop and he pried himself from his seat, touching the breast pocket of his jacket, the slim rectangle of the Canadian passport.

Not Harry Comfort, he reminded himself as he made his way out onto the concourse and down to the airport's lower level. Not Harry Comfort but this other man. Harry of the goofy grin and the bad jokes. Harry who'd sold farm equipment for thirty-odd years and who'd retired with just enough money to see the world. Harry with a tourist's litter in his pockets. A mangled ABC store receipt for sunscreen and plastic sandals. A frayed brochure for sport-fishing trips out of Captain Cook. A phone number, contemplated but never used, for an escort service in Kailua-Kona.

Harry Lyttle, the type on both his driver's license and his credit card read when he handed them to the girl at the rental-car counter. Harry Lyttle of Regina, Saskatchewan. Harry of no regrets.

PERFECT DAY. The first thing anyone said when they spoke of what had happened that morning, as if somehow the affront was worse because of it. As if the blueness of the sky, the sheer limitless clarity against which the events had unfolded, served only to magnify the horror.

In her worst moments, times like this, sleepless AMs with the clock ticking painfully forward, it was that sky Kat thought of over and over again, that brilliant liquid blue into which Max would have jumped.

Like so many others who'd lost someone that day, Kat

hadn't been able to keep herself from looking for clues to her brother's death. Long after the event was over, she'd scoured the Internet for images of bodies falling, hoping and yet not hoping to recognize Max. And, like the lucky ones, she had so far been saved from the proof she so desperately wanted to find.

But he had jumped. Of this Kat was certain. Given any choice at all, Kat knew this was the one he would have chosen, just as she knew that her own fear would have held her back.

In her worst moments, she stood there with him on the lip of that perfectly blue sky. Beneath them was the city, the Hudson flashing like hammered silver in the sunlight. Behind them was the fire.

In her worst moments she could not tell which was more painful: the loss of her brother or the fact that she had failed him so terribly.

Below Kat's window a chorus of male voices caromed back and forth off the street's dark façades. Europeans, Kat thought, though she did not immediately recognize the language. Dutch perhaps, or Danish, something Germanic. The men on their way back from an evening in one of the red-light districts that lay adjacent to the hotel on either side.

A calculation, Kat had thought when Kurtz stopped the Peugeot on the street outside and she realized this was where they were going to spend the night. His own subtle way of saying she was one of them, that this was where she belonged. And a part of her had thought maybe he was right, that she was no better than those women on the Avenue Lalla Yacout.

Kat rolled over on her side and clamped her musty pillow over her head, hoping to quiet not just the voices in the street but the ones inside her head as well. Max's voice and Colin's, the accusations of the dead, and her own voice, cruelest of all, insistent, telling her over and over what she should have seen all along: that she and Kurtz had been sent not to save the boy but to kill him.

Through the paper-thin wall, Kat could hear Kurtz snoring in the next room. Breathe. Pause. Breathe. Pause. And, between each breath, a moment of mortal hesitation, an instant in which it seemed his lungs would fail to catch.

This was her chance, and doubtless the last one she would get. If she left now, she was fairly certain she could find Jamal before Kurtz did. And then what? She had tried to help the boy once before and this was where it had brought them.

No, she reasoned, she would not repeat the mistakes she had made at Bagram. She would not be complicit. Slowly, she sat up and swung her legs off the bed. Moving to the metronome of Kurtz's breath, she collected her things—shoes and jacket and scarf—and let herself out into the hall. She paused for a moment outside Kurtz's door, reassuring herself that he was still asleep, then made her way down the hotel's narrow communal stairwell and out onto the dark street.

IT IS A TERRIBLE THING to wish for the death of another human being, especially one you've come to know in a meaningful way, whose voice you have heard through the walls each morning, whose prayers have marked your day, or whose singing has sheltered you from the cruel cradle of night. That her only joys had come at the expense of fellow prisoners was perhaps the worst of the many humiliations Manar had suffered during her years of incarceration.

"When one of us dies, praise Allah, they let the others out," the woman in the next cell had told Manar not long after her arrival in the desert. Her speech was thin and excited, with an anxious timbre. "The woman on the far end has been dying for some time now. She doesn't know it, but I can hear it in her voice. We must pray that she goes soon."

The voice of insanity, Manar had thought then, turned on each other like the animals they wish us to be. And she had vowed, naïvely, not to give her jailers the pleasure of watching her succumb.

But two weeks later, when the woman finally died, and the guards hauled them all out into the sunlit courtyard for the burial, and Manar was finally able to see the faces of the women with whom she shared the darkness, it was as if she had, for the briefest of moments, been born again. As if the dead woman, who had gone horribly at the end, screaming at the rats that could not wait for her to die, had given them all this gift. As if to squander it would be the worst of sins. And so Manar, like the others, had turned her face to the limpid swatch of Saharan sky.

But there was, Manar would learn, a price to be paid for even this most meager of freedoms. When the guards returned her to her cell and the door was closed and locked, she saw the place as she'd seen it when she first arrived, felt the same breathless panic, the same claustrophobic despair. And in that moment she had prayed to be the next one taken.

"In the name of Allah, the most merciful, the most beneficent," Manar began as she had that day, as she had so many times after, the words now whispered not into the darkness of her cell but of her bedroom. *In the name of Allah, in whom I no longer believe, from whom nothing has been given . . . "please allow me to die."*

Now that the door had been opened, now that she had been allotted her portion of hope, now that the boy, her child, had taken shape in her soul, the pain of his loss was as it had been that first moment, when the nurse had taken him from her arms. This time Manar knew she could not go on.

Iᴛ ᴡᴀꜱ ɴᴇᴀʀʟʏ ꜱᴇᴠᴇɴ when Harry pulled off Route 50 and into the parking lot of the Patriot Shopping Center in Falls Church. Dinner hour, and the Vietnamese noodle shop on the strip mall's far end was doing a brisk business. Harry didn't stop in the lot but pulled around to the back of the long build-ing, where he was relieved to see the discreet PATRIOT SECU-RITY SYSTEMS sign still firmly attached to the familiar gray steel door. He parked the rental car and got out, then made his way to the door and pressed the grimy security buzzer.

A minute passed, and another. The back door of the noodle shop opened and a young man appeared with a heavy black garbage bag. He gave Harry a disinterested look — seen it all before — then tossed the bag into the restaurant's dumpster and disappeared back inside. Most likely he *had* seen it all, Harry thought. Russians, Chinese, Arabs, Americans, just to name a few. There wasn't an intelligence man inside the beltway who hadn't visited the Patriot at least once in his life.

Harry rang the bell and waited again. Half an hour he'd stood here once, waiting for Heinrich to finish whatever it was he was doing inside. The German was not, above all, a man who liked to be rushed. Finally, the door swung open and Heinrich's familiar face, worn even further since Harry had last seen it, peered out from the dim interior.

"Mr. Brown," the German said, his papery mouth breaking into a satisfied smile. "I thought we were done with you." And then, with the flourish of a subject summoning a king to enter his home, he stepped aside. "Come in. Please come in."

Nodding his gratitude, Harry did as he was told.

The shop itself was a marvel of engineering, a human-scale ant farm of sorts, the tunnels and rooms created entirely from electronic scrap and junk. To the untrained eye it all appeared hopelessly chaotic, a garbage pile of mammoth proportions. And yet Heinrich, in his brilliant madness, knew with exact precision where every screw, every microchip, was located.

"This way." The German beckoned, leading Harry into what appeared to be a parlor — a small room carved out of the rubble, furnished with a frayed Persian rug and three sagging armchairs, one of which was occupied by an unmoving gray cat that Harry could only hope was alive.

"To what do I owe this pleasure?" the old man asked when they were both seated.

"Termites, I'm afraid," Harry said.

Heinrich shook his head sympathetically. "Nasty buggers. Hard to get rid of, aren't they?"

"That's why I'm here."

"Yes." Heinrich smiled, satisfied. This was all he needed, all he'd ever needed. Not money, though he happily took their money. But what he really craved was their gratitude, the acknowledgment that he was the best at what he did. And he was.

"I need something today," Harry said.

The German made a clucking sound with his tongue, as a schoolmarm chiding her charges might do. "Always in a hurry."

"It's the business," Harry offered, apologetic.

"Yes," Heinrich repeated. "It is the business." Then he got up shakily from his chair and selected a small box from among the shelves and shelves of similar boxes that lined one wall. "For you, my friend."

TWENTY-FOUR

By the time Harry reached Dong Ba Thin, halfway down the coast, the extent to which he had deluded himself was clear. The road was clogged with southbound traffic, people on foot and others riding in whatever conveyances they could find: oxcarts and trishaws, bicycles lashed together and topped with plywood to form makeshift wagons. It had taken Harry nearly two hours to drive the barely fifty kilometers from Nha Trang, and the collective momentum of the crowd behind him made turning back an impossibility. Once he got to Cam Ranh, he told himself, he would phone Nha Trang and make other arrangements to bring An and her parents south. After all, he had not been the only foreigner in the city. Something would be done, a boat or plane or helicopter sent.

The mass migration had begun to take its human toll. Here and there along the roadside another bloated corpse, its tongue lolling, its face riddled with flies, lay stinking perversely in the tropical heat, while passersby, their cumulative sense of humanity long extinguished, walked unflinchingly by.

Unlike Ambassador Martin, the Vietnamese had given up on Saigon, and the majority of the refugees were heading, wisely, not for the southern capital but for the sea. Cam Ranh, with its massive port, had been deluged by a virtual tsunami of humanity. It was close to dark by the time Harry managed to fight his way to the American consulate and the Agency sub-base in the city's old colonial quarter.

The neighborhood itself was hauntingly quiet. Its residents, mostly foreigners and wealthy Vietnamese, had fled sometime earlier, leaving behind their gated villas and gleaming Mercedes, their perfectly manicured French gardens. In a few of the homes, the inevitable process of looting had begun. As Harry pulled his car into the driveway of the consulate, he saw two young Vietnamese men emerge from the property next door carrying cases of French Bordeaux and Russian caviar. It was, Harry couldn't help thinking, a remarkably nearsighted choice given the current state of affairs.

The consulate itself was deserted, the only evidence of foul play a ravaged liquor cabinet and a dozen hand-smeared crystal tumblers in the downstairs parlor, an ashtray full of spent cigars. Someone's solution to being forced to leave it all behind. Stewed to the gills on brandy and Pimm's. No wonder they were all late getting out of the city.

Harry reached for the phone on the bar and, surprised to find it still in working order, dialed Susan's number in Saigon.

Five rings. Six. Out on the street, there was gunfire, the clatter of breaking glass. And in Harry's ear, suddenly and incongruously, the sound of laughter.

"Carol!" Susan shouted, talking above a din, the unmistakable sounds of a party under way. Carol was one of the other embassy girls. "I told you to get over here."

"No, Susan," Harry corrected her. "It's me."

"Harry? I tried you earlier this afternoon. Sorry about this morning. It was childish of me, really. Dick's fine. Got held up helping clean house in Cam Ranh, but of course you knew that." A pause. "You didn't actually go down there, did you?"

What to say? "No," he told her at last. "Of course not. I just wanted to make sure everything was okay."

"It is," Susan said, somewhat awkwardly.

He hung up and called Nha Trang then, dialed twice and twice let the phone ring and ring. Ten times, eleven, fifteen, twenty. Waiting for An to pick up.

When she failed to answer the second call, Harry emptied the dregs from one of the tumblers and, suddenly overcome by the magnitude of his defeat, poured himself the last three fingers of Johnnie Walker Black.

IRENE HAD CHOSEN THE HOUSE, just as she had chosen everything in it, the faux-antebellum furnishings and the flowered wallpaper. Magnolias bigger then a man's fist in their bedroom, creamy bludgeons of prettiness, and in the bathrooms dainty violets and patio roses. The place was hers entirely, as if by this one great possession she could make up for everything else she would never have, for Harry's long absences and the indiscretions, both real and imagined, that accompanied them.

They had bought the house when they first married, back when an Agency salary could afford such a place, and even then they were lucky to find it. The house itself was unremarkable, a split-level suburban ranch home designed with a family in mind. But the property, nestled just off the beltway in an odd little neighborhood carved out from between two nature preserves, bounded in the back by a thick stand of deciduous woods and a small creek, was a gem.

It was through these woods that Harry picked his way in the failing twilight, tripping over rocks and deadfall, slapping away mosquitoes, grateful, as he had not always been, for the tangle of locusts and dogwoods at the edge of the yard. Certain that Morrow would have someone watching the house, Harry had left his rental car at the end of a seldom-used dirt service road and hiked back through the preserve. But as he drew closer he was surprised to see no sign of surveillance.

Skirting the edge of the property until he was hidden entirely from the street, Harry stepped from the shelter of the woods and crossed the back yard. The landscaping crew had recently been through and the lawn was freshly mowed, the smell of cut grass heavy in the air. The house itself was entirely dark, the black windows reflecting the trees and the evening sky. Moving toward the cluster of potted geraniums on the back patio, Harry rolled the largest planter aside to find the key—his key—hidden underneath.

Thirty-some years in the house, and this was how he had always come and gone. For safety's sake, he'd reasoned. Better, if things went south, not to have a key on him. But even during his Langley postings he had not carried a key, had preferred to slip in like the intruder he'd always felt himself to be. Now, as he'd done so many times before, he opened the back door and let himself inside.

To know a place, Harry marveled, as he stood just inside the doorway amid the kitchen's familiar surroundings, many of them his own gifts of contrition—the stoneware roosters he'd brought back from his Portuguese posting, the brass coffee mill, beautifully embellished, that he'd found in a market in Istanbul—to be entirely intimate with a place and yet to feel like a perpetual outsider: this was perhaps his one great accomplishment.

There was a part of him that wanted to go forward into the house. He was hungry, had eaten nothing but airplane food for nearly twenty-four hours. And there was the Celestron in his study; he had a desperate urge to see it. But he was an intruder, after all, and so he stayed where he was, listening to the ticking of the old mantel clock in the living room, waiting for the sound of Irene's own key in the front lock.

He did not have to wait long. Barely half an hour had

passed before he heard her car in the driveway and the single door closing, the scrabbling of paws on the front door. The dog, who had always hated Harry, smelled him immediately and rushed in, barking.

"Glory!" Irene called from the front of the house. Glory, such a southern name, with that ragged gentility toward which Irene had always aspired. "Quiet, Glory!"

Then the light was switched abruptly on and she was there in the doorway, her face dispassionate as she took Harry in.

"The key," he said, taking a small step forward, setting it on the counter. "You forgot the key."

The little dog moved back, snarling, but Irene held her ground. She had a plastic grocery bag in her right hand. Harry could see the shape of a frozen dinner inside, a large bottle of wine.

He reached into the breast pocket of his jacket and pulled out an envelope. "I brought the papers," he said, setting them down beside the key.

Irene said nothing.

"You look good," Harry commented, and she did. But then she had always been careful to keep herself up. She was dressed in vaguely athletic wear—sleek pants and an expensive-looking Lycra top—as if she had just come from the gym, albeit the kind of gym where people never sweat. He realized then the extent of the crime he'd committed by marrying her.

"What do you want?" she asked wearily. The dog had given up its furor for the time being and was sitting at her feet.

"I need your help," he said. No sense in beating around the bush.

Laughing bitterly, Irene came forward and set the grocery bag down, took out the bottle of wine. "You haven't signed them, have you?" She glanced at the papers as she reached into one of the cabinets for a glass.

Harry shook his head. "They're signed. See for yourself."

She eyed the envelope once again but didn't touch it. She opened the bottle instead.

"It's not about me this time," Harry told her.

"No?" she commented, pouring herself a hefty drink. "It never is."

"It's the boy. The one who called. He's in trouble, Irene."

She closed her eyes and took a long, slow drink of the wine, then set the glass down. "Dick came to see me himself." Her loathing of Morrow was clear in the way she spoke his name. She had a right to hate him, had sacrificed more than her share for the cause. And in the end it was Morrow's cause. "He wanted to put someone on the house, but I told him to go fuck himself."

That explained the lack of surveillance. "I always thought you missed your calling." Harry smiled slightly. "You would have made a hell of a case officer. Better than I am."

"Maybe if I'd been born twenty years later," Irene said without irony.

"Did he mention anything about a phone tap?" Harry asked. He had no doubt Irene's line was bugged. That's why he'd gone to see the German. But he was wagering that the old rules still counted for something, that if Morrow was listening he was doing so off the record and on the sly. If there was a "down line" tap, NSA for instance, there was nothing Harry or anyone could do about it.

Irene shook her head. "No. If the boy calls again I'm to find out where he is and let Dick know. I'm to tell him you're coming and to stay put."

Harry reached into his jacket once again and pulled out Heinrich's box. "You'll need to put it on the line yourself," he told her. "Not my place. You've seen me do it before. It's quite simple, really."

Irene took the box and set it on the counter with the envelope and the keys. All Harry could hope for now was that her hatred of Morrow would outweigh her disappointment in him.

"You can reach me here," he said, handing her a business card from his motel with his room number scrawled on the back.

Irene studied it for a moment, then picked up her wineglass and took another, longer drink. "I want to be clear," she said finally. "If I do this, it won't be for you."

"No," Harry agreed. "I never expected it would be."

Nоt good place for American lady," the taxi driver repeated, in English this time, clearly convinced that Kat had not understood his earlier warnings.

Kat fished ten euros from her pocket and offered it to the man. "There's another twenty if you wait," she told him, opening the passenger door and stepping out. But once she was outside the cab, looking up at Ain Chock's massive iron gate and the ruined hulk of the building beyond, the realization of her folly hit her, along with the full force of her fear.

She should not have come. If she left now, she could return to her room at the hotel and be done with it. Tomorrow she could put Kurtz off, could refuse, in her own way, to help him, as she had that afternoon, when she'd kept her hunch about the young man in the leather jacket to herself. Eventually, Kurtz might come to believe that Jamal had died crossing the strait, and that would be the end of the whole affair.

But when she turned back to tell the driver that she had changed her mind, it was too late; the decision had been made for her. The taxi was already pulling away from the curb, its tires screeching as it leaped forward and disappeared around the first corner.

Kat watched the cab go. Leaving now, she knew, trying to negotiate the city on foot, would be tantamount to suicide.

Her best hope, her only hope, lay inside the walls of Ain Chock. Kat reached up and adjusted her scarf, tucking her hair inside the blue fabric, tightening the knot under her chin, then started through the gate.

Here and there down the courtyard's narrow alleys a fire burned, mitigating the darkness. But mainly the occupants of Ain Chock were, like the rest of Casablanca, fast asleep. As Kat made her way down the settlement's main thoroughfare, two boys, neither of them older than eight or nine, each with an addict's bright ring of gold paint around his mouth, approached her from the shadows.

"Sister!" they called in unison. Their halos were evidently newly acquired; they were wired on paint fumes, their eyes four wild disks bobbing frenetically in the darkness.

Thinking they were as willing and able as any potential guides she would find at this hour, Kat slipped each of the boys a euro coin. "I'm looking for an older boy," she said. "Much older. I saw him here today. He was in blue jeans and a leather jacket." She pantomimed the look for them, trying to convey the young man's attitude, the aggressive stance.

The boys laughed at her attempt—they were still children, after all. But they must have understood something. They looked at each other and declared in unison, "Mahjoub!"

"He stays here?" Kat asked.

The boys giggled again. "Yes," the taller of the two replied.

Kat reached into her pocket, pulled out two more coins, and showed them to the boys. "Take me to him," she said, closing her fist on the money. This payment they would have to earn.

They glanced at each other again, silently communicating their agreement, then scampered forward, stopping to look back at Kat, beckoning her forward.

Kat paused. Just a few meters in and already she could not

see the gate behind her. If she went any farther, she would not be able to find her way out without help.

"This way, sister," the smaller boy called. She could see nothing but the aureole of his mouth flaring in the darkness, the white of his teeth and eyes. "Come! Come!" In English now.

She would be at their mercy, she thought, as she started after them.

It was not easy for Kat to keep up with the pair. Not only were the boys fast; they were skilled navigators, leaping gracefully over the slum's various obstacles in their cheap plastic sandals while Kat struggled along behind, slipping in sewage and rot.

It was a dizzying chase, but one that, thankfully, did not last long. After what couldn't have been more than five minutes, the pair stopped abruptly at the entrance to a short alleyway.

"There, sister." The older boy motioned to a relatively nice shanty several yards away, in front of which a fire was still burning. "There is where Mahjoub stays."

"You're sure?" Kat asked, holding out her still-closed fist.

Both boys nodded.

"Wait here," she began, then she saw the look in their eyes, the craving, and realized the futility of baiting them to stay and guide her out. They had reached their fill of her and her money and were hungry for something else now, not food but the sustenance of escape, in whatever form they could get it. When she opened her fist, they snatched the coins and were gone.

Alone, Kat made her way toward the dwelling the boys had indicated. In comparison to many of its counterparts, it was a solid structure, with a look of near-permanency. The walls were salvaged plywood, the roof sheets of corrugated tin.

Even the fire pit was well constructed, fashioned from the bottom half of a large metal drum, topped with a rebar grill.

Everything used and used and used again, Kat thought, remembering the Afghans who'd combed the base dump at Kandahar—how they had carefully collected and washed the Americans' used MRE containers, salvaging the sturdy black plastic as weatherproofing material.

As Kat drew closer to the shanty, she could hear male voices punctuated by frequent, raucous laughter. It was the sound of abandon, of stories tempered by time from bleakness to humor. Listening, Kat realized that she had never once heard Jamal laugh, that there had been no reason to at Bagram. And yet she knew, knew in her bones before she saw him, that his was among the voices she heard. She stood there for some time, alone in the darkness, listening.

After a while, the plywood door banged open and a figure appeared. It was Jamal. He paused for a moment on the threshold, then stepped away from the structure, unzipped his fly, and pissed into open gutter.

It was not until he was finished that he saw her there, watching him. As he was turning to go back inside, his eyes met hers and the look on his face was not one of relief but of terror.

ANOTHER HOUSE. nicer than Irene's though not as much as one might have thought. Another well-kept yard. Brick and boxwoods. Fireflies flashing in the bushes like out-of-sequence Christmas lights. Behind the living-room curtains a stout figure—a woman, but certainly not Susan. A woman who, even in shadow, managed to evoke a sense of wrathful authority.

A mistake, Harry thought as he watched the figure, whoever she was, disappear into the depths of the house. A mistake to have come, but then he knew that, had known it all along. When he left Irene's, two hours earlier, it had been with the best of intentions. A burger and a beer at the questionable diner next to his equally questionable motel, then a half hour of free cable and sleep. Dead sleep. But five beers later here he was.

He had been inside Dick Morrow's house once, for a Christmas party, and he still remembered every rich detail— the giant Afghan carpets, the carved African fetishes with their genitals on display, the wood, so much wood, and every inch of it burnished and shining like silver for the altar. It was not long after he'd come back from his Kinshasa posting, back when people still considered him a good bet and invited him to things like Christmas parties. He and Irene were engaged at the time, and they had come together.

It was the first time he'd seen Susan since Vietnam, the first time they'd spoken since that evening in Cam Ranh, and Harry, genuinely believing in his affection for Irene, had worked hard to be on his best behavior around Susan. But Irene, perhaps sensing Harry's nervousness, had known nonetheless. In the car on the way home she'd been uncharacteristically quiet, as if contemplating the scope of her future life.

For some time after that, Harry had thought she would leave him. It was when she didn't that he lost all pity for her.

A large SUV turned onto the narrow street. Harry, thinking it might be Morrow, hunkered down in his seat. But the vehicle drove past him and kept going.

When Harry looked back at Morrow's house, he saw the garage door open and the stout figure step out. She had a garbage can, one of those big ones with wheels, but she had picked it up and was carrying it down the driveway with all the graceless dexterity one might use to lift a side of beef or a dead man. When she got to the curb, she set the thing down with a satisfied grunt.

A Russian, Harry thought, a goddamned Russkie in Morrow's house. He was so caught up in the idea of it that he didn't notice the woman look across the street toward his rental car, or the disapproving glance she cast upon him, until it was too late.

They stared at each other for a moment, then she shook her head in that quintessentially Soviet way—two parts resignation and three parts disgust.

Morrow got up from his desk and opened his closet door, took out the spare pillow and blanket he kept for overnights. It was one in the morning and he could not bring himself to go home, could not face another night like the previous one. Susan raging below and Marina on the prowl. They were right, both of them: he was not man enough for what was to come.

Kicking his shoes off, he made a bed for himself on the couch, then opened the liquor cabinet and poured himself a drink. Bourbon and bourbon. From out in the hall came the low whine of a floor polisher, the janitorial crew busy at work.

He was on his second drink when the phone rang, and he almost didn't answer it. He'd never once gotten good news at this time of night, and he wasn't expecting any now. It was the thought that something might have happened to Susan that made him pick up the receiver, and he was both relieved and irritated to hear David Kurtz on the other end of the line.

"She's gone," Kurtz said.

Morrow was still thinking of Susan. It took him a moment to understand what the man meant. The woman was gone, the interrogator. "When?" he asked.

"Sometime last night," Kurtz answered. "But she can't get far. I've got her passport."

"Doesn't make me feel a whole hell of a lot better," Morrow snapped. "Any leads on the boy?"

"Not yet."

Morrow shook his head. There was no use indulging in second thoughts now. "Just find her," he told Kurtz. "Find them both."

TWENTY-FIVE

"I need you to tell me what happened in Madrid. It's important, Jamal. For both of us."

The others had gone just after dawn, leaving Kat and Jamal alone in the shanty. Alone, as they had been so many times in the booth at Bagram. Though this time there was no getting around the fact that Kat needed the boy much more than he needed her.

"You're in trouble, Jamal. But you know that, don't you? It's why you're here."

Jamal nodded. "They killed Mr. Justin."

Kat shook her head. "Justin?"

"In Madrid," Jamal explained. "My American."

"Your handler, you mean? The man you reported to?"

"Yes. The ones who killed him were Americans, too."

"They'll kill you. And me now as well," she told him, wondering to herself just who "they" were. There were so many possibilities. She couldn't even say for sure who Kurtz was working for. Or Morrow, for that matter. That he was from Defense meant almost nothing. "I can help you, but I need to know what happened."

Jamal leaned back against a wooden vegetable crate and closed his eyes, lifting his face to the ceiling. It was a gesture, Kat knew, that could mean one of two things: he was preparing for something, and would either unburden himself and speak or retrench further and refuse to tell her anything.

"Please." The one thing she'd been taught never to say to a prisoner. "Please, Jamal, you have to trust me."

He lowered his head and opened his eyes, looked unblinkingly back at her, a sign of resignation to the truth. "But there is nothing to tell," he said.

THE LIE HADN'T COME to Jamal right away. When he'd first seen Bagheri's picture on the television in the butcher shop, he'd recognized the man immediately—the large pock on his right cheek and the close-set eyes, the mouth that had never once smiled—but it had not even occurred to him to use this knowledge to his advantage. There was no doubt in his mind that this was the same man he'd met in Peshawar, who had helped him flee from the guesthouse owner to whom he'd been offered as payment on a debt by the men who'd brought him from Spain. Bagheri had promised Jamal something better, but had delivered the same as all the others.

Until then, Jamal had known nothing about Bagheri's escape, or the death of the other man, and he had watched the story with interest. He remembered the British soldiers well from the night of his capture. They had not been unkind to him—it was not until he arrived at the American facility that he had been thrown in with the others—and he was surprised to hear that they had been involved in the man's death.

It wasn't until his meeting with Mr. Justin, two days later, that it had occurred to Jamal to lie. Even then the decision to tell the American about Bagheri had not been so much a decision as a reaction. He had offered Mr. Justin Bagheri's name in the same way one might offer a ravenous dog a piece of meat, hoping to preserve his own life with the gesture, or at least put off the inevitable.

The first lie, so small, yet so reckless, not thinking of the lies that would follow, but only of what had to be done in that moment: *Hamid Bagheri is here in Madrid.*

And the look on the American's face when Jamal said this, a depth of greed the boy knew well. The same insatiability Jamal had recognized so many times before, in the face of that first man in Tangier, in Abdullah's face, and Bagheri's.

You have seen him?

Another scrap. *Twice now. At the mosque on the Calle Espino.*

You're certain, Jamal? You're absolutely certain?

Yes. In the name of the Prophet, yes.

He was alone?

The first time, yes. The second time there was another man as well. Thinking: details, one must have details to be believed. *A Saudi.* The lie now unfolding as if of its own free will. Already too late to take anything back.

And, just like that, the American was hooked.

I never meant for anyone to get hurt," Jamal said when he had finished with his story. "But Mr. Justin, he was always pressing and pressing. Jamal, what do you see? Jamal, what do you hear? He said he was going to stop giving me money if I didn't tell him something."

Still and always the pleaser, Kat thought, not for one moment doubting the boy. She had seen the same thing happen more than once in the booth, had experienced it firsthand: that dangerous moment when the prisoner's need to confess and the interrogator's need to hear that confession threaten to overwhelm logic and reason, when the two parties, normally enemies, become willing partners in a deception that is often only nominally about the facts at hand, and sometimes not at all.

Kat and the others had been warned about this over and over, had had their own vulnerabilities constantly drummed into them. No doubt Jamal's American had been taught the same lessons. But it is one thing to understand our shortcomings and quite another to correct them.

The times Kat had been drawn in by false confessions, the shift from disclosure to fabrication had occurred with such simultaneous force and subtlety that neither she nor her prisoner had been aware of what was happening. And in each case, by the time she realized her mistake, neither could tell where the lies ended and the truth began.

"It's okay," she told Jamal. "I understand."

But it was not okay. Not at all. Where she had before seen the narrowest possibility for escape, Kat now saw none.

Jamal's face brightened. "We can explain everything, yes? You will help me."

Kat thought about this for a moment. She did not want to deceive him any further; there had been too much of this already. But she could not bring herself to tell him the truth, either—that his lie had outgrown itself, that no explanation would change that fact.

Kat still did not understand exactly what had happened, what it was about Bagheri's presence in Madrid that could have set the events of the last week in motion. But, whatever the reason, Colin and Stuart were both dead because of it. She thought it unlikely that she and Jamal would be allowed to simply walk away, knowing what they knew.

Perhaps Bagheri knew something about what had happened out at the salt pit. Perhaps the same thing Colin and Stuart both knew. Perhaps the SBS team really had been behind Bagheri's escape, as Hariri had suggested. But none of this explained Morrow's interest in Bagheri, or Kurtz's, or why they would have waited until now to get rid of the two SBS men.

No, she told herself, remembering how she'd found Colin waiting for Kurtz at the Special Forces camp, and the next night in the ICE, Kurtz's face when the SBS team had taken fire, there was something more, something she was missing.

Shaking her head, she looked back at Jamal. "I'm sorry," she said, "but this isn't something I can explain away. We're in trouble, Jamal. Serious trouble."

"But there is no Bagheri," Jamal insisted. "Don't you understand?"

"I do understand, but it's not that simple."

Jamal said nothing.

"Look," Kat told him, "I'll figure something out, but we can't stay here. This is the first place Kurtz will look."

At the mention of Kurtz's name, Jamal's face grew pale.

Kat rose and extended her arm to Jamal to help him up, but Jamal didn't stand. Instead, he reached into the pocket of his pants, pulled out a scrap of paper, and offered it to Kat.

"What is this?" she asked, taking the paper, unfolding it. It appeared to have been torn from a book. There were eight letters in bold type: ES KEPLER. And, below the letters, a hastily scrawled U.S. phone number.

"Mr. Harry," Jamal said. "He will help us. He said so."

Kat contemplated the northern Virginia area code. "Who's Mr. Harry?"

"From Madrid," Jamal explained. "Before Mr. Justin." He made an encouraging motion with his hands. "We can call him."

Kat shook her head. "No, Jamal. I don't think that's a good idea."

But it was clear from the look on Jamal's face that the matter was not up for discussion. "We call Mr. Harry," he said, with uncharacteristic resolve. "Or you go without me." And then, throwing Kat's own words back at her: "You must trust me."

AFTER SIX UNBEARABLE MONTHS back in the States, Harry had finally been posted to Kinshasa. Back to the night-soil circuit, and he'd been happy to go. Relieved to be anywhere besides a desk at Langley.

Irene had been the anti-Susan. A southern girl with a genteel Virginia accent and a sorority pin. Kappa Kappa Gamma, Sweetbriar chapter. A congressman's daughter indulging her diminutive wild streak with a foreign-service job before settling down. She hadn't been a virgin when they met, but close, still uncomfortable with the lights on, still discreetly absenting herself once a month. Always freshly showered and perfectly made up, smelling of lilies and lilacs.

When they were first introduced at the embassy Halloween party, Harry had mistaken her pink twinset and pleated skirt for a cleverly ironic costume. It wasn't until a few days later, when he ran into her in the cafeteria, that he realized this was they way she always dressed.

When Harry was with her, it was as if the last decade—Vietnam and the mess at home—had never happened, as if what had brought them to Africa was not another of Kissinger's dirty wars but a college mixer.

This was what he had fallen in love with: not Irene but the illusion of himself she offered, the person she was not.

IT WAS NEARLY THREE IN THE MORNING when the phone next to Harry's bed rang, jolting him out of an unusually pleasant dream in which he and Char had moved from the Tamarack Pines into a rambling villa in the Kona Hills and were diligently exploring their new home, stopping to have sex in each of the many rooms.

The reality of waking wouldn't have been nearly so painful if it hadn't been for the hangover that accompanied it. On his way back to the motel from Morrow's house, Harry had stopped at a package store and bought a fifth of cheap vodka. It was a decision he'd known he would regret in the morning, and he hadn't been wrong. Though, to be fair, it was hardly morning.

He reached for the phone in the darkness, groping the unfamiliar bedside table, knocking the vodka bottle to the floor as he did so and spilling what little was left of the contents. The smell of the liquor made him gag.

At last his hand found the receiver. "Hello?"

"It's me." Irene.

"Look," Harry began, "you don't have to do this. I underst—"

"He called," she said, cutting him off. Her voice was nervous, electric.

Loving it, Harry thought, as they all did. When it came right down to it, all those things he'd been taught at the Farm about people's weaknesses, about money or shame or sex, were nothing compared to the hook of power, of being on the inside looking out.

"He's in Casablanca," Irene continued. "At the Hotel des Amis, in the medina. I told him you're coming."

Harry didn't know what to say. "There will be questions," he told her. "You'll tell Morrow that I forced you to do this. I threatened you."

"I'm not afraid of Morrow," Irene said, and Harry thought, No? You should be. But he didn't say it.

There was a long silence then, neither of them ready to go, but neither with anything left to say.

"I'm sorry," Harry told her at last.

"Don't be," Irene said.

TWENTY-SIX

"I think you must come now."

It was 6 AM, and Marina's voice was Morrow's wake-up call. The words were ambiguous, but the meaning was clear, and Morrow was up as soon as they were spoken, jamming his feet into his shoes, shrugging into his jacket.

It was daylight by the time he crossed the Key Bridge, heading toward Georgetown, a postcard morning. Down on the Potomac a single scull slid fluidly upstream, the rower moving with machinelike precision. Sweep, dip. Sweep, dip. Legs gliding forward and back, hands crossing and uncrossing. Body sexless from this distance, transformed entirely by the singular concentration the task required.

It's time, Dick, he could hear Susan say. Another morning like this one, another hurried drive. Years earlier, and the details of it were still fresh in his mind. Susan's dress: red with yellow flowers. Her hair pulled back into a neat bun. Her face filled out, softened by the pregnancy.

The memory was so vivid that when he pulled into the driveway now he half expected to see her waiting for him as she'd been that day, her red leather suitcase in one hand, her other hand on her belly. Laughing at him as he leaped from the car. Mouth open, head thrown back, laughing.

But there was no one to greet him this morning. Morrow pulled into the driveway and sat in the Mercedes with his hand on the key, unable to bring himself to turn off the ignition, unable to go inside.

After what must have been at least half an hour, the side door opened and Marina appeared. She was wearing a housecoat and worn blue terry-cloth scuffs, and her hair was tucked, as always, into a cotton scarf. It had been weeks since she'd gotten a full night's sleep, and she looked justifiably exhausted.

She came down the steps and walked to Morrow's open window. "Just like the other one," she said, shaking her head. "Too afraid to come inside." She reached into the car and put her hand on Morrow's hand, turned the ignition off. Her face was almost touching his. Her smell filled the car. It was the odor of days of unwashed sweat and wet wool and boiled meat, a smell that seemed not acquired but somehow native to the woman.

He was going to ask her what she'd meant by her previous comment, but she interrupted him before he had a chance.

"Don't worry," Marina said. "She has just had her morphine. You will not need to speak to her." Then, triumphantly, she released Morrow's hand and moved away.

WHEN KAT WAS IN INTELLIGENCE SCHOOL, she took a class called "Games." The course was legendary, as was the instructor who taught it, a wizened, grandfatherly figure whose heavy Slovak accent and crude forearm tattoo betrayed a past of which he never spoke, and to whom Kat and the other students referred simply as Yoda.

Appropriately, the curriculum of "Games" consisted of just that. Every day for three hours, Kat and the others would struggle through various seemingly unsolvable puzzles while Yoda looked on, offering a rare grunt of approval or, more often, a cluck of displeasure.

His favorite challenges, and by far the most difficult, were a series of three-dimensional wooden puzzles in which various pieces fit together to form sculptures of sorts. What made these puzzles so difficult was the fact that there were many possible solutions, but only one in which all of the pieces could be used.

"Remember," Yoda would say as he paced the room, his long sleeves rolled conspicuously down to his wrists, even at the sweltering height of summer. "Every piece in its place, even the ones that look like they don't fit."

The old man had died not long after Kat graduated, and "Games" was no longer offered. But on more than one occasion Kat had heard Yoda's signature phrase used by colleagues who had graduated long after she had.

Every piece in its place, she thought now as she sat in the window of the hotel room watching the narrow lane below. It was early afternoon and the passageway was clogged with foot traffic—housewives doing their daily shopping and tourists hunting for the ever-elusive deal. Behind her, in the room's single slip of a bed, Jamal was sleeping, as he had been for some time, moving now and again in restless dreams. She still did not know what to make of his Mr. Harry, but her options were slim enough that she was willing to wager a great deal on the boy's judgment. What other choice did she have at this point?

Down in the lane, a man appeared, a European with a build close enough to Kurtz's that Kat's heart seized up for a moment. Then he drew closer, passed beneath the window, and moved on.

Kat watched him disappear into the crowd, then reached into the breast pocket of her jacket for a pen and a scrap of paper. If she could see what the pieces were, she told herself, thinking of her old teacher again, she might just solve the puzzle.

She printed Bagheri's name and circled it. Outside the circle she wrote: *Iranian $, escape?SAS?DOD?CIA?, court-martial testimony.*

Next she made a circle for the dead prisoner. Here she wrote: *Bagheri's traveling companion, killed during SBS interrogation at salt pits, suffocated, asthmatic?*

The third circle was for Colin. Around his name Kat wrote: *witness to prisoner's death?, Stuart's superior, meeting with Kurtz, al-Amir, court-martial testimony, overdose?*

Next she wrote Kurtz's name and the words *Jamal, meeting with Colin, al-Amir.*

The last name she wrote was Stuart's, and around his circle: *suffocated prisoner during interrogation, al-Amir, court-martial testimony, killed by lover? Gay?*

She thought about this last piece of information for a moment. Then, remembering her conversation with Colin's father, she went back to Colin's circle and added *knew Stuart was gay?*

Admittedly, she didn't have much to work with. But then Yoda's wood pieces had never looked like much to begin with, either.

The most obvious connection to start was the court-martial. Colin and Stuart and Bagheri had all been potential witnesses in the trial to determine Stuart's guilt in the death of the prisoner. It was no coincidence that the two SBS men had been killed just days before the court-martial was scheduled to begin. But why the last-minute rush to do so?

If Kat's hunch was right, and the ambush at al-Amir had been set up by Kurtz, then there had been at least one previous attempt to silence the men. But still, the lag time didn't make sense. If the plan to kill Colin and Stuart had been in the works all along, it would have been much quieter to do so months earlier, when the connection to the court-martial was less apparent.

No, the two deaths had something to do with Jamal's reported sighting of Bagheri in Madrid. Perhaps Bagheri knew whatever it was that Colin and Stuart knew concerning the death of the prisoner. Perhaps Morrow and Kurtz were worried that their civilian counterparts would find Bagheri before they did, and that his testimony would force Colin and Stuart to reveal what they knew.

But if this was the case why would Colin and Stuart have agreed to help Kurtz with a cover-up in the first place? The SBS men had nothing but contempt for Kurtz and the other civilians. The Colin Kat had known at Bagram would not have sacrificed himself or his friend for Kurtz's cause. Hadn't he said it himself: *Our only obligations in this place are to ourselves and our friends.*

Kat looked down at her paper again, her eyes coming to rest on Stuart's name, the question she'd penned beneath it: *Gay?*

Kat knew the culture of the Special Forces, if only tangentially. She knew that an admission of homosexuality on Stuart's part would have meant instant expulsion from the group. In the regular military, homosexuality was a subject to be avoided at all costs. In a small group like the SBS team, with its own rigid mores, to even speak of homosexuality was taboo. But Colin had known.

Perhaps Kurtz had known as well. Perhaps Colin had agreed to lie about the events surrounding the prisoner's death in exchange for Kurtz's silence on the subject of Stuart's sexual preference. This Kat could believe.

But what of the prisoner's death? According to the official report, the man had suffocated while being detained with a canvas sack over his head, a practice that was certainly not extreme, and that would not have proved fatal had his health not been compromised in the first place. *They're saying he was asthmatic,* Hariri had told her that night in the ICE, rumors already trickling in. Kat had chalked Hariri's information and the speed with which he knew it up to disinformation, an early attempt to muddy the waters on Stuart's behalf. But if the prisoner really was asthmatic, if this was what had killed him, how could anyone have known so soon?

And what of Hariri's other suggestion, that Bagheri had not escaped on his own? If the Iranian had, in fact, known something incriminating about his companion's death, then it made a certain sense for Kurtz to arrange his escape. Though killing him would have made more sense, and would have been much less risky. No, she was still missing something.

Kat scanned the paper again, the five circles: Colin, Stuart, Kurtz, Bagheri and the dead prisoner, both Iranians. Every piece, she reminded herself, even the ones that look as if they don't fit. She glanced over at Jamal, remembering his story about the women soldiers, how she had dismissed it as fantasy.

Except for the first few times in the booth, when the boy had sketched in the details of his journey and his connection with Bagheri, there had been little time for Kat to actually interrogate Jamal. Instead, all her energy had been focused on preparing him for what lay ahead. Exactly, she now realized, as Kurtz wanted it to be.

A camp where the women were in charge. A camp near Herat, which put it close to the Iranian border. No, Kat told herself, Bagheri had not been kidding.

She rose and crossed the room to where Jamal was sleeping, touched him gently on the shoulder.

He rolled over and blinked up at her, groggy and confused, struggling to get his bearings.

"The camp in Herat," Kat said. "I need to know exactly what Bagheri told you."

I HAVE GIVEN HER MORE THAN USUAL. Marina said as she and Morrow entered Susan's room. Susan was fast asleep in her hospital bed, her eyes locked tight, her breath astonishingly even. On a tray at the bottom of the bed were a handful of morphine patches. A week's supply, at least, unwrapped and ready for use.

In the early days of her illness, before she was confined entirely to home, Susan had taken to wearing bright-colored turbans instead of wigs, and she was wearing one now, the jewel-green fabric twisted elegantly across her bare scalp, secured at the front with a gold clasp. She had had Marina make her face up as well, though here the attempt at beautification had been less successful. Susan's lips were several shades too red against the backdrop of her pale skin, her cheeks rouged in two perfect pink circles. The effect was that of a cheap doll.

Morrow took a tissue from the nightstand by the bed and gingerly wiped Susan's mouth. The gesture, which served only to smear the red off her lips and onto her chin, was worse than futile.

"You will see," Marina told him. "It is easy."

Not always, Morrow thought. But to Marina he said, "Yes, I'm sure it will be." And then, without warning, he was violently ill. He rushed into the bathroom and braced himself over the toilet, retching up a watery bile. Nothing in his stomach except the remnants of the previous night's bourbons.

How Susan had wanted it, he thought then, catching a glimpse of his ragged reflection in the water. No real need for him to be here, except that this was how she had told the Russian it would be. At that moment, he hated her for forcing her death upon him.

"Mr. Morrow?"

"Yes, Marina." He wiped his mouth with the back of his hand and stood. "Everything's fine."

JAMAL SAT UP AND RUBBED HIS EYES. clearly exasperated. "I told you before. He said there would be women. Women soldiers. He said they were Muslims, jihadis. That is all I know."

"What else, Jamal?" Kat said, trying to impress the urgency of the question on the boy. "What did he call them?"

Jamal looked as if he were about to cry. He closed his eyes. It was a gesture, Kat remembered from Bagram, that meant he was recalling something unpleasant. Perhaps the nature of his relationship with Bagheri.

Kat moved back slightly, giving him space to think, to shake whatever dark memories had hijacked his mind.

Jamal's eyes blinked open and slid to the wall above Kat's shoulder. "*Mojahedin.* He called them *mojahedin.*"

"What else?" Kat prompted. She was wary of feeding him the full name, knew that subjects were bound to agree with almost any reasonable suggestion while under the stress of questioning.

Jamal's eyes moved downward, came to rest on hers. "Mojahedin-e Khalq," he said at last, locating the words somewhere deep in his memory. "Yes. That was it."

Kat nodded, scribbled the three-letter acronym MEK on her paper next to Bagheri's name. Not just another piece of the puzzle, she thought, scrounging to remember everything she knew about the group, but an important one.

After fleeing to Europe in the wake of the Iranian revolution, Kat knew, the MEK's first big break had come during the Iran-Iraq War, when Saddam Hussein, shrewdly recognizing it as a potential ally, had armed and financed the group. It, in turn, not only launched terrorist attacks against the Iranian army but also helped Hussein in his brutal campaign against the Iraqi Kurds and Shiites.

For these reasons, among others, the MEK had been labeled a terrorist group by most of the international community, including the United States. But as with so many terrorist organizations, Kat knew, the definition was a fluid one. For many years, when Iran had been America's primary enemy in the region and Iraq her friend, the MEK had found discreet support in Washington. Now the political ground had shifted once again.

Could the MEK have reconnected with its old friends in the United States? Could the group have found a new base in Afghanistan? If so, it was a partnership neither would have wanted made public.

Kat looked down at the paper, at her crude sketch with its tenuous connections. Colin. Stuart. Bagheri. Kurtz. The dead prisoner. She was getting closer, but she still couldn't quite make out how everything fit together.

KURTZ SLID DOWN IN HIS SEAT and watched the solitary figure make its way forward along the street. Cheap leather jacket. Knocked-off jeans. Knocked-off James Dean swagger. Yes, it was definitely the young man he'd seen at Ain Chock the day before, the one who had traded glances with Kat, who had wanted to tell them something but hadn't been able to.

Kurtz waited until the man was just about even with the Peugeot, then popped the door and stepped out, sliding his Beretta from the inside pocket of his jacket.

"Get in!"

The man eyed Kurtz, then turned his head and spit. "Go fuck yourself."

"Get in or I'll shoot you." Simple as that, Kurtz thought, and the man could see it.

Kurtz grabbed the man's arm, twisting it hard, and hustled him into the passenger seat, then closed the door and climbed in behind the wheel. "What's your name?" he asked, laying the Beretta across his lap and turning the key in the ignition.

"Mahjoub."

Kurtz checked his mirrors and pulled away from the curb. "We met yesterday. Do you remember?"

A nod.

"Then you know what I want."

Another nod. "You're looking for Adil's friend, Jamal."

"Very good. He's been here, yes?"

Silence.

Kurtz fingered the Beretta's safety. "Here's the deal, Mahjoub. You tell me what I want to know, and I'll make it worth your while. You don't, and I shoot you. Understood?"

"He left this morning. With the woman, the one who came with you."

Kurtz smiled. Now they were getting somewhere. "Did they say where they were going?"

"No."

Of course not. Kurtz pulled the car to the curb and reached into his jacket, pulled out a hundred-dollar bill. "I'm at the Hotel Noailles," he said, "in the city center. You see them again, you let me know."

Mahjoub nodded, as if what Kurtz was asking was no big deal, as if he did this kind of thing all the time. But when he reached for the money his hands were shaking.

Kurtz lifted the Beretta and aimed it at Mahjoub's chest. "Now get out."

TWENTY-SEVEN

It was not until late that afternoon, after two tattooed ex-convicts in hundred-dollar suits had appeared on behalf of the mortuary and removed Susan's body from the house, zipping her face inside a black plastic bag while Morrow looked on, mumbling awkward condolences, that Morrow truly understood what had happened. Just as Susan's presence in his life had been more physical than spiritual, so in death it was the absence of her body that grieved him most. Even wrecked by illness, she had maintained an almost disciplinary power in the house. Now she was gone, and Marina with her.

Morrow had not seen the Russian leave, but her room had been cleaned out entirely, her closets and drawers emptied, her bed stripped and the linens miraculously washed and folded and put away. It was, Morrow thought, as if she had never been there at all.

True to form, Susan had made a list of people to inform and the order in which to call them, starting with their son, Paul, in New York, on whose voice mail Morrow had left a vaguely urgent message, and ending with Susan's sister in Florida, whom Morrow still could not bring himself to call.

Momentarily bowing to his cowardice, Morrow padded into the library and poured himself a drink. Bourbon again. He had not eaten all day and the first sip hit him hard. He set the glass aside and made his way into the kitchen, opened the refrigerator, and contemplated the paltry contents. Some moldy bread. A bag of shriveled grapes. A dozen cans of Susan's vile energy shakes. And, on the door, year-old condiments—pickles and olives and mustards—most of which predated the diagnosis.

He was trying to decide which of the three drink flavors—strawberry, chocolate, or vanilla—would be the least distasteful when the phone rang.

Paul, he thought, suddenly panicked. He did not know what to say to his son under the best of circumstances, and the task of breaking the news of Susan's death seemed insurmountable. But it would have to be done.

Closing the refrigerator door, Morrow reached for the phone, lifted the receiver to his ear.

"Dick?" Not Paul but Janson on the line. Morrow had called the office earlier that morning to tell his secretary what had happened and that he wouldn't be coming in. "I'm sorry to bother you," Janson said, "but there's some news about Harry Comfort. I thought you'd want to know."

"Good or bad?" Morrow asked.

"To tell you the truth, I'm not sure. Our tail called in earlier today saying they'd lost him. Evidently he walked into some tourist hotel in Kailua night before last and never came out."

"I'd call that bad news."

"I would too," Janson replied. "Except I think we've found him. TSA's got a Harry Lyttle purchasing a last-minute ticket on the red-eye out of Kailua that night. Traveling on a Canadian passport."

"Heading where?" Morrow asked.

"That's the interesting part," Janson said, pausing for effect. "He flew into Dulles yesterday afternoon."

"He's here?"

"Was here. Our same Mr. Lyttle caught another flight this morning. Paris and on to Casablanca." Another dramatic pause. "The boy must have contacted him."

"I thought we were on top of that."

"We are," Janson assured Morrow. "Irene's been quiet since yesterday. Nothing coming in or going out."

"Nothing?"

"Not a peep."

Morrow put his thumb and forefinger to his eyes, squeezed the bridge of his nose. God, he was tired. Wrecked, really. *Just like the other one,* he heard Marina say. *Too afraid to come inside.* Comfort, he thought. After all these years, Harry hadn't been able to stay away.

"He's been to see her," Morrow said grimly. He meant Irene. He meant Susan.

"But we would have heard," Janson insisted.

"Not if he put something on the line."

Silence.

"What time does he get into Casablanca?" Morrow asked.

"About thirty minutes ago."

Morrow didn't say anything.

"What should we do?"

"Start shaking the tree," Morrow told him. "He's going to need help."

"And Irene?"

"I'll take care of her."

Harry had been to Casablanca many times before. In the seventies and early eighties, when Africa Division was his home, he'd had several important contacts in Morocco and had been a regular visitor to the city. He hadn't liked it then, and he didn't like it now.

There was a squalid arrogance to the place that Harry found intolerable. Everything that made Morocco's other cities charming had been replaced in Casablanca by the ugliest kind of Western industriousness: wide boulevards and bland gray façades, women in dark-blue business suits and black leather pumps. And, on the outskirts of the city, the detritus of commerce: ungodly miles of slums.

Even the medina was a contrivance, Harry thought, as he wound his way through the narrow lanes of the old quarter. A relic left untouched by the city's various destroyers. A curiosity piece for tourists to admire. Though at this time of night only the most foolhardy or desperate of visitors would have found themselves here. Harry couldn't help wondering which category he fit into.

It was late and frighteningly dark, the sky a narrow slate overhead, matte black and starless, the passageways groaning with the sounds of sex and death, like some medieval vision of the netherworld come to life. A figure stepped out of a doorway and hissed in Harry's ear, offering something: drugs, a woman, one of any number of gateways to damnation, fruits of the tree, there for the picking.

"Fuck off!" Harry snarled through clenched teeth. No translation needed. He was still hungover from the night before, jet-lagged beyond belief. Halfway around the world from his starting point at the Tamarack Pines and in no mood to be hustled.

The man slunk back into the shadows and Harry continued on, counting the streets as he went, consulting the route he'd laid out for himself in his mind using the walking map he'd bought at an airport kiosk. Three streets, then a left. Four and another left. A blind man tapping his way through the world.

Morrow could hear the dog barking as soon as he started up the walk. The corgi had been sitting on the couch, staring out the front picture window, waiting for someone to harass, when Morrow first drove up. Now the creature was indulging the full range of its ire, darting frantically from one end of the sofa to the other, leaping at the glass like a pit fighter about to take on a formidable opponent. Undaunted, Morrow climbed the front steps and rang the doorbell, noting Irene's Volvo in the driveway.

A chime rang inside the house, three clear tones followed by a fresh outburst from the corgi and the sound of footsteps on the wood floors. A hand drew aside the ivied fabric that covered the door's oval window and Irene's face appeared on the other side of the glass, her expression souring at the sight of Morrow.

She drew the lock and opened the door, keeping the screen closed between them. "Hello, Dick." Her voice was carefully leveled, devoid of any warmth. She was slim and tan, in immaculate tennis whites—a sleeveless shirt and a short skirt that showed off her perfectly preserved body.

"It might be better if we talk inside," Morrow suggested.

"Right here's just fine with me." She turned away from him and to the dog. "Hush, Glory!"

The corgi fell silent.

"I know he's been here," Morrow said.

"Who's that?" Irene asked with practiced coolness. She was not going to make this easy for him.

"What did he tell you? That he could help the boy?"

"I don't know what you're talking about, Dick."

Morrow shook his head. "We know he's in Casablanca. We know he's been in touch with the boy."

Irene crossed her bare arms over her chest. "If you know where he is, why are you wasting your time here?"

"He came to the house, you know," he told her then. "He came to see Susan."

Behind the scrim of the screen her green eyes flickered just slightly, and Morrow thought, This won't be easy for either of us. "It doesn't get old, being the consolation prize?" he asked.

Irene moved to close the door, but Morrow reached inside the screen and stopped her.

"Get off my porch," she said evenly.

"It's foolish of you to protect him like this," Morrow cautioned.

Irene glanced down at his hand on her door with measured disdain. She was not a woman who was easily threatened. "Better a fool than a bastard," she said. Then she shoved the door closed with such sudden and unexpected force that Morrow had no time to counter it.

Jamali Kat put her hands on the boy's shoulders and shook him violently. "Wake up, Jamal!" From the other side of the door she could hear low voices, the muffled commotion of more than one body mounting the stairs.

The boy sat up, his eyes wild in the darkness. "Who is it?"

Kat shrugged, put her finger to her lips to silence him.

The footsteps had reached the upper floor now and were shuffling along the corridor. Kat recognized the voice of the hotel's proprietress, a pied-noir half-breed, from their brief encounter that morning. The woman had charged Kat three times what the room was worth, and Kat, too tired to argue, had let it go.

"*Ici,*" she whispered. *Here.*

Silence, then the sound of the woman retreating down the corridor. Then the man's voice, just outside their door. "Jamal?"

Jamal flung the covers aside and swung his bare feet to the floor. "Mr. Harry!" he called out excitedly, lunging for the door, opening it to reveal a stout and decidedly unimpressive figure.

Christ, Kat thought, noting the man's rumpled clothes and two-day stubble, call in the cavalry and get a skid-row Santa instead.

The man's eyes moved from Jamal to Kat and stopped there, mirroring her own reservations. "You must be Kat. Jamal's told me quite a lot about you."

Kat nodded.

"Not quite what you were expecting, am I?" Harry remarked. "Don't worry. You're not the first woman I've disappointed."

Manar climbed onto a stepstool and ran her hand along the upper shelf of her closet, sweeping aside the paltry detritus of her life—boxes of mementos from the years before, old school books and photographs, things her mother had not been able to bring herself to throw away after Manar's arrest—searching with blind fingers for the shoe box she knew was there. Inside was two months' worth of barbiturates that her mother's doctor had prescribed as sleep aids when Manar had first returned home, and which Manar, unbeknownst to her mother, had discreetly refused to take.

Her decision to keep the pills had not necessarily been a calculated one, in so much as she had not anticipated any specific future in which she would need to take her own life. But her years in the prison had taught her that such desperation was always possible, and that such a tool was not to be discarded.

In her haste to get to the pills, Manar knocked a box off the shelf, sending a cascade of photographs clattering to the floor. They were from the last few years before her imprisonment, snapshots of Manar with her friends from school, Yusuf and others from the student group. Manar bent down and swept the pictures back into the box, embarrassed by what they represented—the ridiculous meetings in the basement of the mosque, their earnest speeches, imagining that they could somehow speak for those who had nothing, that they could even begin to understand those lives, that despair—appalled that someone might find the photographs after she was gone and imagine them to be somehow connected to her death.

She thought about throwing them away, then realized that this act could be construed as meaningful as well, and tucked them back up on the shelf instead. Once she was gone, people could think what they liked.

She found the pills where she'd left them, the shoe box pushed into the rear right corner of the shelf, padded with dust. Her dust, she thought as she took the box down and carried it to her bed, trying to steady her shaking hands. Her skin, the body's sloughings, finer than sand.

There was a time when Manar had been afraid of death, but this was no longer the case. Having lived in such close proximity to it for such a long time, having already been to the point of surrender, she understood that to be afraid was entirely pointless, that when the end did come there was no way not to be ready for it.

She did not believe in the punishments of hell or the rewards of paradise. On the contrary, it was her utter lack of faith that allowed her to proceed as she did. If she had believed, such an act would have been unthinkable, the most final of treasons, the sin against which all others would be measured, the transgression that would have severed her, finally and completely, from her God. But she did not believe.

Still, she had to force herself to open the box, to set each bottle on her dresser, to shake the pills out, one by one, until she was certain there were enough.

TWENTY-EIGHT

"*Fajr,*" Harry remarked, turning his head toward the open window and the sound of the muezzin's song, the day's first call to prayer. "I didn't realize it was so late."

"So early, you mean," Kat corrected him.

He nodded. "Yes, that too." His face, shadowed with several days of gray stubble, looked impossibly old, worn beyond the point of repair.

A man naked in his grief, Kat had thought when she first saw him in the doorway. And it was that which made her trust him completely.

Kat had spent the bulk of the night filling Harry in on the details of their predicament, including her growing suspicions about the prisoner's death at Bagram, Bagheri's subsequent escape, Kurtz's role in the ambush at al-Amir, and Jamal's description of the MEK camp.

"I assure you," Harry said, after listening to Kat's theories, "there are no MEK camps in Afghanistan. You said yourself that Jamal is good at telling people what they want to hear. Maybe the story is simpler than what you are allowing yourself to believe."

"What's that supposed to mean?"

Harry shrugged. "Suppose your British friends were over-zealous in their questioning and killed the prisoner by mistake. Suppose they did help Bagheri escape, to keep him from incriminating them."

"But why not just kill Bagheri, then? That would have been a hell of a lot easier and safer than helping him escape."

"For all we know, they did kill him."

But Kat wasn't buying Harry's theory. "Everything Bagheri told him adds up to the camp being MEK. I mean, that stuff about the women. There's no other explanation. And what about Morrow and Kurtz? What about the court-martial? And Colin and Stuart? Don't tell me their deaths were coincidence."

"It's one thing to say you're going to lie, another to actually do it. Suppose one or both had a sudden attack of conscience and threatened to come clean about the whole incident. Or suppose they got wind of Bagheri's reappearance and got spooked into telling the truth. A lot of people, including Morrow, would have wanted to keep that from happening. A prisoner tortured to death can make people change their minds about war in a hurry."

"I don't know," Kat said, trying unsuccessfully to order the facts in her mind. "Something's still not adding up."

Harry's eyes moved to Jamal once again. "Do yourself a favor," he told Kat, "let it go. You've got other things to worry about now, like what to do with yourself, and with Jamal. Do you have a passport?"

Kat shook her head. In her haste to leave the hotel, she'd left her passport in Kurtz's room, along with her bag.

"It's just as well. You would have needed a new one in any case. You understand that you may have to disappear for a while?"

Kat nodded, but the truth was that she hadn't given much

thought to what would happen next. She certainly hadn't considered the possibility that she might not be going home. She felt as if she'd been kicked in the throat. "What about Jamal?"

Harry was silent for a moment. Aware, Kat thought, as she was, of how little their past good intentions had amounted to, how unlikely it was that this time around would be any different. "I've been thinking. You know, he might still have family somewhere," Harry said at last. "If his mother really was a political prisoner, she would have just disappeared and her family might not have even known the child existed."

"Jamal told you that?" Kat asked. "About his mother, I mean."

"Not in so many words. I'm not sure he even knows. He said something about his mother being taken to the desert by the king. Almost as if it was a privilege. That's the way they did it in those days. Hassan II had special prisons built in the desert for dissenters." Harry closed his eyes, as if trying not to remember something. "Horrible places."

Kat winced, not at Harry's story but at her own stupidity.

"Did he tell you the same thing?"

"Yes," Kat confessed. "I didn't understand. I thought he'd made the story up, to make it all bearable."

"No? Well, in any case, as I said, there could very well be family out there who would take him in." He looked toward the window, through which a thin ribbon of dawn was now visible. "I know people here who can help us. With a passport. With the boy."

You've told so many lies. Harry could remember Irene saying to him once, *that you no longer know what the truth is.*

She'd been right, of course, dead on. Though Harry, who at the time hadn't thought much of the truth, couldn't see what

all the fuss was about. People lied, and in return it was necessary to lie yourself; there was no great mystery to the fact.

But this lie had been different.

Kat wasn't the first person to suggest that the MEK had ex-
panded its operations to include southern Afghanistan. In the
years since September 11, and the subsequent fall of the Taliban, rumors of U.S.-MEK cooperation in the region were frequently discussed within the intelligence community. It was no
secret that there were voices at the Pentagon, Morrow's chief
among them, clamoring for regime change in Iran. A silent
partnership with the MEK would have provided the perfect
tool with which to explore destabilization efforts in the region.

Harry knew for a fact that factions in the Agency had been
proposing a similar program off and on for decades, but had
been shot down by concerns over the MEK's official status as
a terrorist organization. Without the threat of oversight, Morrow and the others in Special Plans could have pulled such a
program off. In fact, Harry would have been surprised if they
hadn't at least tried. Certainly, if the MEK were in Afghanistan,
they were there with the blessing of someone in the Defense
Department.

But this was not what he had told Kat. *I assure you, there
are no MEK camps in Afghanistan.* Not just a lie but a story to
back it up. Better for her, he'd reasoned at the time, knowing
that her ignorance might very well save her life, and the boy's,
if he himself could not. Easier to be honest about what one
doesn't know than to lie about what one does.

Could Bagheri have been working for Morrow? Harry
wondered, as he and Kat made their way down the Rue
Chakib Arsalane to the medina's main gate. It was early still,
but the lanes were already crowded, the air rich with breakfast
smells: hot grease and honey, *beghrirs* on the grill. If Morrow
had struck some kind of deal with the MEK, he would not

have wanted to publicize the fact. Not even to those within the dissident group. If Harry's supposition was right, it was probable that Bagheri's traveling companion hadn't known of his involvement with the Americans.

If the SBS team had unwittingly picked up Bagheri during one of their sweeps, it would have been impossible to release him without casting suspicion on him. Unless, of course, none of his comrades knew he'd been captured in the first place. This would explain the death of his companion, and the army's initial failure to make an official report of the escape.

"Which way?"

Kat's question yanked Harry from his reverie. He stopped walking and glanced up. Directly in front of them, the medina gate opened onto the busy axis of the Place des Nations Unies. Looking through the opening and out onto the traffic-clogged boulevard was like peering directly from the fourteenth century into the twenty-first, and Harry was momentarily disoriented by the powerful incongruity of the vision.

A young Moroccan man—a would-be guide—approached, offering his services.

Kat brushed him off with forceful Arabic, then turned back to Harry. "Gone but not defeated," she remarked, watching the man move off to accost another Western couple. "We'd better go before he changes his mind and comes back."

Harry nodded. "Don't tell me they taught you that in the army?" he asked, heading toward a taxi stand just outside the gate.

"How to get rid of hustlers?"

"No, your Arabic."

"I went to DLI," Kat explained.

Harry signaled to the first driver in line and got an affirmative nod in response. "But you must use it. Arabic gets rusty fast." He opened the taxi's back door for Kat.

Perhaps it was the intimacy of the gesture, or the odd out-datedness of it—how long had it been since he'd held a door for a woman?—but Harry, watching Kat fold herself into the cab, was struck by both a sense of nostalgia and of shame, by the sudden realization of just how much he'd lost, how much of himself he had already forfeited.

"I teach," Kat said when Harry joined her in the taxi's back seat.

"Voyageurs," Harry told the driver, indicating the main train station on the eastern side of town. Then, to Kat. "Language?"

"Yes. And theology."

"Islam?"

Kat nodded. "My specialty is soteriology, that's—"

"The theology of salvation." The old spy smiled. "They don't call us intelligence men for nothing."

Kat returned his smile.

They rode on in silence for some time. Out the window, Harry could see the massive silhouette of the Hassan II Mosque rising from the coast.

"And you?" Harry asked at last. "You believe in all of that?"

"All of what?"

"You know: a jinn on each shoulder, tallying one's works for the day of reckoning; life as a test to see who gets into heaven."

Kat laughed. "It's more complicated than that. But, no, I don't believe in the Muslim version of the afterlife. Or in the Christian one, for that matter. If there is a God, I have to be-lieve we're all saved."

"And if there isn't?"

Kat shook her head. "Then there isn't, and none of it mat-ters."

Twenty years. Harry thought as they passed the train station and turned onto a side street. No, in reality it was more like twenty-five. For the first time, the obvious fact that his old friends might no longer be among the living crossed Harry's mind and he felt a twinge of panic. Then the familiar storefront slid into view, the old sign Harry remembered unchanged except by time and the elements: M. RAFA, PRINTING.

"Here?" the driver asked, pulling to the curb. Even he was reluctant.

"Yes." Harry fished a wad of crumpled dirhams from his pants pockets and paid the man, then stepped out onto the sidewalk. "You speak any other languages besides Arabic?" he asked Kat, as they started for the shop's front door.

"High-school Spanish and the worst Pashto you've ever heard. Why?"

"Just thinking about your passport." Harry opened the door and a string of bells sounded overhead, announcing their arrival.

A middle-aged Moroccan man in an ink-smeared printer's apron appeared from the rear of the shop. He was short and round about the middle, but powerfully built, his arms thick and muscular. His graying hair was cropped close to his skull, his beard trimmed into a neat goatee. A pair of delicate, wire-rimmed spectacles perched on the bridge of his nose.

"Mustafa?" Harry asked, marveling at the kindness the last two decades had shown his former acquaintance.

The man stepped forward and offered an ink-blackened hand. "Mustafa the son," he said. His grip was firm, his English nearly perfect, the accent British public school. He made a point of shaking Kat's hand as well. "You are looking for my father, perhaps?"

"Yes," Harry said, remembering the younger man from his previous visits. "Is he in?"

Mustafa the son shook his head solemnly. "My father is no longer with us, *subhan'allah*." He peered over his glasses at Harry. "I remember you. You are the American, yes. Mr. . . . ?"

But Harry didn't offer his name. "I'm sorry for your loss," he said.

Mustafa bowed just slightly. "Thank you," he said. "But you have not come merely to offer your condolences. My father may be gone, but I assure you his business is very much intact. You need something for the lady, I think."

"A passport," Harry told him. "English-speaking, preferably. Something with a few miles on it: EU, Asia, nothing suspicious. With a Tangier entry stamp."

Mustafa nodded. "It can be done."

"How soon?"

"One week. Five thousand euros." He wiped his palms on his apron, leaving two dark streaks behind.

"One thousand, and we'll have it by this afternoon."

Mustafa balked. "You know that's impossible."

"Two thousand."

"Three, and the document is in hand by six this evening."

"Three," Harry agreed.

Mustafa smiled at Kat. It was a crook's smile, obsequious and leering at the same time. "We will need a picture, yes?"

JAMAL OPENED THE FRONT DOOR of the Hotel des Amis and scanned the narrow street before wading out into the slow-moving river of humanity. It was nearly noon, well past the time by which Kat had promised to return, and Jamal was too hungry to wait for her any longer. His belly complaining, he stepped out into the crowd and started for the food stall he'd both seen and smelled from the window of the hotel room.

Twenty meters, he told himself, remembering Mr. Harry's warning about leaving the room. And what could possibly happen to him in such a short distance? This was his home, after all, his cradle and, if fate so wished, his grave. He had already made up his mind that no matter what happened he would not be leaving again.

Zid! Zid! From behind him came the cry of a donkey driver. The crowd jostled together, bodies moving in unison to let the creature pass. Bodies like his own, Jamal thought, marveling at the unusual sensation of belonging, at the oddness of the few European faces.

He reached the little food kiosk and stopped, momentarily stunned by the range of choices, unable to decide between the soft *sfenj* and the flaky *rghaif*, both still hot from the fryer, drenched in honey and butter, or the delicate half-moons of the gazelle's horns, with their thick layer of icing. Greedily, he chose all three, stuffing one of the crescent-shaped pastries into his mouth while the merchant packed the others into a paper bag.

His hunger dulled, he paid the man and turned to go, slipping into the crowd's upstream current and allowing himself to be carried back toward the hotel. Twenty meters or not even, he thought. Already he was halfway back. And then, moving toward him in the oncoming press of bodies, he saw a familiar face.

Mahjoub, he thought, Adil's friend from Ain Chock. Jamal ducked his head, but it was too late. As he elbowed his way forward toward the hotel's door, Jamal glanced back and saw that the man had stopped to watch him go.

For the first few moments upon waking, the only thing Manar could think was that she was back in the prison. The inside of her throat was raw and sore, as if some object had been forced into her and then withdrawn. Her chest and abdomen were bruised and tender, her back resting uncomfortably on cold tiles.

Perhaps, she thought with relief, the last few years had not happened at all. Perhaps it had merely been some long, extended dream. Memory resolving into shape. She had never really left the desert, had not been wounded by hope and the forfeit of hope.

Then a voice came to her. "Sister? Wake up, sister!" Then a hand, a warm palm on her forehead, and she understood that she had failed.

She opened her eyes and saw Asiya kneeling beside her. The housekeeper's djellaba was damp at the chest, soiled with vomit, her hands red and shaking. Her scarf had slipped back from her forehead, and her hair was loose and disheveled.

Manar had a dim memory of the last seconds before she'd drifted off, of trying to force down the pills before sleep and paralysis overcame her. How many had she managed? Ten? Fifteen? Whatever the number, it had not been enough.

She raised herself up just slightly and grasped the housekeeper's hand. "Who knows?" she asked, suddenly wild with panic.

"No one, sister," Asiya assured her. "We will tell no one."

TWENTY-NINE

Sitting in the courtyard of Abdul Moussaoui's villa just south of the Parc de la Ligue Arabe, drinking fresh mint tea and listening to the sound of water in the basalt fountain and the gentle laughter of the home's unseen female inhabitants, Harry could scarcely imagine the existence of anything beyond the windowless walls. That was the point of such architecture, of course: to separate the luxuries of civilization from the arid outer world, to protect the family and its guests. But Harry had never been entirely comfortable with the opacity of Arab life. He knew that what happened behind the locked doors of these homes was not always pleasant, and that evil could be sheltered as easily as good.

How many had disappeared from this very spot, leaving only the dregs of their tea behind, how many had heard the soothing gurgle of the fountain and mistakenly thought it signaled their reprieve, Harry could only guess. But he was not naïve enough to be fooled by Moussaoui's genial smile and Hermès slippers into thinking him untainted by the horrors of the previous regime.

Once, Harry remembered, after a South African arms

dealer they'd been working with had shorted them on a ship-
ment, Moussaoui had the man's Moroccan lover picked up by
the secret police and tortured to death. Harry had seen the pictures of the girl—Moussaoui made sure everyone got a look—
and it was her face he was thinking of, the eyes swollen shut,
the nose flattened to one side, the left cheek stippled with four
small bruises, one for each knuckle, as he watched Moussaoui
perform the ritual of lighting a fresh Cohiba.

"I'm telling you this as a friend," Moussaoui said, once the
cigar was burning to his satisfaction. "People know you are
here. I received a call from Pete Janson this morning. He said
you'd be coming to see me."

Morrow, Harry thought. After all these years, Janson was
still doing his dirty work. He couldn't help wondering if
Mustafa the son had gotten a similar call. Rafa's name would
have cropped up on the same short list as Moussaoui's.

There was a noise on one of the upper balconies, and Harry
glanced up to see an Asian woman in maid's attire carrying a
stack of folded linens.

Moussaoui chuckled. "It's the life of a pasha, no? Even I am
embarrassed sometimes."

Harry took a sip of his tea, wishing desperately that it was
vodka. "The boy," he prompted Moussaoui. "We were talking
about the boy."

"Yes. The boy." Moussaoui leaned back in his chair and
sucked appreciatively on his cigar, producing a large and aro-
matic cloud of smoke. "There were not as many cases like this
as you would imagine. I remember only two or three in my
time. Though undoubtedly there were others I was not aware
of. When did you say he was born?"

"Nineteen eighty-three," Harry said, quoting the boy's file.
"Give or take a year."

"You're not going to make this easy for me, are you?"
Moussaoui observed.

Harry tried to smile. Dirty hands all around, he reminded himself. That girl's death on his conscience as surely as if it was his fist that had broken her nose.

"I'll make some phone calls," Moussaoui said. "Discreetly, of course. See if I can turn anything up. It shouldn't take more than a few hours. You can call me later this afternoon." He produced a business card from a pocket with a phone number printed in small black type, then rose and gestured to the way out. "My driver can take you somewhere?"

Harry contemplated the offer.

"Yes," he told Moussaoui at last. "I would like to see the Blue Mosque."

AN HOUR, TWO AT MOST. Harry had told Kat when he'd dropped her off at the gate of the medina. He hadn't volunteered where he was going and she hadn't asked. There was a kind of inviolable sadness about the man that she couldn't breach. All his failings on his sleeve.

Inside the medina, the few befuddled tourists who hadn't yet been picked up by guides moved cautiously forward past souvenir stalls and spice shops, shadowed by the Al-Djemma Mosque's minaret. Up on the flat rooftops a garden of rust-pocked satellite dishes bloomed, their faces turning in unison, like morning glories to the sun. Farther down the lane, above the poultry merchant's cages and the limp and flightless bodies of the dead, a Coca-Cola billboard loomed in red and white, the script familiar even in Arabic.

Kat paused briefly outside a clothing shop on the Rue Centrale, shuddering at the racks of loose-fitting dresses visible from the street, the bright colors and fabrics struggling to lend an air of individuality where none was possible. Inside, a woman in a full chador, her hands in black gloves, her face hidden behind a *niqab,* was browsing through a rack of children's clothing, while a girl of three or four tagged along behind.

Mother and child, Kat thought, watching the pair with horror, the woman gliding through the shop, silent and substanceless as a ghost. The girl stopped to do a ballerina's twirl and her hair swung dark and lush against her back.

It seemed foolish to be afraid of this woman, and yet Kat was, not of her necessarily but of what she represented. There was something perverse in such utter abandon of self, in allowing one's identity to be consumed entirely, as Kat's mother had allowed herself to be. Offering herself, piece by piece.

The woman looked up from her shopping then, and Kat, feeling herself caught, turned quickly from the window and hurried along the street.

It was almost noon when Kat finally returned to the hotel. Nearly time for *Asr,* she thought, already measuring the day in prayers instead of hours, anticipating the muezzin's call. She let herself in the front door and climbed the narrow steps to the second floor.

When Kat opened the door to their room, Jamal was sitting by the window, staring down at the lane below. His eyes, when he swung his head toward the door, were wide with panic, his face ashen.

"It's okay, Jamal," she told him gently, forcing a reassuring smile. "It's just me." Then, noticing the grease-stained paper bag on the table, she winced. "You went out?"

Jamal nodded.

"Did something happen?" She locked the door behind her and stepped forward. "What happened, Jamal?"

"Nothing," he insisted. But his face, flushed, said otherwise.

A child, Kat thought, a child who'd been caught doing something he knew he shouldn't. "It's okay, Jamal," she repeated. "I'm sure it's okay."

But he was crying.

Kat reached out her hand and laid it on his shoulder. It was, she realized, the first time she had touched the boy. Physical contact had been strictly forbidden at Bagram, such a gesture entirely unthinkable.

His body beneath her fingers was even frailer than she had expected, his bones grazing the skin, brittle as spun glass.

He took a deep breath and shuddered, then turned his face up to hers. "I was hungry," he said.

Kurtz? Janson's voice on the phone was clipped and nasal, the words chopped short, punctuated by the telltale ping of the satellite transmission. "You still there?"

A bad sign, Kurtz thought, that it was Janson calling and not Morrow, notice that Morrow was washing his hands of the whole affair. Kurtz pressed the phone closer to his ear. "What do you have?"

From his seat on the patio of the Café National, Kurtz could see the Avenue Lalla Yacout in all its sun-struck squalor, the neglected Art Deco façades and the sagging balustrades, works of art in wrought iron and stucco, the aspirations of French culture left to the care of drug addicts and whores. Directly across from the café, in the doorway of the Wafa Bank, two boys were hustling the tourists who came and went from the ATM.

"There's a man named Rafa," Janson said. "Runs a print shop out near Voyageurs. It's a family business. We used to work with his father. You know him?"

"I've heard of him." Kurtz leaned back in his chair, watching the boys work. They had a system going, a divide-and-conquer routine that appeared to be serving them quite well. No doubt they shared a part of their profits with the bank manager in return for such a choice spot.

"Well, our Mr. Rafa claims he got a visit from two Americans this morning. A young woman and an older man looking for a passport."

Kurtz sat up. "Who's the man?"

Janson paused, another bad sign. "His name is Comfort. He retired this past spring, out of the Madrid office. I can't imagine you would have known him. He was a bit of a dead weight at the end. You know the type, gin blossoms and the pre-lunch shakes. Endless stories about the old days."

Kurtz shuffled through the Agency Rolodex in his head, failing to locate the name. He'd never been especially familiar with the European Division. "What's he doing here?"

"Apparently he developed some kind of friendship with the boy. Slipped him his home number before he left."

"You're joking!" Kurtz had heard rumors of this kind of thing happening, but he'd never actually believed them.

"I wish I was," Janson said.

A perfect pair, Kurtz thought, Kat and this sentimental spy. "So she's found the boy, then?"

"It looks that way."

"And the boy found his . . . what's his name again?"

"Comfort. Harry Comfort."

Kurtz managed a laugh. "Fits, doesn't it?" But Janson wasn't listening.

"Rafa's got them coming back at six to pick up the passport. I told him to expect you. He should be quite accommodating."

"What should I do about Comfort?"

This time Janson didn't hesitate. "Find out what he knows and put him out of his misery."

Sᴛᴀɴᴅɪɴɢ ɪɴ ᴛʜᴇ ᴠᴀsᴛ ɢʀᴀɴɪᴛᴇ ᴄᴏᴜʀᴛʏᴀʀᴅ of the Hassan II Mosque, surrounded on all sides by the most perfect expressions of geometry, Harry couldn't help wondering what Kepler, whose life work had been the unification of mathematics and the divine, would have thought of the structure.

Like all good Christians of his age, Kepler had both feared and hated the Moors; one of his greatest discoveries, the Supernova of 1604, he had interpreted as a harbinger of the downfall of Islam and the return of Christ. But Harry suspected that even Kepler would have been awed by the elegance of Hassan II's vision, by the flawless repetitions of shape and line, the archways moving forever outward, the rectangular minaret towering above it all like some primitive phallus.

Here, Harry thought, watching a group of schoolchildren navigate the mosque's massive tiered esplanades, each with room for several thousand adults, was a place meant to obliterate the individual, to merge the singular into the vast and infinite whole. Here was the Roman Forum of prayer, room for a hundred thousand worshippers. An Army of God at the ready.

There was a gust from the Atlantic, and Harry felt momentarily light on his feet. A wave surged forward and broke against the seawall, spraying a group of teenage girls who had gathered for a photograph, sending them shrieking and laughing, their bright-colored *hijabs* flapping recklessly in the breeze.

Suddenly Harry understood, as he had not allowed himself to understand before, that things were going to end badly for him. He would die as he had so often feared he would, faithless and unredeemed, in some foreign city to which he had no claim.

"Before the universe was created," Harry said to himself, conjuring the text of the *Mysterium Cosmographicum,* "there were no numbers except the Trinity, which is God himself. For the line and the plane imply no numbers: here infinitude itself reigns."

It was a passage in which he had at times found solace or even release but which now sounded as hollow as the wind in the mosque's empty *haram.*

THIRTY

It was a warm afternoon, even for September, the palm trees along the Boulevard Sour Jdid tousled and dry, the colonial buildings brilliant in the sea-light, white and sun-scoured as beached bones. Harry, who for some foolish reason had chosen to walk back from the mosque to the medina, was sweating profusely as he crossed the Place de l'Admiral Philbert and stepped into the old post-office building. It was not the healthy perspiration of an athlete but the rancid sweat of a body unused to exertion and in desperate need of a drink.

He stood just inside the doorway for a moment, letting his eyes adjust to the dim interior lighting, scanning the dark depths of the building for the public phones he knew were there. He located them at last, made his way back, and slipped into one of the empty booths, pulling the glass panels of the ancient folding door closed behind him before fishing Moussaoui's card from his damp shirt pocket and carefully dialing the number printed on it.

Moussaoui answered quickly, cutting the second ring short with a curt *"Allo?"*

"It's me." With the door closed, Harry could smell himself,

his own funk mingling with that of the booth. Decades of unwashed bodies.

"I believe I have something for you," Moussaoui said, sounding proud of his own resourcefulness. "I spoke with a friend who worked as a doctor at Oukacha Prison during the time frame you've given me. He recalls several incidents like the one you described, but only one in which the child was a boy. May of '83. The boy was sent to an orphanage. The Ain Chock Charity House."

Harry gripped the receiver. "Do you have a name?"

"The mother's name was Manar Yassine. Unmarried. She was transferred to a facility in the South almost immediately after the child's birth. There appear to be no records after that."

A death sentence, Harry thought. Worse. "Her family didn't know about the child?"

"Of course they knew." Moussaoui was slightly defensive. "The Yassines are a respectable family. The arrest of their daughter would have been humiliating enough. They would not have taken the child."

Of course not. Jamal, born out of wedlock and in prison, would only have served as a reminder of the ways in which his mother had dishonored them. If they had not wanted him then, it was hard to imagine they would want him now. Still, Harry could try. "Do you have an address?" he asked.

Moussaoui hesitated. "Tell me. What is it about this boy? You are in love with him?"

Harry laughed grimly. "How long have you known me, Abdul?"

TIME TO MOVE ON, Kurtz told himself, snapping the sample case shut, slipping the last of the spare magazines into his jacket pocket. He'd paid for three nights' lodging when he'd first arrived, but after just two the place and its staff had become uncomfortably familiar. Tonight he would find somewhere different to stay. Something out near Voyageurs, perhaps.

Hoisting the case and his small bag, he stepped to the window and scanned the street below, as was his habit. The two boys were still at their post at the Wafa Bank ATMs. Their competition had increased since Kurtz first observed them from the café, but they were still doing well. Making a killing for someone. Directly across the street, several doors down from the bank, a slouched figure stood in the doorway of an apartment building, smoking and watching the hotel. Mahjoub.

Kurtz was mildly surprised to see the young man. After their ride the previous night, Kurtz had wondered if his methods hadn't been just a bit too brutal. Apparently, the money he'd offered had been enough to overcome whatever missteps he'd made.

Leaving the room key on the bedside table, Kurtz let himself out into the hall, then made his way down the stairs and out onto the street. He didn't go to Mahjoub, but, after confirming that the young man had seen him, turned in the opposite direction. He walked away, slowly and deliberately, then ducked into the narrow service passage that ran along the side of the hotel.

It didn't take long for Mahjoub to catch up. Kurtz could hear the hard soles of the young man's boots on the concrete almost immediately. A few seconds later, a wary silhouette appeared at the mouth of the passage.

"In here!" Kurtz hissed.

Mahjoub glanced behind him, then stepped forward. "I've seen the boy," he announced clumsily, a dog returning a stick he'd been thrown.

"Where?" Kurtz asked.

"In the medina. This morning. I saw him go into the Hotel des Amis." A smile then, anticipating his pat on the head.

"A hundred dollars." Kurtz, reaching into the back pocket of his pants, fitting his hand around the stock of his Beretta, smiled back. "Wasn't that the agreement?"

Mahjoub nodded, then stepped closer, just as Kurtz wanted him to do.

A snitch for money, Kurtz thought, as he brought the gun forward and up. There was nothing worse. He squeezed the trigger and the silencer flashed, illuminating Mahjoub's face — a look of confusion, then the blank stare of death.

Now it really was time to move on.

WHERE THE HELL HAVE YOU BEEN? Kat asked angrily.

Harry glanced over Kat's shoulder at Jamal, then motioned for her to join him in the hallway.

"It's been over five hours," she hissed, following him out of the room. "I thought something had happened to you."

Harry pulled the door closed behind them. "I found his mother. I was right; she was sent to a dissenters' prison after he was born."

"Where is she now?"

"Disappeared," Harry whispered. He reached into his jacket and produced Moussaoui's business card, upon which he'd scribbled the name, Yassine, and the Anfa address Moussaoui had given him. "Her parents," he explained.

Kat took the card and glanced down at the smeared writing, then back up at Harry. "What's wrong?"

"They knew," Harry told her, lowering his voice. "The family knew about Jamal."

Kat shook her head. "I don't understand." But then she did.

Harry saw the expression on her face change from bafflement to comprehension to disgust. "I'm going to pick up your passport," he told her. "You'll take Jamal to Anfa."

"What makes you think his family will help him now?"

"Nothing," Harry answered honestly. "But it's the best we can do."

He pulled his remaining cash from his pocket and counted out enough for cab fare to the print shop and back, then pressed the rest of the money into Kat's hands.

"What are you doing?" she asked.

"We'll meet at the Hassan II Mosque," he told her. "Eight o'clock. If I'm not there by eight-fifteen, I want you to leave without me."

"No," Kat protested. "We'll all go together. We can ride out to meet Rafa now and come back to Anfa afterward. There's no hurry."

But Harry was already turning toward the stairwell. "Eight," he repeated, and then the lie, for his own benefit as much as hers. "I'll be there. I promise."

THIRTY-ONE

The street was like so many others in the city's wealthier neighborhoods: whitewash and black ironwork, leggy poinsettias breaching high garden walls, shutters folded grimly in on themselves. On the sidewalk, children and servants came and went, nannies pushing strollers or gripping their charges' little hands, old women in *abayas* carrying bread for the evening meal.

Kat stopped in front of a tall iron gate and took Harry's business card from her pocket one last time, confirming the address.

"This is the house?" Jamal asked with trepidation.

Kat had not yet told the boy why they were here, only that there was someone Harry wanted them to see, someone who might be able to help them. "Your mother lived here once," she said, "before you were born."

"She worked for these people?"

"No, Jamal."

The boy peered through the gate at the front courtyard and the imposing house beyond, struggling to understand.

"She grew up here," Kat said, pressing the gate's brass buzzer. "This was her home."

A woman's voice erupted from the intercom, a garbled greeting in rough Moroccan Arabic.

"Madame Yassine?" Kat asked.

There was a click and then silence. Kat was about to ring the buzzer again when a second voice warbled out at her, this one more cultivated than the last.

"This is Madame Yassine."

"My name is Katherine Caldwell," Kat said in her most respectful Arabic. "I would like to come in and speak with you if I could."

"Speak to me about what?" the woman asked, after a lengthy pause.

"It concerns your daughter, Madame."

Another pause. "What about my daughter?" The voice was wary now.

"If I could just come in," Kat pressed.

Silence.

Kat glanced up at the house and saw a figure move behind the front window, then disappear again. "He is your grandson, Madame!" Kat called out, loudly enough to be heard inside without the help of the intercom. "His name is Jamal!" She looked down at the boy and saw him staring back at her, frightened. "It's okay," she told him. "She will let us in." How could she not?

The speaker clicked again, and for a moment, hearing the static, Kat was flooded with relief. She put her hand on the gate, ready to push it open, but it was still locked.

"I'm sorry," the first, rougher voice said. "Madame would ask that you do not come here again."

Mr. Comforti Rafa greeted Harry at the front of the shop, smiling like the cheap whore Harry knew he was. "Come in. Come in. I am just putting the finishing touches on your document." He nodded obsequiously, showing Harry the top of his bald head, and motioned to a thick curtain that separated the front of the shop from the rear. "You can wait back here. It is much more comfortable."

Harry stepped forward as instructed. "I don't recall telling you my name before."

Rafa flinched, then quickly recovered himself. "But of course you did," he said, camouflaging his error with another smile. "How would I have known it if you had not?"

How, indeed. Harry returned the man's lunatic grin. "Of course. I'm afraid this business has made me a bit jumpy."

Rafa nodded sympathetically, then parted the curtain and held it for Harry to pass. "There." He pointed to an intricately carved cedar partition beyond which Harry could see a small sitting area furnished with pillows and ottomans. "I will join you in a moment."

Death at its most gracious, Harry thought as the curtain fell behind him and he heard Rafa moving away. He stepped around the partition and took a seat on one of the ottomans. A low table—a traditional brass plate set atop a wooden tripod—was set with a teapot and two glasses. And who would be joining him? Harry wondered. Not Rafa, surely, for Harry did not think the printer had the discipline required to kill another man, no matter what the wage. No, Morrow would have sent someone he trusted for this task.

Harry poured himself a glass of tea and sat back to wait. Tea and more tea, he thought, the great weapon of the Arab world. If the West fell, it would fall not to bombs or guns but to the politesse of the tea table, the endless bargaining to which Europeans would never be more than baffled guests.

Through the partition, Harry saw the curtains move aside. A figure approached, a man, a Westerner, in standard Agency uniform: rumpled khakis and a tropical shirt, a lightweight safari jacket with multiple pockets. In his right hand was a silenced pistol. A Beretta, Harry noted appreciatively, though the man himself looked to be nothing more than a thug.

Harry spread his arms and gestured to the table, as if he were the host of their little party. "Join me?"

To Harry's surprise, the man came forward and sat down opposite him, letting the Beretta rest between his legs.

"I understand you and I have something in common," he said.

Harry bristled. "I doubt that very much, Mr. . . . . ?"

"Kurtz," the man said, and then, returning to his earlier train of thought. "Our former employer, I believe."

"A slim thread, no?"

"Thicker than one might think," Kurtz replied.

Harry took a sip of his tea. It was achingly sweet.

Kurtz gestured over his shoulder toward the front of the shop. "You really should pick your friends more carefully," he remarked.

"My business associates as well, it would seem," Harry countered. He leaned forward and set his tea down on the table, moving with careful deliberation, keeping the Beretta in sight. If he was going to die, he wanted at the very least to see death coming. "Tell me," he said. "What happened with Bagheri?"

"Now, why should I tell you that?" Kurtz asked.

Because you're going to kill me, Harry thought, because it hardly matters now. He shrugged. "Professional courtesy. That, and the fact that I know where Bagheri is."

"A trade, then?"

Harry nodded. "I already know most of the story. It's the end I can't quite figure out. Am I correct in assuming that Bagheri was already working for you when he was picked up by our British friends?"

Silence, which Harry took for assent.

"That Bagheri's traveling companion did not know of his

affiliations; that the only way to return Bagheri to his friends in the MEK without arousing suspicion was to arrange for the other man's death and Bagheri's subsequent escape."

Kurtz relaxed slightly, content to continue with the game. Confident, Harry thought, of its ultimate outcome.

"The Iranian's condition," Harry continued. "Did Bagheri know his companion was asthmatic, or was that just luck?"

Kurtz smiled. "A bit of both, I would say."

"Here's where things get hazy for me. I can only assume Bagheri was not all he appeared to be, that he did not return to his friends, as had been the bargain. I must also assume that, as with all such intrigues, there was money involved."

"Janson said your mind was not all it used to be," Kurtz countered. "But it appears he was wrong. Yes, there was money involved. A lot, as you might imagine."

"But you did not pursue Bagheri then. Did you think he had died?"

"There were reports, yes. There was no reason to question them at the time. Afghanistan, as I'm sure you know, is a dangerous place. Our assumption was not unreasonable."

"Until Jamal told you otherwise. Though it wasn't you he told, was it?"

"No." Kurtz smiled. "Perhaps if it had been you, and not your replacement, the situation would be different."

"Surely."

"You are very good at this," Kurtz remarked. "But you have yet to tell me anything I don't know. That's the nature of a trade, is it not? Or have you already forgotten how these things work?"

"I have not forgotten," Harry said. "Unfortunately, there is nothing I can tell you that you don't already know."

"Don't be coy," Kurtz snapped, his brutishness getting the better of him. "I could kill you now and lose nothing for it. I know where the boy is, and, from the look on your face, the woman as well. They are at the Hotel des Amis, am I right?"

Harry smiled, then picked up his tea and took a measured sip. "I'm afraid your information is outdated."

"You're lying."

Harry shrugged. "I want to talk to Morrow."

"You know that's impossible."

Harry glanced at the Beretta, acknowledging the gun's presence and what was meant by it. "Do what you like," he said. "But I will only talk to Morrow."

SISTER! WAKE UP!"

Manar rolled over on her side and drew her knees into her chest, trying to ignore the urgent pounding on her door and the housekeeper's frantic voice.

"Please, sister! Please, you must get up!"

"Go away!" Manar rasped, reluctantly opening her eyes. The shutters on her bedroom window were closed, but bright daylight was visible through the slats. Afternoon or perhaps even morning, Manar thought regretfully. She could not say how long she had been asleep, only that the prospect of waking was unbearable.

For a moment all was quiet, then Asiya's voice came again, a whisper this time: "If you do not let me in, I will call for your mother."

Manar pushed the sheets aside and swung her feet to the floor. "Leave me in peace or I will find a reason to have you dismissed!" she called angrily, making her way across the room and flinging open the door. "Have you forgotten your place in this house?"

Asiya stared defiantly at Manar, then grabbed her arm and forced her toward the window. "Quickly!" she barked.

Manar tried to free herself, but the housekeeper's grip was painfully, stubbornly strong. They reached the window and Asiya undid the latch with her free hand.

"There!" she exclaimed triumphantly, pushing open the shutters, motioning to the front gate. "He has come. The boy has come!"

Manar looked down at the garden wall and the street beyond. On the sidewalk just outside the gate stood two figures, a woman in a blue head scarf and a young man—a boy, really—with Maghreb coloring and a slight build.

"Do you not see?" Asiya asked, incredulous.

Manar did see. The boy turned and it was the same gesture she had seen through the doorway at Ain Chock. His shoulders swinging as she had seen Yusuf's do so many times, the movement perfectly duplicated.

"Do you not see that he is your son?"

THIRTY-TWO

"It's Comfort, sir." Kurtz's voice was preemptively defensive. Careful to take his own fault out of whatever equation was at hand.

"What is it?" Morrow set aside the glossy brochure the man at the funeral home had given him to study, with its silk-lined twenty-year caskets and its gold-filigreed urns. Susan had always been clear about the way she wanted her burial handled. During the early stages of her illness, she'd made Morrow promise that it would be done as simply and as inexpensively as possible. He had agreed with her then, but now the thought of her naked body in a cardboard box made him physically ill.

"He wants to talk to you. He claims he knows where Bagheri is."

"You have him there now?"

"Yes, sir."

"Good," Morrow said. "Put him on."

"Yes, sir."

There was a jarred handover of the phone, then the sound of uneven breathing on the other end of the line.

"It's a little late for a pardon, isn't it?" Morrow said wearily.

"I don't want a pardon. I want you to leave the boy out of this, and the woman as well."

"Oh, redemption," Morrow corrected himself. "Too late for that as well."

"They don't know anything."

"You've said that before."

"Yes," Harry agreed, "and I was right. Bagheri was never in Madrid, or anywhere else for that matter. The boy made the whole thing up. That idiot they sent to replace me threatened to cut him off if he didn't produce something spectacular. So he did."

Morrow didn't say anything. Harry was right, no doubt, and Morrow believed him. These things happened, but the lie had outrun itself now. "What about the woman?" he asked. This was the real worry.

"She won't be any trouble," Harry said.

"I met her," Morrow reminded him.

"She doesn't know anything," Harry insisted. "I've made sure of that."

"No? But you do, don't you? That's the problem."

They were both silent, each contemplating the truth of this last statement.

Morrow glanced at the brochure on his desk. What did it really matter, he wondered—two more living, two more dead—when at the end it all came to this?

"Susan's dead," he said wearily. It was a relief to speak the words to someone who would understand what they meant. Like an act of confession, Morrow thought, each man able to offer the other absolution.

Harry cleared his throat, as if he were about to speak, but didn't.

"She was ruined at the end, you know," Morrow said. "The cancer ruined her."

"WAIT! PLEASE, WAIT!"

Jamal stopped and looked back at the house.

A woman, a dark figure in a cotton *abaya*, stood in one of the upper windows. She waved her arms and pointed to the front gate. "She is coming!" she called. "Please, do not go."

Jamal glanced at Kat.

She nodded encouragingly.

"She is coming!" the woman called from the window once again.

The villa's front door opened and a woman appeared. She was small and thin, dressed in a simple brown burnoose. Her feet and head were bare; her hair long and loose around her shoulders, matted on one side, as if from sleep. Moving quickly, she came down the steps and crossed the small court-yard, then stopped just inside the gate, fumbling with the lock.

"It's okay," Kat said, putting her hands on Jamal's shoulders, urging him gently forward.

But Jamal did not move. He had rehearsed this moment so many times, in so many ways, but now that it was upon him he did not know what to do.

My mother, he told himself, knowing it to be true without question. Yet she was not as he had imagined. She was tiny and small-boned, delicate as a bird, her hair shot through with gray, her bare feet long and slim, as were his own.

The gate opened then and she was through it and upon him, pushing his head down, probing his hair with her fingers, searching for something. He could feel her lips on his ear, her breath as she spoke:

God is great.

I testify that there is no god except God.

I testify that Muhammad is the messenger of God.

Come to prayer.

Come to salvation.

And the second prayer, this one in his left ear:

There is no strength nor power but in God.

When she had finished, she released him and took a step back. "Your name, my son," she said. "What is your name?"

Silence.

Then, at last, the American spoke for him. "His name is Jamal."

HARRY CLOSED HIS EYES AND TRIED, as he had so many times before, to conjure that first afternoon at the Hotel Duc. It wasn't the act of sex that he wanted to remember, for even he could not have sentimentalized that first awkward coupling. What Harry was hoping to re-create were the moments in the bar before intimacy altered everything, and which he now understood to have been the most, and perhaps the only, authentic moments he and Susan had shared.

There was Susan, her eyes raw from crying, her cotton sundress just skimming her tennis-club thighs, the eyelets hinting at what was beneath. Brown skin and white slip. And everything else—the fine blond trail that led downward from her navel, the two small hollows at the base of her spine—as yet unimaginable.

Sometimes, he thought, intimacy is the worst of saboteurs. Though other times, as with Char, the opposite is true; one comes to love a person not in spite of her faults but because of them. And this not out of pity but out of awe—a kind of reverence for the human condition, a reverence for one's own condition.

"Yes, sir," Harry heard Kurtz say, in response to whatever Morrow had told him. His tone was one of disappointment, that of a bully whose plans have been thwarted by someone more powerful than he. "No, sir. It won't be a problem." Then the call was over.

They would live, Harry understood. Jamal and the woman would live, though he would not.

Funny, he thought, that after all these years of anticipating the end he could have been so wrong. His awareness at the moment was not logical but personal. Instead of becoming a part of something larger than himself, it was as if he was returning to a place he knew well. He could feel Char's warm thigh against his cheek, the thick mat of her pubic hair on his forehead. Her skin smelled of its usual anointment of oils: sandalwood, clove, cinnamon, jasmine. Like a body perfumed for death.

There was a single soft click as the Beretta engaged, but the sound was distant, almost incidental. The sound of a twig breaking underfoot. An inevitable consequence of our presence in this world.

Iᴛ ᴡᴀꜱ ᴍᴏʀɴɪɴɢ, but just barely, the moon still bright overhead, its hammered face a near-perfect circle, like a nickel coin, thumb-worn on one edge. In the distance, Taza and its ramparts hung against the high plateau of the Rif foothills, a watchman's tin lamp flickering in the darkness.

City of the conquerors and the conquered, Kat thought, recalling the history of the Taza Gap. This barren and forbidding place through which countless armies had passed on their way to the towns and cities of the lowlands. First the Romans and then the Arabs. Later, the great Moroccan dynasties: the Almohads and the Merenids and the Alawites. Later still, the French.

They had been on the road for more than six hours, moving slowly eastward across the dark countryside, toward Oujda and the Moroccan frontier, toward the vast and, Kat knew, un-policeable desert borders of the African north. Algeria. Libya. Egypt. Nations in name only. Divisions on a map where none could truly be made. Ahead of them, the ragged earth curved upward to embrace the first, paltry smudge of dawn. Black land against blue-black, star-stippled sky.

Soon the bus would stop for the day's first prayers. The other passengers would file out into the cold and darkness. And Kat, having chosen to come this far, would be obliged to join them.

In the window beside her, Kat's reflection blinked silently back. Two eyes and nothing more. The space once defined by her head and face now black and formless behind her *niqab*. It was, Kat thought, as if she had ceased to exist. And, in a way, she had.

She had not gone to the mosque the night before, as she and Harry had agreed they would, but had made her way from Anfa to the medina instead, to the dress shop on the Rue Centrale, where she had stopped that morning to watch the young girl and her mother.

She had thought it unlikely that Harry would return, had taken the nature of their last encounter as tacit acknowledgment of this fact. But her choice had been made without Harry in mind. She would not be going home, at least not now, not yet. Not until she had completed the journey she had begun three years earlier.

Kat's decision to cover herself had been a practical one. As terrifying as the prospect of wearing the full veil was, she knew the *niqab* would allow her to travel unmolested. When she finally did put it on, she had felt not defeat but relief. There was, she realized, an unexpected power in anonymity, a freedom that came with the camouflage of the veil, as if she were neither in the world nor of it but something else entirely. A ghost among the living. A silent witness.

Kat checked herself in the window, pulling her black gloves tight across her forearms, bringing the heavy fabric of her *abaya* down over her forehead and shoulders. Up ahead, where the bus's headlights swept forward, illuminating the shoulder of the road, Kat could see two figures, two women dressed as she was, moving gracefully through the salat.

Not an obliteration of self, she thought, watching them kneel and bend forward, touching their heads to the earth, but self in its purest and most potent form, unencumbered by the hallmarks of identity. One as an expression of all.

The bus slowed, then pulled to a stop just in front of the women's car. The driver popped the door and the other passengers stood, shuffling forward with their kilims. Yes, Kat thought, she had made her choice, just as Harry had made his, and Colin his.

She was still not certain what had happened between him and Kurtz that last night in the Special Forces camp, what, exactly, Colin had agreed to. She had reconciled herself with the fact that the details of the Iranian's death would always be a mystery to her. But this she did know: that whatever lies Colin had told he had told out of loyalty to Stuart, that his allegiance had been not to cause or country but to his friend. Any other explanation, Kat knew, would have required him to be someone he was not.

"Sister?"

Kat lifted her head to see a young Moroccan woman standing over her. She was tall and unexpectedly beautiful, wearing snug designer jeans and an elegant jacket. Her face was bare, her hair loose beneath her casually pinned head scarf.

She motioned toward the front of the bus, which was empty by now. "You will not join us?" she asked, looking slightly puzzled.

Kat nodded her thanks and stood, shuffling forward down the narrow aisle. Outside, the passengers had gathered together on a dusty patch of earth. Several of the men were busy filling buckets of water from a large plastic barrel in the bus's hold. The two women were still praying, dipping like dancers through each *rakat,* their black robes flapping like nationless flags in the wind.

Kat reached the doorway and stopped on the threshold, contemplating the long step down, the distance to be traveled into the cold and the wind and the darkness. An obligation, she told herself, thinking about her brother and that long, weightless, graceless fall. *Fard,* the Arabic word for those things to which we are duty-bound. And for a brief moment she understood: that love itself is an obligation, one to which we must submit, and that in order to do so we must abandon the larger part of our self. Then she stepped, and felt the gravity of descent, the earth pulling her down.

"Sister!" one of the women called, motioning for Kat to join them. "Here, sister!"

She moved to them and then among them, pulling off her socks and gloves, unsheathing her hands and feet, baring herself as if for a lover. Their breath hung thick in the bitter morning air, an intimacy of odors: saffron and coriander, damp wool, and sweet perfume. And the smells of the female body: blood and sex, sour milk.

Kat bent over the bucket with the others and plunged her hands to the wrists in the icy water, readying her body for the act of worship, preparing herself, as we all must, to receive whatever grace might be given.

ACKNOWLEDGMENTS

My sincerest thanks to all the usual suspects: Simon Lipskar, Dan Conaway, and the whole crew at Writer's House; Mark Tavani, Jane von Mehren, and all the immensely talented people at Random House who have had a hand in this book; Bill Massey and everyone at Orion. Thanks also to my family and friends, especially my husband, Keith, who has always encouraged me to trust myself, and my dear friend and fellow exile, Julie Tisone, without whom I might not have survived to write this book.

THE YEARS OF LEAD

Characters rarely spring fully grown from my imagination. In general, the people who inhabit my books have inhabited my real life in some form or other. Often they are products of my research, individuals whose identities I have borrowed and shaped to fit my needs. Sometimes they pass opportunely into my world, the template for a hero or a villain when I need one. Occasionally they are modeled on people I met years ago and have been unable to forget, passing acquaintances whose stories were so gripping that they refuse to be silenced. This was the case with the character of Manar Yassine, in *The Prince of Bagram Prison*.

In the late 1980s, while bumming my way across Europe, I had the extreme good fortune to share a house in the French Pyrenees with a group of young Moroccan men. As an undocumented worker, my employment options were limited, and one of the first jobs I had was working the grape harvest, or *vendange*, in a remote village near the Spanish border. It didn't pay much, but food, lodging, and a generous ration of cheap wine were provided. I was barely nineteen at the time, and living with the Moroccans was my first intimate brush with a non-Western culture. In many ways, the experience was surprisingly unremarkable. Most of the men had come to France on student visas and were studying at the regional university. The atmosphere in the house was not unlike that of a college dorm. During the day we worked; in the evenings they cooked and we ate and drank together. For the most part, the men treated me like a younger sister. They were open and friendly yet respectful, certainly more respectful than the European men I had encountered up to that point. But there was one man in particular, Bernoussi, who seemed, if not disapproving, at least wary of me, and to whom the others showed a solemn deference. Eventually, I would come to learn that he had been a political prisoner in his native country. A victim of the brutal regime of Morocco's King Hassan II, Bernoussi had been arrested at a student protest and detained for several years. Upon his release, he fled Morocco for France.

Sadly, Bernoussi's experience was not an unusual one. The reign of Hassan II, which lasted from 1961 until his death in 1999, is commonly referred to by many Moroccans as the Years of Lead, for the violent state repression of various dissident groups that characterized it. Though Hassan was a staunch ally of the West, like many of his counterparts in the region he maintained power through intimidation, using a vicious network of security and interior ministers and secret police to silence his critics. So fierce were his tactics that, in a chilling demonstration of his ruthlessness, he regularly ordered his own sons beaten in front of his court. Prominent dissenters and political activists, including many pro-democracy activists, were routinely "disappeared." Hundreds of anti-government protesters were killed and thousands imprisoned and tortured for their participation in demonstrations or labor strikes. Independence movements in the Rif Mountains and the Western Sahara were brutally crushed. Secret detention facilities, like the notorious Tazmamart, in which prisoners were held for years in coffinlike underground cells, were constructed clandestinely in the desert, out of view of international human-rights groups. Like Bernoussi—and the character Manar Yassine—many of those detained or killed during this time were students.

To call Bernoussi's presence in my life fleeting would be to vastly overstate our relationship. I can say with confidence that he probably has no recollection of me. Yet the impression he made was great enough that, two decades on, I felt the need to tell a version of his story through Manar. Curiously, what has stayed with me all these years, what I have gone back to again and again, is not Bernoussi himself but myself as seen through his eyes.

In the years since, especially in the wake of September 11, and the deepening rift between the Western and Arab worlds, I have found myself contemplating Bernoussi's wariness of me and the reasons for it. There were times when I took his reticence for hostility, a reaction to an American foreign policy that supported leaders like King Hassan II. But I have traveled enough now to know that, as much as we may think otherwise, people from other countries are remarkably able and willing to separate the actions of a government from its citizens, and that the vast majority of the world does not hold the American people responsible for the decisions of our leaders. If anything, I believe it was my innocence of which Bernoussi was afraid—that unique combination of naïveté and privilege with which I navigated the world, living as a lark the life that hundreds of thousands of Turkish and African immigrants to Europe live out of necessity.

Looking back, I cringe at my behavior, at the extent to which I took for granted the hospitality of my Moroccan housemates, who certainly could not afford to be as generous as they were. That I lived with them without once considering the deep-seated cultural differences between us, or the implications of my physical presence in their midst, is shameful to me now. They were not particularly pious men, but they were Muslims, and the fact that they accommodated me as they did was, in hindsight, remarkable. How terrifying my ignorance must have been to Bernoussi, my incredulous curiosity about what he had been through, the host of outrage and good intentions on my sleeve. Bernoussi was, above all, someone who understood the consequences of his actions, who had suffered deeply for his convictions and knew intimately what it meant to be powerless. I, on the other hand, understood nothing yet was, by virtue of birth and the passport in my pocket, entitled to everything.

At the time I lived with Bernoussi and the others, the situation in Morocco had already begun to change. Hassan II was growing old and his power waning. But it would be another sixteen years—seven years after Hassan's death—before the monarchy officially recognized the human-rights abuses that had occurred during the Years of Lead. In November of 2003, Hassan's son, King Mohammed VI, in keeping with his many attempts to present a face of modernity and reform, established the Equity and Reconciliation Panel, a seventeen-member independent body that was headed by a former political prisoner, to investigate sixteen thousand cases of human-rights abuses that had occurred under Hassan II's rule. Two years later, on January 6, 2006, in the wake of calls for an official apology following the IER's finding, Mohammed publicly acknowledged for the first time nearly ten thousand instances of murder, disappearance, torture, and rape. "I announce the comforting news," he said, "with the hope that the merciful angels will carry it to the soul of my venerated father and the hearts of all the victims, the persons who had been wronged and their families, that we have sympathy and solicitude for them." Though far from an apology and far from complete—the king's critics claim that the number of victims was much higher than the ten thousand acknowledged, and that his policies, which call for blanket amnesty for those who committed atrocities, are ineffectual—Mohammed's statement and his initial decision to set up the panel were the first of their kind in the Arab world.

Despite his outward efforts to reform the monarchy, Mohammed's reign has so far been less than perfect. Critics rightly denounce the king's lavish lifestyle in the face of the rampant unemployment and overwhelming poverty that grip most of the country. The constitutional monarchy he instituted is viewed as largely a symbolic step toward democracy. Abuses still occur, especially in regard to the ongoing conflict in the Western Sahara region. But there can be no doubt that his reign represents a step forward for human rights in the region. One consequence of the comparative openness of Mohammed's rule has been the publication of a number of accounts of those imprisoned during the Years of Lead, including Malika Oufkir's *Stolen Lives: Twenty Years in a Desert Jail;* Ahmed Marzouki's *Tazmamart Cell 10;* and Tahar Ben Jelloun's stunning work of fiction, *This Blinding Absence of Light,* which chronicles the ten-year imprisonment of a Moroccan army officer in Tazmamart. These books, which are all available in English, offer intimate glimpses into the lives of political prisoners under King Hassan II, and I highly recommend them for anyone who wants to learn more about the human consequences of this unfortunate era in Moroccan history.